# ☆☆ Forbes
### TRAVEL GUIDE

CHICAGO

## ACKNOWLEDGMENTS

We gratefully acknowledge the help of our representatives for their efficient and perceptive inspections of the lodgings listed. Forbes Travel Guide is also grateful to the talented writers who contributed to this book.

Some of the information contained herein is derived from a variety of third-party sources. Although every effort has been made to verify the information obtained from such sources, the publisher assumes no responsibility for inconsistencies or inaccuracies in the data or liability for any damages of any type arising from errors or omissions.

Neither the editors nor the publisher assume responsibility for the services provided by any business listed in this guide or for any loss, damage or disruption in your travel for any reason.

Front Cover image: ©iStockphoto.com/sborisov
Back Cover image: ©City of Chicago/GRC
ISBN: 9781936010981
Manufactured in the USA
10 9 8 7 6 5 4 3 2 1

# CONTENTS

**✩ Forbes**
TRAVEL GUIDE

## CHICAGO STAR PROPERTIES

# STAR ATTRACTIONS

If you've been a reader of Mobil Travel Guide, you will have heard that this historic brand partnered in 2009 with another storied media name, Forbes, to create a new entity, Forbes Travel Guide. For more than 50 years, Mobil Travel Guide assisted travelers in making smart decisions about where to stay and dine when traveling. With this new partnership, our mission has not changed: We're committed to the same rigorous inspections of hotels, restaurants and spas—the most comprehensive in the industry with more than 500 standards tested at each property we visit—to help you cut through the clutter and make easy and informed decisions on where to spend your time and travel budget. Our team of anonymous inspectors are constantly on the road, sleeping in hotels, eating in restaurants and making spa appointments, evaluating those exacting standards to determine a property's rating.

What kinds of standards are we looking for when we visit a property? We're looking for more than just high-thread count sheets, pristine spa treatment rooms and white linen-topped tables. We look for service that's attentive, individualized and unforgettable. We note how long it takes to be greeted when you sit down at your table, or to be served when you order room service, or whether the hotel staff can confidently help you when you've forgotten that one essential item that will make or break your trip. Unlike any other travel ratings entity, we visit each place we rate, testing hundreds of attributes to compile our ratings, and our ratings cannot be bought or influenced. The Forbes Five Star rating is the most prestigious achievement in hospitality—while we rate more than 5,000 properties in the U.S., Canada, Hong Kong, Macau and Beijing, for 2011, we have awarded Five Star designations to only 54 hotels, 23 restaurants and 20 spas. When you travel with Forbes, you can travel with confidence, knowing that you'll get the very best experience, no matter who you are.

With our City Guide series, you can also count on a local perspective, in the form of a fresh, witty, insider voice. We employ local writers and inspectors who are well-connected in their respective cities to give you the very latest information on what's going on around town. As you are reading these pages, we hope you get a real flavor of the city and that you feel even more inspired to visit and take it all in. All of our books in the City Guide series include vibrant photos and easy-to-use maps to help you find your way to the city's best attractions. We understand the importance of making the most of your time. That's why the most trusted name in travel is now Forbes Travel Guide.

## STAR RATED HOTELS

Whether you're looking for the ultimate in luxury or the best value for your travel budget, we have a hotel recommendation for you. To help you pinpoint properties that meet your needs, Forbes Travel Guide classifies each lodging by type according to the following characteristics:

★★★★★These exceptional properties provide a memorable experience through virtually flawless service and the finest of amenities. Staff are intuitive, engaging and passionate, and eagerly deliver service above and beyond the guests' expectations. The hotel was designed with the guest's comfort in mind, with particular attention paid to craftsmanship and quality of product. A Five-Star property is a destination unto itself.

★★★★These properties provide a distinctive setting, and a guest will find many interesting and inviting elements to enjoy throughout the property. Attention to detail is prominent throughout the property, from design concept to quality of products provided. Staff are accommodating and take pride in catering to the guest's specific needs throughout their stay.

★★★These well-appointed establishments have enhanced amenities that provide travelers with a strong sense of location, whether for style or function. They may have a distinguishing style and ambience in both the public spaces and guest rooms; or they may be more focused on functionality, providing guests with easy access to local events, meetings or tourism highlights.

Recommended: These hotels are considered clean, comfortable and reliable establishments that have expanded amenities, such as full-service restaurants.

For every property, we also provide pricing information. All prices quoted are accurate at the time of publication; however, prices cannot be guaranteed. Because  rates can fluctuate, we list a pricing range rather than specific prices.

## STAR RATED RESTAURANTS

Every restaurant in this book has been visited by Forbes Travel Guide's team of experts and comes highly recommended as an outstanding dining experience.

★★★★★Forbes Five-Star restaurants deliver a truly unique and distinctive dining experience. A Five-Star restaurant consistently provides exceptional food, superlative service and elegant décor. An emphasis is placed on originality and personalized, attentive and discreet service. Every detail that surrounds the experience is attended to by a warm and gracious dining room team.

★★★★These are exciting restaurants with often well-known chefs that feature creative and complex foods and emphasize various culinary techniques and a focus on seasonality. A highly-trained dining room staff provides refined personal service and attention.

★★★Three Star restaurants offer skillfully prepared food with a focus on a specific style or cuisine. The dining room staff provides warm and professional service in a comfortable atmosphere. The décor is well-coordinated with quality fixtures and decorative items, and promotes a comfortable ambience.

Recommended: These restaurants serve fresh food in a clean setting with efficient service. Value is considered in this category, as is family friendliness.

Because menu prices can fluctuate, we list a pricing range rather than specific prices. The pricing ranges are per diner, and assume that you order an appetizer or dessert, an entrée and one drink.

## STAR RATED SPAS

Forbes Travel Guide's spa ratings are based on objective evaluations of more than 450 attributes. About half of these criteria assess basic expectations, such as staff courtesy, the technical proficiency and skill of the employees and whether the facility is clean and maintained properly. Several standards address issues that impact a guest's physical comfort and convenience, as well as the staff's ability to impart a sense of personalized service. Additional criteria measure the spa's ability to create a completely calming ambience.

★★★★★Stepping foot in a Five Star Spa will result in an exceptional experience with no detail overlooked. These properties wow their guests with extraordinary design and facilities, and uncompromising service. Expert staff cater to your every whim and pamper you with the most advanced treatments and skin care lines available. These spas often offer exclusive treatments and may emphasize local elements.

★★★★Four Star spas provide a wonderful experience in an inviting and serene environment. A sense of personalized service is evident from the moment you check in and receive your robe and slippers. The guest's comfort is always of utmost concern to the well-trained staff.

★★★These spas offer well-appointed facilities with a full complement of staff to ensure that guests' needs are met. The spa facilities include clean and appealing treatment rooms, changing areas and a welcoming reception desk.

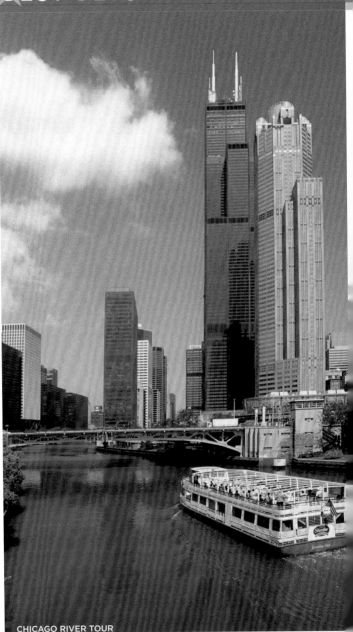

CHICAGO RIVER TOUR

# SWEET HOME CHICAGO

Things change fast in the Windy City, with new restaurants, shops and even multi-million dollar sights (as anyone who's seen the incredible Millennium Park can attest) opening every day. Whether it's your first time in Chicago or your fiftieth, there's certain to be a new skyscraper, celebrity chef creation or cutting-edge art gallery you need to experience. Here, a short list of the very best to see, do and taste in Chicago right now.

## WHAT ARE THE TOP HOTELS?

Don't be surprised if the Five Star **Four Seasons Hotel Chicago** *(page 96)* has a file on you. The staff meets every morning to go over who's arriving that day and what they might need, whether it's something you requested prior to your visit or something they know by scrolling through their huge database of guests. It's this flawless service that makes a stay here feel exquisitely relaxing. It also doesn't hurt that the hotel recently underwent a thorough revamp, and is just steps from the city's best shopping.

The Five Star **Peninsula Chicago** *(page 99)* mixes Old World opulence with modern-day ease. The hotel's graceful service befits the dignified atmosphere of this gem. But the Peninsula's crown jewels are also its most delicious. While the trendy Shanghai Terrace serves inhalable Asian-inspired fare and cocktails, the reputable Avenues is still a force to be reckoned with in the city's fine-dining scene.

You might be confused when you walk into Four Star **Trump International Hotel and Tower** *(page 104)*. Is it a hotel? Is it a condo building? It's both, and the understated but upscale lobby is a precursor to everything else this well-done hotel has to offer: A sophisticated but relaxed lounge; a gorgeous, fine dining restaurant; lavish rooms where every detail has been taken into consideration (down to the Sub-Zero refrigerators); and amazing views from everywhere.

Located high atop Water Tower Place along Michigan Avenue, **The Ritz-Carlton Chicago** *(page 99)* recently underwent a major renovation, giving rooms a sophisticated and modern makeover. The new Deca restaurant on the 12th floor is a chic place for cocktails and bistro fare.

The city's newest hotel, the **Elysian** *(page 96)*, is adorned with chandeliers inspired by Coco Chanel's jewelry and features only ten rooms per floor, which include fireplaces, terraces, and white Carrera marble bathrooms. The elegant Parisian-style building has a cobblestone motor court, a Greek-columned spa, handsome bar and two fantastic restaurants.

## WHAT ARE THE CAN'T-MISS SIGHTS?

When **Millennium Park** *(page 32)* opened in the summer of 2004, it was several years overdue and millions of dollars over budget. But for Chicagoans, it's hard to stay mad about the delays and cost after seeing the park's tremendous role as a civic center. Throughout the year, tourists and locals mix and mingle over the park's weekly concerts (many of them free), and public art exhibitions and expos. The park is also home to the lovely, peace-inducing Lurie Garden; the interactive, wet-and-wild Crown Fountain; and everyone's favorite reflective bean-shaped sculpture, Cloud Gate.

Other cities might vie for the title of skyscraper capital of the country, but the truth is, these awe-inspiring structures were invented in the Windy City at the turn of the century after the Chicago Fire. If you're mad for Mies der Rohe, that is), all you have to do is walk through Chicago's Loop and look up; or take a tour, like the **Chicago History Museum's Architecture River Cruise** *(page 48)*, which winds through the Chicago River and gives you a rundown of the city's most significant buildings.

Likewise, Chicago is peppered with public art, beyond the confines of Millennium Park. A walk through the **Loop** *(page 34)* showcases the city's wealth in public art, as would a trek to the city's neighborhoods (for example, the West Loop has The Haymarket Memorial on Desplaines Street between Lake and Randolph streets, and the South Loop has *Arris* at Cermak Road and Calumet Avenue). Even the El can bring you closer to public art: Many of the city's CTA stations feature mosaic murals and pieces by local artists, such as Juan Chavez and Corinne Peterson's *Hopes and Dreams* (Roosevelt station on the Red Line, South Loop).

From the observation deck at the 103rd floor of the **Willis Tower** *(page 37)*, formerly the Sears Tower, you can see up to 40 miles out in either direction on a clear day. The **John Hancock Observatory** *(page 29)* is no slouch, either. Take the elevator to the 95th floor Signature Room Lounge, where you can get vistas for the cost of a slightly sugary cocktail. (Ladies, check out the view from the bathroom.)

You've seen *Ferris Bueller's Day Off* and the spoofs of the farmer couple in the *American Gothic* painting—now experience the **Art Institute of Chicago** *(page 31)* in the flesh. The new Renzo Piano-designed Modern Wing, opened in 2009, is simply stunning and one of the city's best new attractions. Whatever you do, set aside an afternoon to take in this massive museum, which boasts an impressive collection of Impressionist and post-Impressionist pieces, plus 20th century classics.

## WHAT ARE THE TOP EXPERIENCES?

If you enjoy the great outdoors, there's nothing like summer in Chicago. The season ignites three months of celebration, during which Chicagoans cram in every outdoor activity possible before they have to hibernate again for the winter. The city's many street festivals are alfresco shindigs held every weekend, celebrating everything from folk music (Chicago Folk and Roots Festival at Welles Park) to local eats at the massive **Taste of Chicago** *(page 163)*. The hot weather also ushers in another only-in-Chicago experience: **Lollapalooza** *(page 163)*. The three-day music extravaganza brings big-name acts such as Lady Gaga and hometown heroes Wilco to Grant Park and, of course, fans from all over the country follow them. For a real taste of Chicago in the summer, head to **Green City Market** *(page 46)*, the city's only sustainable market, where you can shop alongside the area's top chefs for the freshest-of-the-fresh fruit and vegetables.

A short trek from downtown to Wrigleyville is a small distance to go for a bit of history—a visit to **Wrigley Field** *(page 157)*. The home of the Chicago Cubs baseball team was built in the early 1900s, and it remains one of the city's most beloved landmarks; possibly more beloved than the ill-fated Cubbies themselves, who haven't won a single World Series in 100 years and counting. Win or lose, games at Wrigley are a cherished part of Chicago summers, and it's not hard to see why: It's a thrill to sit with the loyal Cubs bleacher bums, chow down on a ballpark dog and watch Derrek Lee hit one out of the park. A huge highlight is seeing which celebrity guest will pop in to sing *Take Me Out to the Ball Game*—it could be anyone from Bill Murray to Vince Vaughn stepping up to the microphone. Can't get tickets?

MARINA CITY

Head to Wrigley anyway and watch the game from one of the watering holes surrounding the park; the neighborhood setting is half the fun.

If baseball isn't your thing, go see the daytime diva everyone seems to adore before her last show wraps in September 2011. TIckets to see Oprah have always been hard to come by, so if you want to see her in action at **Harpo Studios** *(page 33)*, be sure to plan ahead. You can also shop Oprah's favorite things at her store near her studio.

When day turns into night, the city just gets hotter. One place in particular that heats up is the area in the Gold Coast where Division, Rush and State streets come together. Here, a mix of locals and tourists crowd the pricey restaurants, bars or clubs. Another nightlife hub that's growing in popularity is the six-corner intersection in Wicker Park where Milwaukee, North and Damen avenues meet. All sorts of party people roam the neighborhood, ducking into clubs, music venues and hotter-by-the-minute restaurants.

Ready-for-primetime comedy is a Chicago legacy. **The Second City** *(page 152)* and **iO Chicago** *(page 152)* have turned out some of the best jokesters around, including Tina Fey and Steve Carell. At Second City, you'll get top-notch topical sketch shows, while iO will give you laugh-out-loud improv, an art form invented in Chicago.

## WHAT ARE THE BEST FOOD EXPERIENCES?

Chicago has come a long way from the days when it was known as the "Hog Butcher for the World." Nowadays, the city's dining scene is known much more for its role in the molecular-gastronomy movement—hot spots like Five Star **Alinea** *(page 82)* and **Moto** *(page 77)* give Ferran Adrià a run for his money. Meanwhile, stalwarts like Five Star **Charlie Trotter's** *(page 83)* confidently remain at the very top of the country's contemporary American list. And Chicago chef **Rick Bayless** *(page 66)* is more popular than ever, thanks to winning the first season of *Top Chef Masters*. His newest place **XOCO** *(page 66)*, which serves delicious tortas, has a continuous line out the door.

BUCKINGHAM FOUNTAIN

Of course, if you've come for the fulfilling, gooey goodness of deep-dish pizza, you won't be disappointed. Just pack your patience when you visit the legendary **Pizzeria Uno** *(page 71)*; the waits are usually long (Uno claims to have invented deep-dish pizza in the '40s), but the pie is worth the wait. If you simply cannot stick it out, then try other deep-dish spots like **Gino's East** *(633 N. Wells St., River North, 312-943-1124; www.ginoseast. com)* and **Giordano's** *(Prudential Plaza, 135 E. Lake St., 312-616-1200; www.giordanos.com)*. Or try one of the many places that have been popping up which serve woodfired pizzas, such as **Great Lake** *(page 86)* or **La Madia** *(page 67)*.

Though the city has plenty of outstanding vegetarian options—from the upscale **Green Zebra** *(page 87)* to the Indian food counters on the Far North Side's Devon Avenue—Chicago is still largely a carnivore's paradise. Witness the city's famous steakhouses, which are always packed cheek to jowl. You can't go wrong whether you chow down at classics like **Gibsons**, *(page 56)* where you can expect a lively atmosphere and full-flavored steaks, or at newer places such as **David Burke's Primehouse** *(page 63)*.

On the other end of the spectrum—but no less delicious—are Chicago's renowned Italian beef sandwiches. These messy sandwiches (thinly sliced roast beef and au jus served on an Italian-style roll with giardiniera or sweet peppers on top) are said to have originated in the city in the 1930s. Nowadays, you can try this drippy, delicious throwback at **Al's #1 Italian Beef** *(169 W. Ontario St., River North, 312-943-3222; www. alsbeef.com)* and **Portillo's** *(100 W. Ontario St., River North, 312-587-8910; www.portillos.com)*. Another Depression-era classic that's still as popular as ever is the hot dog. But not just any frank will do—locals line up for the gourmet dogs at **Hot Doug's** *(page 60)*, which offers a Chicago-style hot dog with all the trimmings, with a side of addicting duck fat frites.

## WHAT'S THE BEST NIGHTLIFE?

Chicago nightlife suffers from bipolar disorder. On one hand, you have the Midwest's famous no-nonsense, pragmatic attitude, which manifests itself in dive bars, come-as-you-are live-music hubs—such as **Smartbar** *(page*

## WHERE IS THE BEST SHOPPING?

Until you have walked the **Magnificent Mile**, you won't really know just how huge of a shopping destination this section of Michigan Avenue is. Walk north on Michigan between the Chicago River and Oak Street, and your closet will lack for nothing. From reliable chains like Gap, Guess and Aldo; to high-end department stores such as Neiman Marcus and Bloomingdale's; to niche shops like the Apple Store and Niketown, you'll be hard-pressed to go home empty-handed.

If you're searching for something homegrown, break away to buzzing neighborhoods such as **Wicker Park**, where you can often buy local designers' goods at boutiques such as **Habit** and **Eskell**.

When it comes to shopping for clothes, girls might prefer to hit **American Girl Place** to outfit their dolls instead. Aside from the new wardrobe, girls can pamper their Samanthas and Kayas with a cut at the doll hair salon, afternoon tea at the café and family portraits at the photo studio—all are available at the massive Chicago shop, the company's first flagship store.

*155).* On the other hand, you have an irrepressible appetite for drinking and dancing the night away. (It's not for nothing that house music was born here.) You could go from lounging with the hip-and-hot at **J Bar** *(page 139)* to dancing at **Le Passage** *(page 137)* to sipping the city's best-mixed cocktails at **The Violet Hour** *(page 147),* all in one night.

If you're looking for that beloved local institution known as the dive bar, you won't have to look far. These holes-in-the-wall are usually tucked into any residential neighborhood, and many sport generic Old Style beer signs out front and the words "Zimne Piwo" or "Cerveza Fria" (cold beer in Polish and Spanish, respectively). Here, beer is cheap and plentiful, and the crowd varies from blue-collar regulars to hipsters, all seeking a low-key spot to drink and congregate with friends. Some, such as **Empty Bottle** *(page 153)* and **The Hideout** *(1354 W. Wabansia Ave., Bucktown, 773-227-4433; www.hideoutchicago.com)* have turned into destinations for music aficionados. By and large, many remain no-frills: perfect for when all you need is a cold one, and no pretense.

If it's summer, you don't want to be holed up—and for that, Chicago teems with beer gardens and bars with patios from which you can tipple and people-watch under the sun to your heart's content. Popular spots include **Sheffield's** *(page 140)* and **Nick's Beergarden** *(1516 N. Milwaukee Ave., Wicker Park, 773-252-1155; www.nicksbeergarden.com)*. Chances are that if you simply walk around neighborhoods like Lakeview or Wicker Park, you'll practically trip over an alfresco patio down any street.

MICHIGAN AVENUE BRIDGE

# WHAT'S THE EARLY HISTORY OF THE CITY?

Tucked in the heartland of the country, Chicago holds its own on both a national and international level. As the home of the skyscraper and an always-thriving cultural scene, this jewel by the lake is both gritty and cosmopolitan at once. Its short and storied history reflects the city it has become today: The Haymarket Riot of 1886 demanding legalized workers' rights happened here, and to this day, Chicago has a reputation as a hardworking, blue-collar town. The skyline, one of the most recognizable anywhere, continues to make global headlines by pushing forward with some of the world's most boundary-shattering architecture.

Centuries before buildings jutted into the sky, Chicago's lakeside location proved auspicious. The first Native Americans who found the spot recognized its strategic positioning long before French explorers Marquette and Joliet "discovered" it in the 1670s. The Chicago River, around which the city grew, was relatively small, but it provided the shortest portage from the Great Lakes—the largest body of fresh water on Earth—to the river systems connecting with the Mississippi, making it an ideal port for trade. The first permanent European settler of record here was Jean Baptiste Pointe DuSable, a Frenchman whose mother had been a slave taken from Haiti. (The DuSable Museum of African American History, in the Bronzeville neighborhood on the city's South Side, is named after him.) DuSable established a trading post on the north side of the river in the 1790s, but was driven away for a time by the Indian wars that followed the Revolutionary War. Not long after came the Fort Dearborn Massacre of 1812, a brutal battle resulting in the killing of more than 50 U.S. soldiers, women and children by Native Amerian tribes seeking to reclaim the land. Walk just south of the Michigan Avenue Bridge today, and you'll see the spot where the fort—abandoned by the soldiers and civilians who only made it a mile and a half away before the Native Americans caught up with them—once stood. The tribes' victory was short-lived, as Fort Dearborn was rebuilt and Europeans continued their mass migration here. By the 1830s, Native Americans had been driven across the Mississippi and forced out of the area, and the settlers started taking over. Chicago soon became the hub of a new national rail system, and the rest of the country's connection to the prairie, where both goods and people of all kinds came and went.

# HOW DID THE CITY REBUILD AFTER THE FIRE?

Just as Chicago was establishing itself as an important city, the Great Fire of 1871 set the city ablaze. Most historians now doubt that the inferno began as legend has it, by Mrs. O'Leary's cow kicking over a kerosene lamp. (Theories of the actual cause range from someone knocking the lamp over while trying to steal milk or while playing a craps game in Mrs. O'Leary's barn. Some aerospace scientists have even argued that the fire was caused by a meteor shower.) Regardless of how the fire started, it blazed on October 8, and three days later, driven by strong winds, had burned three and a half square miles—virtually all of Chicago—to the ground. Among the few buildings left standing was the Water Tower at Chicago and Michigan avenues, a then-modern sandstone structure containing a 135-foot-high standpipe that was constructed just two years earlier. The fire was considered one of the greatest U.S. disasters of the 19th century, but the almost immediate rebuilding that followed transformed Chicago from a poorly planned city into a bigger and better international hub of commerce. Between 1872 and

1879, more than 10,000 construction permits were issued here. With land in short supply and prices for lots at a premium, architects started thinking vertically. Wooden structures were banned within city limits by then, so they turned to steel, and by 1882 Chicago was home to the steel-framed, 10-story Montauk Building—the first to be called a skyscraper.

There was plenty of work in rebuilding the city after the fire, but a growing rift was deepening between business- and working-class segments of the population. Calls for legalized workers' rights, including a maximum eight-hour workday, started to flare. In 1886, the infamous Haymarket Riot took place at the corner of Randolph and Desplaines streets. A melee sparked by protesters resulted in the killing of 11 people and eventually led to the creation of May Day, a workers' holiday still observed the first day of May through much of Europe. (The eight-hour workday, however, is but a dream for many of Chicago's modern-day workers.)

Toward the end of the 19th century, Chicago began to earn a more cosmopolitan reputation. In 1893, with a new metropolis in place, the Chicago World's Fair (also known as the World's Columbian Exposition) gave the city a chance to strut its stuff. (One of several legends has it that a journalist who wanted New York to host the fair made a statement to "pay no attention to that windy city," earning Chicago its most popular nickname.) More than 27 million people from all parts of the world came to visit during the fair's six-month run, getting a firsthand look at new inventions like the Ferris wheel.

It was 200 new architectural gems built for the fair and designed in large part by local greats Daniel Burnham and Frederick Law Olmsted in the beaux arts style that gave Chicago a new level of international prestige. Still, the picturesque setting also provided a backdrop for tragedy: H.H. Holmes, considered the country's first serial killer, lured victims to his "World's Fair Hotel," which he built just for the expo. Inside was a gas chamber, dissection table and crematorium to dispose of bodies. Holmes admitted to 27 murders, though only nine were ever confirmed. (You can read more about how the lives of Holmes and Burnham horribly intertwined in Erik Larson's best-selling book *The Devil in the White City*.)

After the turn of the century, the city's racial makeup began to shift. Previously, the population predominantly consisted of white immigrants from Germany, Ireland, Poland and Scandinavia. But during World War I, African-Americans from the South began arriving in search of wartime industrial jobs. There was work to be had (in his 1916 poem *Chicago*, Carl Sandburg referred to the city as both "Hog Butcher for the World" and "City of the Big Shoulders" because of the thriving meatpacking industry and the strong willingness of the people here to bear the burden of this work). But for many African-Americans, jobs were not as plentiful as they had hoped. Tensions brewed and ethnic groups established strong territorial boundaries throughout the city. The eight-day Chicago Race Riot of 1919 was sparked by conflict between working-class whites and African-Americans—many of them war veterans who felt they deserved equal pay and the better housing they saw their white counterparts getting. By the riot's end, 38 people were dead, and more than 500 injured.

## HOW DID MODERN CHICAGO TAKE SHAPE?

By the 1920s, Prohibition-era gangsters like Al Capone had made Chicago synonymous with crime and corruption. Bootleggers made money hand over fist while police looked the other way, thanks to their handsome

CHICAGO BUNGALOWS

payoffs. Violence reached a peak when the rivalry between South Sider Al Capone and North Side gangster George "Bugs" Moran led to the St. Valentine's Day Massacre in 1929, when seven men—several from Moran's gang—were shot to death in a garage on Clark Street, presumably on Capone's orders. Today, there is no historical marker of the site, just an inconspicuous patch of grass. But the Biograph Theater—another landmark that became infamous in that era as the site where notorious bank robber John Dillinger was killed by the FBI in 1934—is still standing not far away and is now home to the renowned local Victory Gardens Theater.

One of the good things to come from the illegal speakeasies of the '20s was the birth of Chicago's jazz scene. (One of Al Capone's henchmen had a 25 percent stake in the legendary Green Mill Jazz Club at one time.) Louis Armstrong made his name in Chicago, coming up from New Orleans in 1919 to be a part of Joe "King" Oliver's band. Piano player Earl Hines soon joined him, and the records they made together revolutionized jazz.

In the early '40s, at the height of World War II, scientists secretly worked in an underground bunker beneath a football field on the University of Chicago campus, conducting experiments that led to the creation of the atomic bomb. That invention in turn led to the abrupt mushroom-cloud end to World War II in August 1945, when nuclear bombs were dropped by the United States on the Japanese cities of Hiroshima and Nagasaki.

The World War II years also produced another surge of movement north by Southern African-Americans, but this time, more found work. At the same time, music legends like Howlin' Wolf and Muddy Waters brought the blues to the South Side. When Elvis Presley duplicated their sound in the '50s, rock 'n' roll earned a spot in mainstream culture. In 1955, Chuck Berry recorded *Maybelline* at Chess Records, located at 2120 South Michigan Avenue—later immortalized in the Rolling Stones' song named for that address. (In 1965, the Stones again used the studio to lay down the basic tracks of *Satisfaction*, one of that era's biggest hits, just a year after Frank Sinatra sang about Chicago being *My Kind of Town*.)

CHICAGO LAKE FRONT

The '50s saw the expansion of nearby suburbs, and protests over Vietnam and civil rights hit Chicago hard during the '60s. Local riots following the assassination of Martin Luther King, Jr. left fires burning for days on the city's West Side. The 1968 National Democratic Convention was overshadowed by a battle between protesters and the police, augmented by the National Guard. Mayor Richard J. Daley (father of current mayor Richard M. Daley) promised that "law and order would be maintained," but protestors chanted, "The whole world is watching!" while violent street conflicts were broadcast on the newly powerful medium of television. Eight of the protestors—national figures Abbie Hoffman, Jerry Rubin and Bobby Seale among them—were charged with conspiracy in connection with the protests that eventually led to the notorious "Chicago Seven" trial. (Seale wound up being tried separately; the others were acquitted on the charge of conspiring to incite a riot, though five were convicted of incitement as individuals.)

## WHAT IMPACT DID URBAN RENEWAL HAVE?

Gentrification—and in some cases, a lack thereof—has been a significant part of Chicago's more recent history. Notorious public housing projects such as Cabrini Green—built near downtown between two affluent neighborhoods over a 20-year period ending in the 1960s—represented a model of "urban renewal" upon its completion. But Cabrini Green became a synonym for everything that could go wrong with this idea. "White flight" heightened the segregation of public housing, and almost simultaneously, factories providing the majority of work in the neighborhood closed and laid off thousands of people. Furthermore, the budget-crunched city cut back on services like transit, police presence and regular maintenance of the area. Vandalism and crime rose, leading law-abiding residents with any financial means to move away and leave the area to the poorest citizens, ripening it for increased problems. By the 1980s, the complex was so crime-riddled that even police were said to fear Cabrini Green.

But the project's prime location made it a diamond in the rough during

## WHAT ARE CHICAGO'S NICKNAMES?

Chicago has more nicknames than P. Diddy, including the Windy City, the City of the Big Shoulders and the City of Neighborhoods. The reason is that Chicago is all of these things and more—so here's how to keep the names straight.

### WINDY CITY

The origins of the Windy City moniker are unclear, but the most widely accepted theory is that it was a jab at the city's boastful, long-winded politicians. Nowadays, people use it to refer to the city's cutting winter winds that blow off Lake Michigan.

### THE SECOND CITY

The population of Los Angeles has surpassed that of Chicago, but the Second City nickname remains. The nickname is usually used to signify Chicago's second-billing status to New York, but don't mention that to proud Chicagoans—they'll insist that their hometown is second to none.

### CITY ON THE MAKE

Nelson Algren's 1951 essay is a love letter—a booze-soaked, beautifully imperfect love letter—to the city. In it, he famously wrote that "like loving a woman with a broken nose, you may well find lovelier lovelies. But never a lovely so real."

### CITY OF THE BIG SHOULDERS

Poet Carl Sandburg gave Chicago this nickname as a nod to the hard-working people who toiled away in its industrial heyday. (In the same poem, Sandburg gave the city another nickname, "Hog Butcher for the World.")

### CHI-TOWN

Chi-Town is simply a slang way of saying Chicago. Chicago native Kanye West raps, "Two words, Chi Town, South Side…" in his 2004 song *Two Words*. Many local radio DJs use the nickname, and some businesses include it in their names.

---

the housing boom that began in the '90s. In 1995, the federal Department of Housing and Urban Development took over management from the city and demolished many of the buildings to create a new, mixed-income approach in the neighborhood. New construction now includes everything from rental apartments and condos to a seniors-only complex and swanky single-family homes. Crime is down, but only time will tell if what's officially called the "Plan for Transformation" will improve things in the long term.

Meanwhile, other neighborhoods throughout Chicago continue to experience rapid change. The Southwest neighborhood of Pilsen—originally home to Czech immigrants and more recently to the city's largest Mexican-American community—became a haven for starving artists in the '90s because of its proximity to downtown and as an alternative to more expensive gallery districts. Developers soon caught on to the prime locale, and now families who have lived in the area for decades face moves from what is now an unaffordable neighborhood. Similar situations are occurring in other parts of the city, including longtime German neighborhood Lincoln Square on the Far North Side and Ukrainian Village on the near Northwest Side.

FARMER'S MARKET AT DALEY PLAZA

## HOW LONG HAVE THE DALEYS RULED CHICAGO?

Mayoral Term Limits? Not here. Chicago—a city known for a "vote early, vote often"-style of politics, is the largest U.S. city without them. Due to this, someone with the last name Daley has held the office here during 42 of the last 56 years.

The first, Richard J. Daley, was elected in 1955 and remained mayor until his death in 1976. Considered the last of the bosses of big-city politics, Daley was known as tough and hard-nosed even by loyalists, and racist, corrupt and cruel by his harshest critics. His son, Richard M. Daley (not-so-affectionately dubbed Richard II), was elected in 1989 and remains in office today despite his own brushes with corruption. The father-son combo are the only Chicago mayors to serve more than five terms. They're also the most influential duo to shape the city's modern political history.

During what many consider his "reign," Richard J. Daley was one of the most powerful politicians in the United States. His Chicago Democratic machine—a tightly run ship of controlled patronage positions—was pivotal in getting John F. Kennedy his narrow victory in Illinois during his 1960 run for president. (Chicago and the state of Illinois have always had a reputation for crooked politics, the most famous recent example being ex-Governor Rod Blagojevich's Senate-seat-selling scandal.) The Sears Tower (now Willis Tower), McCormick Place and O'Hare International Airport were all built during his tenure, as were some controversial expressways that critics said divided the city along racial lines. When the 1968 Democratic Convention came to Chicago and thousands of Vietnam War protesters came along with it, the infamous violent conflicts that ensued between police and the public were blamed on Daley. His own party criticized him during the convention for the "Gestapo-style" tactics police used, but his image managed to recover and he won re-election again in 1971.

Though his years in office were tumultuous, Richard J. is still credited with helping Chicago avoid the decline many other American cities endured during the 1960s and 1970s. Before his death from a heart attack in 1976, his efforts to revitalize downtown and largely keep the city's middle class from fleeing to the suburbs helped Chicago escape the fate of places like Cleveland, Detroit and New York.

It was 13 years later when Richard M. took the helm as the head of the city, and he's had his own stronghold on it ever since. He tends to run largely unopposed—mayoral elections seem barely noticed in Chicago, and he garnered more than 70 percent of the vote in 1999, 2003 and 2007. When Daley completes his current term, he'll beat his father's record of 21 years in office. Charges of bid-rigging, a corruption investigation by high-powered U.S. District Attorney Patrick Fitzgerald and even the covert destruction of small lakefront airport Meigs Field in the dark of night seem to be easily forgiven by voters. (Though the recent loss of the 2016 Olympic bid may leave the mayor, who staked his legacy on it, bruised.) They'd rather think about the fact that the Mayor has given them treats like lush Millennium Park and how he has revived just about every part of the city, from the South Loop to the notorious Cabrini Green projects (where you will now find attractive mixed housing).

## WHAT TIES DOES BARACK OBAMA HAVE TO CHICAGO?

Barack Obama first came to Chicago in 1985, at the age of 24, to work as a community organizer in poor neighborhoods. He left to attend Harvard Business School and then returned to work as an associate intern in Chicago with the country's oldest law firm, Sidley Austin. It was here that he met the future First Lady, then Michelle Robinson, who was assigned to be his mentor. By 1992, the two were married and had set up permanent residence on the South Side of Chicago and had two daughters, Malia and Sasha. Obama went to work practicing law as a civil rights attorney, teaching at the University of Chicago Law School and heading up Project Vote in Illinois, registering almost one-half of the 400,000 African-Americans in the state. In 1997, he ran for the Illinois State Senate and served seven years, leaving to become the third African-American to be elected to the U.S. Senate.

Obama first announced his plan to run for president in early 2007. His national headquarters occupied the 11th floor of a building located in Chicago at 233 North Michigan Avenue. He received many endorsements from fellow politicians, including Chicago Mayor Richard M. Daley, but one of his biggest supporters was Chicago talk show host Oprah Winfrey. After Obama defeated Senator Hillary Clinton to become the Democratic presidential nominee, Oprah headlined a $2,300 per-person fundraising event for him at the Sheraton Hotel & Towers.

On November 4, 2009, Barack Obama's election night celebration was held in Chicago at Grant Park. When the gates opened at 8:30 p.m., over 200,000 people (including, famously, a teary-eyed Oprah Winfrey and Jesse Jackson) poured into Hutchinson Field to hear him give his acceptance speech. It was a night that locals and people from all over the world will never forget. Banners were put up all over the city celebrating Chicago's hometown hero.

The Obamas still keep their residence in Hyde Park and the First Family still makes time for their city. In July 2009, the President—a die-hard White Sox fan—took time out of his busy schedule to travel to Busch Stadium in St. Louis to throw out the ceremonial first pitch at the MLB All Star Game. And in April 2010, when he threw out the first ceremonial pitch for Washington D.C.'s Nationals on Opening Day at Nationals Park, he wore a Nationals jacket—and a White Sox cap.

DOWNTOWN EL TRAIN

## WHAT ARE THE CITY'S GREEN INITIATIVES?

Say what you will about Mayor Richard M. Daley—and plenty of his critics do—but one thing most Chicagoans seem pleased with is his initiative to make the Windy City one of the greenest places in America.

More than half a million trees have been planted amidst the asphalt, highways and miles of concrete here since 1989, when Daley was first elected. In warmer months, workers seem to sprout up everywhere planting trees, pruning bushes and potting flowers. At different times during the growing cycle, an army of gardeners hits the city overnight to transform the planters with tulips in spring, lush greenery and flowers in summer, and mums and hardier plants in fall. You'll find greenery along roadsides, over underpasses, and in all kinds of high-traffic and high-profile places about town, plus a few of the less tony neighborhoods, too.

There's always been an attention to greenery in Chicago, whose official motto became "Urbs in Horto" (Latin for "City in a Garden") in 1837 when the city incorporated. In 1909, famed architect Daniel Burnham developed a plan for a string of parks connected by wide boulevards dubbed Chicago's "Emerald Necklace," akin to similar green-space plans in Boston and New York City.

Daley's plans go beyond keeping the city looking pretty. Environmental efforts include an extensive green roof program, started with a lush garden planted atop City Hall (consisting of more than 100 species of indigenous plants)—it's the first municipal green roof in the country. Today, it's estimated that there are more than four million square feet of high-in-the-sky gardens completed or under construction here, thanks to the Chicago Green Roof Grants Program. The roofs—which work as natural insulators, improve air quality and reduce rainwater runoff—dot Chicago atop everything from McDonald's locations and the Apple store to new office towers and private residences, many planted with the city's financial assistance or incentive.

Daley has said his goal is to see Chicago eventually use renewable energy for a quarter of all municipal operations. To do that he's lured solar-panel manufacturers to move to the city and ordered local government departments to do things like buy energy-efficient vehicles and forbid them from idling for more than five minutes, as well as repave alleys with asphalt that better absorbs water. Though it ironically sits on a former illegal dump site, the Chicago Center for Green Technology offers free seminars to the public, distributes rain barrels, and is home to organizations and businesses with an environmental bent. (Greencorps Chicago, the city's community gardening and job-training program, is here.)

There's still plenty of room for improvement. The city's recycling program—launched by beloved Mayor Harold Washington in the late 1980s—is considered a giant flop, with the overwhelming majority of garbage still not being fully recycled. (The city is trying to rectify the problem by launching new initiatives, including the Blue Cart program.) And Daley's blind eye to the high air pollutants coming from coal-burning power plants on the Southwest Side has raised eyebrows for years. Just mention the CTA to a local, and they're likely to launch into a tirade on what a dilapidated mess that system is (slow trains, buses that run on diesel). Daley's solution is to encourage people to bike everywhere, adding 25 miles of new bicycle lanes on various city streets, 200 miles of signed routes and 2,500 new bicycle racks. Recently, the Chicago Transit Authority also purchased 58 hybrid buses, which result in more fuel efficiency. The city also purchased new rail cars to replace some of the oldest cars.

DOWNTOWN CHICAGO

# CHICAGO STYLE

The nation's third largest city is notorious for its harsh winters and its love of sports. But there's much more to Chicago than subzero temperatures and professional sports. The city is headquarters for major international businesses from Boeing to Sears, and is home to a thriving media industry as well as finance and insurance hubs. Scores of ethnic neighborhoods make up the fabric of the city, and a rich history of scrappy (and sometimes unscrupulous) political figures give it a gritty edge. So what makes Chicago so unique? Read on for a snapshot of the Second City.

## WHAT KIND OF BUSINESSES MAKE CHICAGO THEIR HOME?

No longer the epicenter of the nation's meatpacking industry, Chicago now keeps its economy humming in other ways. Aviation has an anchor in Chicago, with the world headquarters for Boeing and United Airlines located in the Loop. One of the city's main sectors is food processing, which includes confections. Although big-time brands such as Brach's and Fannie May have stopped producing sweets in the city, the chocolaty aroma in River West comes from the nearby **Blommer Chocolate Factory** (*600 W. Kinzie St., River West, 800-621-1606*), confirming that the city still retains the "national candy capital" title.

Chicago is also a hub for the printing and publishing industries. It's the source for nationally distributed magazines, catalogs, educational materials, encyclopedias and specialized publications, ranking it second only to New York in the publishing industry.

The city's location in the middle of the country makes it a national transportation and distribution center, thanks to a substantial industrial base and a major inland port. Chicago also gets a boost from the finance and insurance sectors, as it is home to the Federal Reserve Bank, the Chicago Board of Trade and the Chicago Mercantile Exchange.

## WHERE ARE THE ETHNIC NEIGHBORHOODS?

Chicago's many ethnic enclaves retain their distinct character in a way that doesn't happen in other metropolises. Pilsen and Little Village, for example, are home to a vibrant Mexican-American community. Located on the Southwest Side, these conjoined neighborhoods are peppered with taquerías and bakeries—try a slice of classic Mexican tres leches cake at **Bombon Bakery** (*3748 W. 26th St., Little Village, 773-277-8777*). The **National Museum of Mexican Art** (*1852 W. 19th St., Pilsen, 312-738-1503*), as well as the numerous galleries that dot the area—especially around the Chicago Arts District (18th and Halsted streets in East Pilsen)—make the area an artists' hub.

A few blocks east of Pilsen is Chicago's **Chinatown** (*Wentworth Avenue and Cermak Road*). All along Wentworth and Archer avenues, you can find shops literally brimming with tchotchkes and wares, such as paper umbrellas, lanterns, jade statuettes and woks. Dining options are just as diverse—head for **Lao Szechuan** (*2172 S. Archer Ave., Chinatown, 312-326-5040*) for tongue-singeing Szechuan fare, or **Phoenix Restaurant** (*2131 S. Archer Ave., Chinatown, 312-328-0848*) for Sunday dim sum.

For a taste of Swedish heritage, head to the North Side's Andersonville. Locals wait in long lines at the **Swedish Bakery** (*5348 N. Clark St.,*

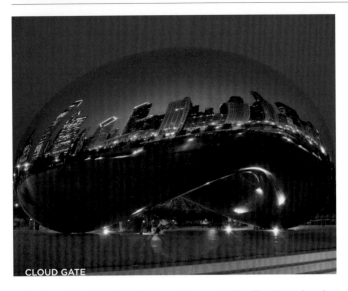

CLOUD GATE

*Andersonville, 773-561-8919)* to snatch up goodies like streusel and flourless chocolate cake. Crowds also pack **Ann Sather** restaurant *(5207 N. Clark St., Andersonville, 773-271-6677; www.annsather.com)* for a traditional breakfast of Swedish pancakes with tart lingonberries.

## WHAT'S THE BEST WAY TO BLEND LIKE A LOCAL?

If you want to fit in with the natives, you have to talk the talk. Chicago's inhabitants have words of their own for everyday things. Say "soda" and "sneakers" and you will probably be met with blank looks; instead use "pop" and "tennis shoes" (or "gym shoes"), respectively. The greater Chicago area is called Chicagoland in news broadcasts, but natives just refer to the outskirts as "the 'burbs." And Chicagoans don't refer to highways by their numbers, but by their names, such as the Kennedy (I-90), the Eisenhower (I-290) and the Dan Ryan (I-90/I-94).

Be sure to note that Chicago-ese has detailed diction: "Da Mare" (Chicagoan pronunciation of "the mayor") and "Hizzoner" ("his honor") are both nicknames for Mayor Daley. "Sassage" refers to the meaty pizza topping, while "sammitch" is a sandwich.

Beef up on Chicago-specific vocab, too. An "Italian beef" is roast beef cooked in its own juices and served on an Italian roll. You can order it "hot," with spicy giardiniera sauce; "wet," dunked in meat juice; or "sweet," with peppers. "The El" is what everyone calls the train system. Though it's short for "elevated train," the underground El trains get the same moniker. The "Friendly Confines" is another name for Wrigley Field. "Trixies" are native to Lincoln Park, and the twenty- or thirty-something ladies can be recognized by their bleach-blond hair and preppie attire, and are usually seen flirting with overgrown frat-boy types. (They're called Chads, by the way.)

## WHAT IS THE FASHION IN CHICAGO?

The Windy City's residents have never been known for their fashion sense. But that's changing. In 2006, Mayor Richard M. Daley, himself a fan of fedoras and rumpled suits, appointed a director of fashion arts and events and formed the Mayor's Fashion Council, a group of designers and industry leaders brought together to help promote local designers and boutiques. The council hosts the yearly **Fashion Focus Chicago**, the city's answer to New York's Fashion Week, and maintains **Chicago Fashion Resource** to connect well-dressed consumers with the city's designers and independent shops. Even though you'll see many locals decked out in not-so-flattering orange and navy Bears gear, with all of these initiatives, Chicago is aiming to become a major player on the fashion stage.

## WHICH MOVIES HAVE BEEN FILMED IN CHICAGO?

The city has long been a destination for filmmakers to shoot movies, and was the backdrop for Hitchcock's *North by Northwest* (1959), and *A Raisin in the Sun* (1961) starring a young Sidney Poitier. The '80s ushered in a made-in-Chicago film renaissance led by teen-flick king, the late John Hughes, who grew up in nearby Northbrook, Illinois. Hughes' *Ferris Bueller's Day Off*, *The Breakfast Club* and *Sixteen Candles* all were shot in the Windy City.

Meanwhile, another iconic '80s film, *The Blues Brothers*, showed the nitty-gritty city, including Maxwell Street Market. And *The Untouchables* relived Chicago's gangster past of Al Capone in the Brian de Palma film.

Today, the tape keeps on rolling in Chicago. Jennifer Aniston and Vince Vaughn filmed *The Break-Up* (2006); Angelina Jolie shot *Wanted* (2008); and Christian Bale donned the Batsuit for *Batman Begins* (2005) and *The Dark Knight* (2008). Part of the movie *Public Enemies* (2009), starring Johnny Depp in the role of gangster John Dillinger, was also filmed here and the movie had its world premiere downtown. Several movies were also filmed here in 2010, including *Transformers 3*, *The Dilemma*, starring Vince Vaughn and directed by Ron Howard, *Little Fockers* and *Nightmare on Elm Street*.

MUSEUM OF CONTEMPORARY ART

# SIGHTS TO SEE

No matter how old you are or what you like to do, you won't experience a dull moment in Chicago. The city has world-class museums (the Art Institute of Chicago and Field Museum among them); inviting parks; amazing architecture; and colorful neighborhoods inhabited by famously friendly Midwesterners. Add to that the sparkling, expansive Lake Michigan, and you have a magical place.

## GOLD COAST/STREETERVILLE

The name speaks for itself. The Gold Coast shines with world-class retail (the gilded northern edge of Michigan Avenue and Oak Street) and gorgeous mansions (especially along Astor Street). Homeowners in this tony residential neighborhood know the area's pedigree and oblige by maintaining gorgeous homes north of Division Street and east of State Street, while ladies who lunch gather at old-fashioned hang-outs like the Drake Hotel and shop at Chanel. Streeterville, the neighborhood just south of the Gold Coast, is a gentrifying mish-mash of chains and shops along Michigan Avenue and '70s-era hole-in-the-wall bars, with graduate schools for Northwestern University, University of Chicago and Loyola University thrown into the mix.

### JOHN HANCOCK CENTER

875 N. Michigan Ave., Gold Coast, 312-751-3681, 888-875-8439;
www.hancock-observatory.com

It may not be the first or even the second or third tallest building in Chicago, but the world-famous Hancock, which towers over the city at 1,127 feet, still holds the record for being the world's highest residence (condos begin on the 49th floor). Zoom up to the always-packed 94th-floor observatory for a view that can extend to four states on a clear day. Then check out the city's only open-air skywalk to feel the famous Chicago wind. Don't worry about taking a plunge; though the skywalk is windowless, NASA-tested stainless-steel screens will prevent you from falling. Before you leave, be sure to skim the wall murals to read about how the city went from the ashes of the Great Chicago Fire to a booming metropolis. For a less-touristy option, visit the 95th-floor Signature Room's bar (www.signatureroom.com) to enjoy the same stunning vista of the city as you sip a cocktail.
*Admission: adults $15, children 3-11 $10, children under 3 free. Daily 9 a.m.-11 p.m.*

### MUSEUM OF CONTEMPORARY ART

220 E. Chicago Ave., Gold Coast, 312-280-2660;
www.mcachicago.org

Housed in a rather uninspired building between Lake Michigan and the Water Tower, the MCA is home to 2,345 pieces in its permanent collection, including work by Dan Flavin and Lee Bontecou. The interior space can be daunting, with wide hallways and an unusual eyelid-shaped staircase with a fish pond at the bottom that is worth viewing on its own. But despite its size, the MCA won't take long to see (perhaps an hour or two to review the museum's first-rate contemporary experimental works) before you'll want to grab some lunch at the museum's café, operated by chef Wolfgang Puck of Spago fame. If you're around on the first Friday of the month, the museum holds a happening event where, for a $16 admission ($11 for advanced tickets), you can check out the latest exhibit, enjoy live entertainment, nibble on tasty Wolfgang Puck hors d'oeuvres and sip cocktails (you can purchase extra drink tickets). Local singles pack the joint on First Fridays, which has become a meat market for culture vultures on the prowl.

*Admission: adults $12, seniors and students $7, children 12 and under free. Free Tuesday. Tuesday 10 a.m.-8 p.m., Wednesday-Sunday 10 a.m.-5 p.m. First Fridays: $16; first Friday of the month 6-10 p.m.*

## NAVY PIER
**600 E. Grand Ave., Streeterville, 312-595-7437, 800-595-7437; www.navypier.com**

Nearly 200 navy planes remain submerged in Lake Michigan as a result of the training once done at Navy Pier. Reborn in 1995 after years of disuse, the tourist-packed pier and lakefront area have become as emblematic of Chicago as the skyscraper. The pier contains a mall (nothing notable there) as well as a 3-D IMAX theater, a small ice-skating rink, the Chicago Shakespeare Theater, the Smith Museum of Stained Glass Windows (seriously, it's a lot better than it sounds), and the Chicago Children's Museum (head here quickly, as the museum is planning to move into its own 100,000-square-foot structure in Daley Bicentennial Plaza at 337 E. Randolph St. in the next few years). The museum has plenty of hands-on but not-so-messy exhibits for the kids, including Dinosaur Expedition, which re-creates a trip to the Sahara to dig for fossils. There is also an urban "neighborhood" for toddlers to practice driving a city bus or shopping for groceries. Adults can have fun at the outdoor beer garden or on any number of dinner cruises that leave from the docks, which offer a lakeside view of the pier's 150-foot-high Ferris wheel and the Chicago skyline beyond.

*Memorial Day-Labor Day, Sunday-Thursday 10 a.m.-10 p.m., Friday-Saturday 10 a.m.-midnight; Labor Day-November, Monday-Thursday 10 a.m.-8 p.m., Friday-Saturday 10 a.m.-midnight; November-March, Monday-Thursday 10 a.m.-8 p.m., Friday-Saturday 10 a.m.-10 p.m., Sunday 10 a.m.-7 p.m.; April-Memorial Day, Sunday-Thursday 10 a.m.-8 p.m., Friday-Saturday 10 a.m.-10 p.m.*

## OLD CHICAGO WATER TOWER AND PUMPING STATION
**806 N. Michigan Ave., Gold Coast, 312-742-0808**

After the Great Chicago Fire of 1871 roared through the city, the Old Chicago Water Tower and Pumping Station were the only public structures left unscathed. The Water Tower now houses City Gallery (*Monday-Saturday 10 a.m.-6:30 p.m., Sunday 10 a.m.-5 p.m.*), which features Chicago-themed photography exhibits. The Pumping Station is now the base of the Chicago Water Works Visitor Center and the Lookingglass Theatre Company (*312-337-0665; www.lookingglasstheatre.org*), which was co-founded by David "Ross from *Friends*" Schwimmer (who also writes and directs here). Try to catch a Lookingglass production by Tony Award-winning director Mary Zimmerman. Her visually stunning shows, such as *The Arabian Nights* and *Argonautika*, set the place on fire (metaphorically speaking, of course).

# LOOP/WEST LOOP

Chicago's heart is in the Loop. It's home to the city's government, commerce and civic cultural venues. Visitors typically start their tour of the city in the shadows of the Loop's towering skyscrapers, sometimes from inside an El train, which lumbers through it. Keep in mind that after 5:30 p.m., office

THE ART INSTITUTE OF CHICAGO

drones head home and the area becomes a bit quiet, despite recent efforts by the city (Millennium Park, Theater District revitalization) to lure locals and tourists after dark. The West Loop encompasses the area west of the Loop across the Chicago River, including Greektown; the Randolph Row restaurant stretch; and the gritty-trendy Fulton Market, Chicago's answer to New York's Meatpacking District. The area is home to Harpo Studios, right off Washington Boulevard, where *The Oprah Winfrey Show* is filmed until the show's final episode on September 9, 2011.

## THE ART INSTITUTE OF CHICAGO
111 S. Michigan Ave., Loop, 312-443-3600; www.artic.edu/aic
The Art Institute is best known for its vast stock of Impressionist works. But with the spring 2009 opening of The Modern Wing, it now also houses collections of modern art, photography, and architecture and design. With this addition of 264,000 square feet, the Art Institute is the second-largest art museum (in square feet) in the United States at approximately 1.2 million square feet. Among the museum's permanent collection of approximately a quarter million pieces (in ten curatorial departments) are iconic works such as *American Gothic*, *A Sunday on La Grande Jatte* and *Nighthawks*. The Modern Wing has its own full-service entrance.
*Admission: adults $18, children, seniors and students $12; children under 14 free. Free admission from 5 p.m.-8 p.m. on Thursdays. Monday-Wednesday 10:30 a.m.-5 p.m., Thursday-Friday 10:30 a.m.-8 p.m., Saturday-Sunday 10 a.m.-5 p.m.*

## CHICAGO CULTURAL CENTER
78 E. Washington St., Loop, 312-744-6630; www.cityofchicago.org
While locals head to the Cultural Center for the free art exhibits, daily concerts and other performances, visitors go to gape at its magnificent Tiffany stained-glass dome, which is the biggest in the world. If you zoom your camera in on the center of the 1897 dome, which was refurbished in 2008, you might be able to make out the signs of the zodiac. After craning

CHICAGO CULTURAL CENTER

your neck to see the dome, make like a native and see if any of the art offerings are worth a look—or just escape the downtown crowds with a quick bite at the center's Randolph Café.

*Monday-Thursday 8 a.m.-7 p.m., Friday 8 a.m.-6 p.m., Saturday 9 a.m.-6 p.m., Sunday 10 a.m.-6 p.m.*

## GRANT PARK
### 337 E. Randolph St., Loop

Grant Park's Buckingham Fountain is best known for its role in the opening credits for the TV show *Married...With Children*, but don't dismiss the beloved Chicago site as a tourist trap. Come on the hour to see one of the world's largest fountains and its elaborate 20-minute water display (Daily 8 a.m.-11 p.m., the last starting at 10 p.m.), which features colored lights and music at dusk and a water jet stream at the center that shoots 150 feet high (mid-April to mid-October, weather permitting). Grant Park also hosts many popular outdoor festivals in the summer, including the Taste of Chicago, a massive annual event that offers samples from hundreds of the city's restaurants, and Blues Fest, a yearly celebration featuring preeminent blues artists. Music fans also flock to Grant Park each August for Lollapalooza, a three-day extravaganza that's featured big-name acts such as Lady Gaga and Kings of Leon.

## MILLENNIUM PARK
### Michigan Avenue near Randolph Street, Loop;
### www.millenniumpark.org

Widely regarded as one of the best public works projects in the city's recent memory, Millennium Park is fast becoming synonymous with Chicago. Once an eyesore filled with railroad tracks and parking lots, it's now home to the Frank Gehry-designed Jay Pritzker Pavilion (which displays the architect's well-known style of curved steel and hosts free concerts all summer long), and Crown Fountain, which is a set of two large faces (the likenesses of 1,000 Chicagoans rotate through the display) opposite one another

## WHAT IS THE BEST WAY TO SEE CHICAGO IN ONE DAY?

Start your day early with a cup of Chicago's own **Intelligentsia** coffee at the **Monadnock Building** (*53 W. Jackson Blvd., Loop, 312-922-1890; www. intelligentsiacoffee.com*), then head to **Millennium Park** to see your reflection in "The Bean" and check out the "spitting" faces at Crown Fountain. Next-door neighbor **the Art Institute of Chicago** will give you a chance to look at more works. See the man behind the sunflowers in Vincent van Gogh's *Self-Portrait*, and you'll notice the artist's seemingly mismatched dirty-blond hair and red beard. Also take a peak at Monet's *Stacks of Wheat* series, which depicts the eponymous wheat through different seasons. Be sure to leave time to explore the spectacular Modern Wing, which was competed in May 2009. If you are more interested in dinasours or diamonds than art, the **Field Museum** is also nearby, as is the **Shedd Aquarium**.

When you're ready for lunch, The Modern Wing has three eateries, including **Terzo Piano**, headed by Spiaggia chef Tony Mantuano. Or grab some upscale pub grub at **The Gage**, which is across from **Millennium Park** on Michigan Avenue.

Head back north and stroll along the **Magnificent Mile**. Stop in the Hancock Center's **Signature Room** for a drink and some of the best views in the city before catching dinner in any of the **Gold Coast** restaurants.

that spit water into a play area that kids love to splash around in when the weather is warm. In fact, today the park is one of the city's most popular attractions, especially its stainless-steel sculpture Cloud Gate, which acts as a fun-house mirror from underneath and reflects the city's skyline on the outside. Just don't ask locals about the sculpture by name (they won't have any idea what you're talking about)—everyone calls it "The Bean" because the sculpture is shaped like a kidney bean.
*Daily 6 a.m.-11 p.m.*

## MONADNOCK BUILDING
**53 W. Jackson Blvd., Loop, 312-922-1890;**
**www.monadnockbuilding.com**
It's funny that the Monadnock Building is considered a masterpiece in the Chicago School of architecture, because it's like two very separate buildings in one: John Wellborn Root designed the northern section, the tallest commercial building to be supported primarily by brick walls; and firm Holabird & Roche designed the southern section, which uses steel-frame construction. There's also the seemingly incongruous design mix of Chicago School simplicity with Egyptian elements. Put it all together, and you have a visual representation of one building tradition's end and the beginning of another. Today in the Monadnock you'll find a mix of tenants, including old-school Frank's Barber Shop, the city's finest cup of joe at Intelligentsia and women's boutique Florodora.

## THE OPRAH WINFREY SHOW
**1058 W. Washington Blvd., West Loop, 312-591-9222; www.oprah.com**
Oprah moved to the Windy City in 1984 to be on TV morning show *AM Chicago*, and the city has considered her as one of its own ever since. If you're an Oprah fan, you'll likely be on the hunt for tickets to see one of her final shows. The show's 25th season, which ends in September 2011, will

# WHAT ARE THE CITY'S BEST PUBLIC ART WORKS?

Some of the city's most famous artwork is spread out across parks and plazas, making Chicago widely acclaimed for its commitment to public art. What's better than free art? The fact that you can reach all of these by foot in an afternoon stroll.

❶ Start with **The Four Seasons** (*JPMorgan Chase Tower, Dearborn and Monroe streets, Loop*). Russian artist Marc Chagall is known for his paintings, but Chicagoans know him for his 14-foot-high, 10-foot-wide and 70-foot-long mosaic mural. This is a bright spot among downtown's business offices; the piece is adorned with hand-chipped stone and glass pieces in more than 250 pastel colors. Chagall used elements from his surrealist paintings to depict six city scenes in the mural, with couples embracing, suns shining and birds flying.

❷ Walk north on Dearborn Street three blocks until you hit Washington Street, where the **Picasso** (*Daley Plaza, 50 W. Washington St., Loop; www. thedaleycenter.com*) stands tall. When this 162-ton, 50-foot-high steel sculpture by Pablo Picasso was unveiled in 1967, residents scratched their heads. They couldn't figure out what the heck it was. (Picasso didn't help by leaving it untitled.) Your reaction will likely depend on your own love or hate for modern art. Though many at the time deemed it an eyesore, "The Picasso" jump-started an interest in public art and prompted the city to add more pieces to its outdoor gallery. People still wonder what the abstract sculpture is supposed to be—a woman? A horse? A woman who looks like a horse?

❸ Head west on Washington Street for about five blocks and when you get to Michigan Avenue, **Cloud Gate** (*Millennium Park, 55 N. Michigan Ave., Loop; www.millenniumpark.org*) won't even need an introduction. Millennium Park, just across Michigan Avenue, is home to this 66-foot-long, 33-foot-high stainless-steel kidney bean-shaped installation, whose official title is Cloud Gate. To locals, it's "The Bean." Gaze at the 110-ton behemoth to see Michigan Avenue's buildings and the blue skies above them reflected brightly in seamless silver. Or walk under its 12-foot-high arches to see your own reflection (and that of those around you) stare back like a kaleidoscopic mishmash on the Bean's shiny underbelly. This marks British artist Anish Kapoor's first site-specific installation in the U.S. and it's one of the city's newest works. Completed in 2004, "The Bean" is an essential part of an art lover's diet.

❹ Make your way a few steps southwest of Cloud Gate, and you'll practically trip over **Crown Fountain** (*Millennium Park, 55 N. Michigan Ave., Loop; www.millenniumpark.org*). This pair of 50-foot glass blocks project gigantic faces across from one another as they "spit" water into a shared shallow reflecting pool. Instead of using traditional gargoyles for his modern 2004 fountain, Spanish artist Jaume Plensa decided to feature the faces of 1,000 Chicagoans, each appearing one by one on large LED screens. The water is on from mid-spring through mid-fall (weather permitting), when kids splash around in the pool, while the faces peer from the towers all year long.

Public Art Walking Tour

❻ In ancient Greece, people met at the Agora, or marketplace. Polish artist Magdalena Abakanowicz's installation, **Agora** (*Grant Park, Michigan Avenue at Roosevelt Road, South Loop*) is also a meeting place, where you can interact with the 106 nine-foot-tall headless, armless humanoid figures. The work represents the relationship of Chicago's people to its city, with the figures dwarfed by the high-rise buildings behind them. From afar the headless "people" look all the same, but up close the iron-case figures show individuality in their wrinkled and tree bark-like surfaces.

JAY PRITZKER PAVILION AT MILLENNIUM PARK

be its last. Tickets have always been hard to get but here are some tips: Call the Audience Department, but have your dialing finger ready and don't let busy signals stop you. The phone lines close during the summer but reopen in early August. Also, call the reservation line during off hours, as it's most busy after a broadcast. You can also try getting last-minute tickets through the show's website—screeners are always looking for people to attend shows based on the day's topic. You must be 18 years or older to attend a taping and have a valid photo ID. If all else fails, you can simply check out The Oprah Store (*37 N. Carpenter St., 312-633-2100*) where you can take home O's favorite things.

## RICHARD J. DALEY CENTER AND PLAZA
### 50 W. Washington St., Loop
Named after the city's former mayor (who was current mayor Richard M.'s father), the building is literally rusting away—it's built from a compound that uses rust to strengthen the building's façade and give it its brown color. You won't want to go in the building, given the traffic courtrooms and civic offices inside, but outside is a plaza dominated by an untitled 50-foot sculpture by Pablo Picasso, the artist's personal gift to the city. The plaza is kept busy by farmers' markets in the warmer months and festivals in winter, including the perennial Christkindlmarket (*www.christkindlmarket.com*), an alfresco German market leading up to Christmas, which is a great place to sip hot apple cider and eat potato pancakes as you admire the tall, sparkly Christmas tree in the plaza.
*Farmers' Market: May-October, Thursday 7 a.m.-3 p.m. Christkindlmarket: November 27-December 24, times vary.*

## ROOKERY
### 209 S. LaSalle St., Loop
The Rookery is the city's oldest high-rise and widely considered the master-piece of famed architects John Wellborn Root and Daniel Burnham, who

## WHAT ARE THE CAN'T-MISS FIRST VISIT SIGHTS?

**Lake Michigan**: One of the city's biggest surprises is its great beaches. Locals love hitting Lake Michigan's 26 miles of free lakefront during summer. On a typical sunny Saturday, you'll see hundreds of Chicagoans at the beach, soaking up the sun, playing volleyball, running and barbecuing.

**Millennium Park**: Millennium Park has become synonymous with Chicago, home to the Frank Gehry-designed Jay Pritzker Pavilion, Crown Fountain and stainless-steel sculpture Cloud Gate, which acts as a fun-house mirror and reflects the city's skyline.

**Willis Tower Skydeck**: The Sears Tower may have a new name, but it is still the tallest building in America (and currently the second tallest in the world).

housed their offices in this grand 1886 building. The structure represents a transition between the use of masonry and metal construction techniques, with the outer walls supported mostly by masonry piers and the inner frame built of steel and iron. In 1905, Frank Lloyd Wright injected some of his trademark Prairie School design into the building when he remodeled its gorgeous glass-domed, two-story lobby. He added white marble and gold-leaf trim and let more light seep through the dome, all of which make it a bright, airy space that gleams when the sun hits it.

### WILLIS TOWER

**233 S. Wacker Drive, Loop, 312-875-9696; www.theskydeck.com**

No other building says Chicago more than the Sears, er, Willis Tower. The name may have recently changed but this iconic building is still the tallest building in America (and currently the second tallest in the world) and defines the city's skyline at 1,450 feet and 110 stories high. The Skydeck on the 103rd floor gives a view of 40 to 50 miles out on a clear day, enabling you to see Michigan, Indiana, Illinois and Wisconsin. It also offers interactive multi-language kiosks and exhibits. The recently added Skydeck Ledge features glass boxes extending four feet from the Skydeck that deliver a stomach churning view of the city 1,353 feet below. Although there are displays on the building's history to keep you busy while waiting to snag an elevator to get to the Skydeck, avoid the long, long lines by heading here before the observation deck opens, or after 5 p.m., when it tends to be less crowded. *Admission: adults $15.95, children 3-11 $11, children under 3 free. April-September, daily 9 a.m.-10 p.m.; October-March, daily 10 a.m.-8 p.m.*

## SOUTH LOOP/PRINTERS ROW

The South Loop is a condo-riddled neighborhood that, up until about fifteen years ago, was a no man's land of abandoned warehouses. Rapid gentri-fication in the form of new restaurants and slick new buildings led to its current status as some of the hottest blocks in city real estate (even Mayor Richard Daley lives in the neighborhood). Printers Row is a small portion of the South Loop—technically, it's just the stretch of Dearborn Street between Congress Parkway and Polk Street. This two-block area was the Midwest's printing hub in the late 1800s, and it boasts some architectural fans dreams: The Dearborn Street Station and the Pontiac and Donohue buildings are all beauties.

# WHAT IS THE BEST WAY TO SEE CHICAGO IN THREE DAYS?

Begin your second day in Chicago at the **Willis (Sears) Tower**, arriving before it opens at 10 a.m. to get a jump on the lines to zip up to the observatory. At 1,353 feet, the observatory offers a view of Michigan, Wisconsin and Indiana when the clouds are at bay. After seeing Chicago by land, look at it by sea—or rather, river. Hop on a riverboat tour along the **Chicago River** to see the city's famous architecture. Grab lunch at River North pizzeria **La Madia**, which often has great specials.

After lunch take a walk through the **Lincoln Park Zoo**, one of the country's only free zoos. There you can see the usual bears and lions and the not-so-usual snow leopards and sloths. You'll have time to kill before seeing a nighttime improv show at the legendary **Second City** (be sure to purchase tickets in advance because shows consistently sell out). Spend that waiting time wandering through the great nearby neighborhoods of **Lincoln Park** and **Old Town**. Armitage Avenue is an excellent independent-boutique thoroughfare in Lincoln Park. While you're in Lincoln Park, stop by **1154 Lill Studio** *(904 W. Armitage Ave., Lincoln Park, 773-477-5455; www.1154lill.com)* to customize your own purse. For a Chi-Town souvenir, forget tacky tchotchkes and instead head to **Art Effect**, an eclectic shop that carries everything from clothing to ibride trays to a parking meter alarm. Stop at **Adobo Grill** *(1610 N. Wells St., Old Town, 312-266-7999; www.adobogrill.com)*, a Mexican eatery next door to the Second City theater that has delicious guacamole and margaritas. You'll want to arrive at Second City early to wait in line for a table or even just a chair; seating is first-come, first-served, so early fans of comedy will get the best tables. But don't jet out once the show is over; the jokesters put on a free improv set after the last performance every night but Friday.

For your last day, plan ahead and get tickets for bleacher seats at **Wrigley Field**. As you cheer on the Cubbies, resist the urge to order a ballpark dog—save your appetite instead for authentic Chicago hot dogs with the works at the **Wieners Circle** *(2622 N. Clark St., Lincoln Park, 773-477-7444)*. Be sure to ask nicely; the sassy staff is known to dish out insults with the cheese fries (no doubt their patience was strained long ago by drunken Cubs fans and the area's weekend revelers).

To see a less-touristy side of the city, travel southwest to **Bucktown** and **Wicker Park**. Fashionistas will point their Choos in the direction of **p.45** to browse racks of clothing from 3.1 Phillip Lim and local designer Lara Miller. For dinner, try **Coast Sushi Bar** *(2045 N. Damen Ave., Bucktown, 773-235-5775; www.coastsushibar.com)* for some of the city's best sushi (bring your own booze); or **Restaurant Takashi** for immaculately prepared contemporary American/Japanese fare. Then head to **HotChocolate** *(1747 N. Damen Ave., Bucktown, 773-489-1747; www.hotchocolatechicago.com)* for delicious hot chocolate with housemade marshmallows. The Black & Tan (one part hot fudge, two parts medium hot chocolate) is so rich, it'll count as dessert.

Try to reserve tickets for a show at the renowned **Steppenwolf Theatre** or a production from the city's many storefront troupes (ones to check out: in-your-face **Profiles Theatre**, *4147 N. Broadway, Uptown, 773-549-1815, www.profilestheatre.org;* or the rockin' **House Theatre of Chicago**).

FIELD MUSEUM OF NATURAL HISTORY

## ADLER PLANETARIUM

1300 S. Lake Shore Drive, South Loop (Museum Campus),
312-922-7827; www.adlerplanetarium.org

If a fear of flying took you out of contention for a career as an astronaut, then head to the Western Hemisphere's first planetarium. Interactive exhibits like Shoot for the Moon, which features Apollo 13 astronaut Jim Lovell's fully restored Gemini 12 spacecraft and some of his effects, will let you envision what your life might have been like. Stargazers should make their way to the Doane Observatory for a look through the largest public telescope in the area, but to appreciate the heavenly Chicago skyline instead, step onto the North and South terraces.

*Admission: adults $10, Chicago residents $8, children 3-14 $6, Chicago residents 3-14 $5. Monday-Friday 10 a.m.-4 p.m., Saturday-Sunday 10 a.m.-4:30 p.m.; mid-June-Labor Day, daily 9:30 a.m.-6 p.m.*

## FIELD MUSEUM OF NATURAL HISTORY

Roosevelt Road and Lake Shore Drive, South Loop (Museum Campus),
312-922-9410; www.fieldmuseum.org

Lurking in the grand Stanley Field Hall that greets visitors at this historic museum is Sue—at 42 feet long and 13 feet high at the hips, it is the most complete, best-preserved and largest Tyrannosaurus rex fossil ever discovered. Unearthed in South Dakota in 1990, Sue (named after the woman who found her) is no plastic replica (though the creature's skull is so heavy the real thing is housed upstairs while a stand-in graces the actual body), and the skeleton's placement near the entry is a reminder of the museum's commitment to displaying authentic remnants from nature's past. Spread out over 400,000 square feet, the museum also holds popular exhibits on ancient Egypt as well as artifacts and wilderness scenes from all parts of the globe. The museum's newly renovated Grainger Hall of Gems features rare jewels, gold objects and designer creations, including a collection from Tiffany & Co.

*Admission: adults $15, seniors and students $12, children 3-11 $10. Daily 9 a.m.-5 p.m. Additional charge for special exhibits.*

## PRAIRIE AVENUE HISTORIC DISTRICT
### 1800 and 1900 blocks of South Prairie Avenue, South Loop

Chicago's wealthiest denizens set up mansions in this South Side neighborhood after the Great Chicago Fire of 1871. Biz whiz Marshall Field and inventor George M. Pullman were among a select few who had Prairie Avenue addresses. Many of the houses were demolished in the 20th century, but a few remain. The Glessner House (*1800 S. Prairie Ave., 312-326-1480; www.glessnerhouse.org*), built by Henry Hobson Richardson for businessman John J. Glessner, has a Romanesque Revival-style façade and is one of the last remaining Prairie Avenue mansions. Walk around inside to see more than 6,000 artifacts, including Arts and Crafts Movement furniture and rare art glass. Built in 1836, the Clarke House Museum (*1855 S. Indiana Ave., 312-326-1480*) is the city's oldest building and it remains standing, having survived fires and two moves. The Greek Revival structure was owned by hardware dealer Henry B. Clarke and shows what life was like for a middle-class family in Chicago before the Civil War.

*Single-house admission: adults $10, seniors and students $9, children 5-12 $6, children under 5 free; combo admission: adults $15, seniors and students $12, children 5-12 $8, children under 5 free. Free Wednesday. Glessner tour: Wednesday-Sunday 1 p.m., 3 p.m. Clarke tour: Wednesday-Sunday noon, 2 p.m.*

## SHEDD AQUARIUM
### 1200 S. Lake Shore Drive, South Loop (Museum Campus), 312-939-2438; www.sheddaquarium.org

More than 32,000 animals swim, slither or crawl around this underwater wonderland, which is one of the largest and best indoor aquariums in the world. You can't miss the Caribbean Reef, a circular 90,000-gallon habitat filled with sea turtles, moray eels, sharks, rays and plenty of colorful fish, where you can watch a diver feed the sea creatures while speaking to guests. Head over to Wild Reef, where only five inches of glass separate you from more than two dozen sharks. Don't miss the new Fantasea water show where you can see dolphins, belugas and penguins perform stunts.

*Admission: adults $24.95, children 3-11 $17.95. Labor Day-Memorial Day, Monday-Friday 9 a.m.-5 p.m., Saturday-Sunday 9 a.m.-6 p.m. Memorial Day-Labor Day, daily 9 a.m.-6 p.m*

# OLD TOWN/RIVER NORTH/RIVER WEST

River North lies just west of Streeterville, and in spirit, it's not much different: the area is a tourist's haven for its preponderance of deep-dish pizza places like Pizzeria Uno, but it's also home to more upscale restaurants and lounges, boutique hotels, dress-code-enforcing clubs and tons more shopping. On the western edge of River North—under the El train tracks, on Franklin Street between Chicago Avenue and Kinzie Street—major chains give way to established art galleries. In-the-know Chicagoans take it across the river to River West for a more urban setting and less crowded but chic restaurants such as Japonais, though the neighborhood is largely residential. Old Town, which is north of River North, is also a residential area with some historic gems and includes the Second City improv theater, the Chicago History Museum, and plenty of neighborhood restaurants.

BROOKFIELD ZOO

## CHICAGO HISTORY MUSEUM

1601 N. Clark St., Old Town, 312-642-4600; www.chicagohs.org

As Chicago's oldest cultural institution, the Chicago History Museum predates the Great Chicago Fire of 1871. And the CHM gets better with age. A major 2006 renovation provided new galleries, which feature shows such as Chicago: Crossroads of America. The comprehensive permanent exhibit looks at the city's many neighborhoods, and its disasters and innovations. The CHM tries to go beyond stuffy historical documents with past exhibits like Chicago@40: The Band and Its City, an homage to the legendary soft-rock band, and Chic Chicago: Couture Treasures from the Chicago History Museum, a collection of dazzling gowns worn by local fashionistas, including the first couture dress designed for an uncorseted woman as well as modern designer pieces by the likes of Versace.

*Admission: adults $14, seniors and students $12, children 12 and under free. Free Monday. Monday-Saturday 9:30 a.m.-4:30 p.m., Sunday noon-5 p.m.*

## CHICAGO TRIBUNE TOWER

435 N. Michigan Ave., River North, 312-222-3232, 800-874-2863; www.chicagotribune.com

When the Chicago Tribune needed a bigger space in 1922, the newspaper held a contest challenging architects to create the world's most beautiful office building for the prosperous paper. The unanimous winning entry: A distinctive 36-story Gothic skyscraper topped with dramatic floodlights from New York City architects John Mead Howells and Raymond M. Hood. To ensure the tower's grandeur, embedded into its lower elevations are fragments from well-known buildings throughout the world, including a chunk of the Great Wall of China. Although you can't tour inside the tower, which now serves as the Tribune Company's headquarters, its ground-level radio room lets the public peek at live broadcasts of WGN talk radio, and you can peruse the Chicago Tribune Store *(312-222-3080)* to buy an

# WHERE IS CHICAGO'S GREATEST ARCHITECTURE?

The Great Fire of 1871 leveled nearly everything in Chicago, so the city had to rebuild from scratch. It needed a new architectural vision and construction technique (wood buildings weren't so resilient the last time around), all of which set the stage for innovation. The ensuing building boom in the 1880s attracted creative architects, and that's when the city's reputation as an architectural hub started.

Almost 130 years later, Chicago maintains that reputation. The world's best architects, including Ludwig Mies van der Rohe, Frank Lloyd Wright and Frank Gehry, passed through the city, leaving their marks in the form of towering structures of steel, glass and concrete. The city continues to be at the forefront with architects like Renzo Piano and Frank Gehry, who left their mark on the Art Institute's Modern Wing, and Millenium Park. Here are some of the most celebrated architectural wonders:

### FRANK GEHRY: PRITZKER PAVILION
**Millennium Park, 55 N. Michigan Ave., Loop; www.millenniumpark.org**
Gehry's 2004 Pritzker Pavilion is a remarkable sight. The 120-foot-high outdoor bandshell shows the architect's trademark use of bright steel to make buildings look like free-form sculpture. The stainless-steel layers curl upward from the stage like shaved chocolate, and a steel criss-crossed trellis covers the venue seating and lawn below. Known for his contorted steel structures, Gehry made this one of his most accessible and functional buildings. His adjacent BP Bridge echoes the unique design.

### BURHAM & ROOT: RELIANCE BUILDING
**32 N. State St., Loop**
Chicago became the birthplace of skyscrapers because of buildings like this Burnham & Root 1890 masterpiece. Its glass-covered exterior makes it a precursor to today's glass-and-steel skyscrapers. The exterior looks like it's all windows, but between them you'll see narrow piers, mullions and spandrels, all covered with cream terra cotta and Gothic ornamentation. It's a prime example of the Chicago School of architecture; it combines columns of steel to house airy façades of glass. Today, the building houses the Hotel Burnham and Atwood Café, and is often sketched by students from the nearby Art Institute.

### HOLABIRD & ROOT: CHICAGO BOARD OF TRADE
**141 W. Jackson Blvd., Loop**
Holabird & Root created this imposing Art Deco behemoth in 1930, an unapologetically vertical structure marking an abrupt end to LaSalle Street. Head into the two-story lobby to really see its Art Deco beginnings, with its clean lines forming intricate yet orderly geometric designs. If you're wondering what is on top of the building, it's Ceres, the Roman goddess of agriculture—a symbol of the exchange's beginnings in the agricultural commodities business.

ROBIE HOUSE

### LOUIS SULLIVAN: SULLIVAN CENTER
1 S. State St., Loop

The former Carson, Pirie, Scott and Company Building has changed its name to honor its architect, Louis Sullivan. The 12-story structure was constructed for the Schlesinger and Mayer Department Store between 1898 and 1904 and is considered one of Sullivan's most important. After Carson's took over the building in 1904, a 12-story south addition by Daniel Burnham was made and an eight-story south addition followed by Holabird and Root in 1961—a succession of great Chicago architects competing and complementing each other's styles in one building. The white terra cotta façade is most remarkable for Sullivan's amazingly intricate, curvy cast-iron ornamentation. The space was just renovated to house restaurants and shops.

### LUDWIG MIES VAN DER ROHE: CROWN HALL
3360 S. State St., Bronzeville

One of the Modernist architect's masterpieces is a literal lesson to the people who work and study inside of it, as it's the location for the Illinois Institute of Technology's College of Architecture. Mies had the foresight to accommodate the changing needs of the students. He created a 120-foot-long, 220-foot-wide and 18-foot-high clear-span building without any columns, a flexible space where temporary partitions can be changed as needed (though school officials nixed student requests to use the space for keggers). Mies, who was head of the school's architecture program in 1938, also designed nearly 20 campus structures for the Illinois Institute of Technology, the largest collection of the architect's buildings.

### FRANK LLOYD WRIGHT: ROBIE HOUSE
5757 S. Woodlawn Ave., Hyde Park; www.gowright.org

In 1910 Frank Lloyd Wright, the grandfather of American architecture, created this home in his signature Prairie style. Named for the prairie landscape of his Midwest youth, this style is characterized by sweeping horizontal lines, dramatic overhangs, art glass windows and an open floor plan—all of which can be seen at the Robie House (entry is by guided tour only; to reserve a spot, visit *www.gowright.org*).

authentically Chicago trinket (like the Tribune logo mug etched with an image of the top of the tower, or a framed poster of the front page of the *Chicago Tribune* announcing Barack Obama's presidential victory).
*Store hours: Monday-Friday 9 a.m.-5:30 p.m., Saturday 10 a.m.-4 p.m.*

## HOLY NAME CATHEDRAL
**735 N. State St., River North, 312-787-8040;**
**www.holynamecathedral.org**
Built in the 1870s to replace a church destroyed in the Great Chicago Fire of 1871, the cathedral's gothic architecture sits uneasily against the Magnificent Mile's modern skyline. But Holy Name Cathedral has grown up with Chicago and has been a spiritual home to the city's Roman Catholic population. It is the seat of the Roman Catholic Archdiocese of Chicago and was host to a mass by John Paul II in 1979. Open the 1,200-pound bronze doors (don't worry, they open easily thanks to a finger-touch hydraulic system) and peek inside the church to see five galeros—the red, broad-brimmed hats worn by cardinals—suspended from the ceiling. A galero used to be raised to the ceiling of a cardinal's cathedral upon his death and left there until it decayed as an example that all earthly glory passes. Also check out the stained-glass windows; made in Milan, they tell a story of humankind's movement from darkness into light. The western windows are dominated by dark shades of blue and red, but lighten up until they become primarily white and gold behind the altar and crucifix. The cathedral is also a part of Chicago's macabre lore, since it was the site of a battle between Al Capone-era mobsters over turf. Bullet holes remain in a Philippians inscription, now covered by stairs.
*Mass schedule: Weekdays 6 a.m., 7 a.m., 8 a.m., 12:10 p.m., 5:15 p.m.; Saturday vigil 5:15 p.m., 7:30 p.m.; Sunday 7 a.m., 8:15 a.m., 9:30 a.m., 11 a.m., 12:30 p.m., 5:15 p.m. The building is open a half hour before the first Mass of the day through 7 p.m.*

## MICHIGAN AVENUE BRIDGE
**At the Chicago River between Michigan and Wabash avenues, River North**
Motorists drive on Michigan Avenue Bridge daily, but they're too busy cursing the traffic to stop and appreciate the striking gateway to the Magnificent Mile, which connects the North and South Sides of the city. Built in 1920 by Edward Bennett, the bridge was designed not just for better transportation but also to enhance the waterfront as part of architect Daniel Burnham's 1909 Plan of Chicago. The landmark bridge later got an esplanade in 1926 and sculptures in 1928. The southwest bridge tower houses the McCormick Tribune Bridgehouse & Chicago River Museum *(376 N. Michigan Ave., River North, 312-977-0227; www.bridgehousemuseum.*

---

### WHAT ARE THE BEST PLACES FOR FAMILY FUN?
**Adler Planetarium:** A visit here is a must, if only because it is the Western Hemisphere's first planetarium. Interactive exhibits include a fully restored Gemini 12 spacecraft.

**Navy Pier:** The tourist-packed pier and lakefront area offers all kinds of entertainment, including a Ferris wheel, fireworks displays, IMAX theater and much more.

CHICAGO SKYLINE FROM NAVY PIER

*org).* Not atmospheric enough for you? There are often street performers playing saxophones or drums on either side of the bridge, adding a fitting soundtrack to the hustle and bustle.

*McCormick Tribune Bridgehouse and Chicago River Museum: adults $4, seniors and children 5-12 $3, children 5 and under. May-October, Thursday-Monday 10 a.m.-5 p.m.*

### WRIGLEY BUILDING

400 N. Michigan Ave., River North, 312-923-8080; www.wrigley.com

Sitting on the north bank of the Chicago River, the Wrigley Building signals the start of the Magnificent Mile. The white terra-cotta building with its distinctive clock tower is particularly stunning when it stands in contrast against the night sky. Built to house the headquarters of William Wrigley, Jr.'s chewing gum empire, the building is actually two structures connected by ground-level and third-floor walkways. To create the building, Graham, Anderson, Probst and White used the Seville Cathedral's Giralda Tower in Spain as a template for its shape while employing French Renaissance-style ornamentation. Inside there's not much to see, because it's mostly business offices, and unfortunately, there are no free samples of Wrigley's gum or tours to be had.

## LINCOLN PARK

Pretty does it in Lincoln Park—this mainly residential neighborhood is home to some of the most gorgeous two- and three-flats in the city and picture-perfect tree-lined streets, as well as acclaimed restaurants such as Alinea and Charlie Trotter's. Culture is not far behind (Lincoln Park is home to Steppenwolf Theatre Company), and shopping won't be outdone here, either—Barneys Co-Op, local chocolatier Vosges Haut-Chocolat, Kiehl's and more dot the landscape along Halsted Street and Armitage Avenue.

LINCOLN PARK LAGOON

## LINCOLN PARK
2400 N. Stockton Drive, Lincoln Park, 312-742-7529

Lincoln Park, also the name of the neighborhood in which it is located, is the largest of Chicago's parks. On its grounds, which reach from North Avenue to Hollywood Avenue, you'll find numerous beaches and the lakefront jogging/biking trail. It's also the home of the Lincoln Park Zoo *(2200 N. Cannon Drive, 312-742-2000; www.lpzoo.org)*. At only 35 acres, it's not as big as its suburban Brookfield counterpart, but its park surroundings make it a scenic place to visit, plus it's free and open year-round. Check out ZooLights in the wintertime, when the zoo puts out Christmas lights in animal shapes and serves warm drinks while kids visit Santa. Just past the zoo's north border is the Lincoln Park Conservatory *(2391 N. Stockton Drive, 312-742-7736; www.chicagoparkdistrict.com)*. The free botanical garden offers four houses within its glass-domed structure: the Palm House, Fern Room, Orchid House and Show House, which hosts annual flower shows. If you head to the south end of the park, you'll see Green City Market *(www.chicagogreencitymarket.org)*, Chicago's only sustainable green market. The market features more than 40 vendors hawking everything from baked goods (get a slice of whatever pie is in season at Hoosier Mama Pie Co.) to produce (buy juicy peaches from Mick Klug Farms) and flowers (pick up lilies from The Flower Garden). After you gather your treats, watch the chef demos to learn how pros from noted restaurants whip up culinary masterpieces. In winter, the outdoor market sets up shop indoors at the Notebaert Nature Museum. *Lincoln Park Zoo: Admission: Free. April-May, daily 9 a.m.-5p.m.; Memorial Day-Labor Day, Monday-Friday 10 a.m.-5 p.m., Saturday-Sunday 10 a.m.-6:30 p.m.; September-October, daily 10 a.m.-5 p.m.; November-March, daily 10 a.m.-4:30 p.m. Lincoln Park Conservatory: Daily 9 a.m.-5 p.m. Green City Market: Mid-May-October, Wednesday and Saturday 7 a.m.-1 p.m.; November-late December, Wednesday and Saturday 8 a.m.-1 p.m.; January-April, days and times vary.*

## WHAT ARE CHICAGO'S TOP MUSEUMS?

**The Art Institute of Chicago:** The Art Institute has always been known for its vast stock of Impressionist works, but the spectacular new Modern Wing has put it on the contemporary art map (and made it the second-largest art museum in the United States).

**Field Museum of Natural History:** The Field Museum houses the best-preserved and largest Tyrannosaurus rex fossil ever discovered. Spread out over 400,000 square feet, the museum also holds popular exhibits on everything from ancient Egypt to diamonds to Jacqueline Kennedy during The White House years.

**Museum of Contemporary Art:** The MCA is home to 2,345 pieces in its permanent collection and includes first-rate contemporary experimental works.

## LAKE MICHIGAN
Lakefront, Lincoln Park, 312-742-7529; www.chicagoparkdistrict.com
One of the city's biggest surprises is its great beaches. Locals love hitting Lake Michigan's 26 miles of free lakefront for a respite during the scorching summers. On a typical sunny Saturday, you'll see hundreds of Chicagoans soaking up the sun, playing volleyball, running in the sand, barbecuing in designated grassy areas and, of course, swimming. Although there are tons of entry points to the beach in various neighborhoods, the hub is North Avenue Beach, which has a boat-shaped beach house; a restaurant (Castaways Bar & Grill, *1603 N. Lake Shore Drive, 773-281-1200; www.stefanirestaurants.com)*, complete with live music from cover bands on weekends; and an outdoor gym. Fitness fiends also will find that the lakefront is a great place to work out; the 18-mile trail is perfect for jogging, rollerblading or biking. If group sports are more your thing, try to pick up a game at the sand volleyball courts and tennis courts that line the trail. In the summer, the best of Chicago's local theater companies put on Theater on the Lake, at Fullerton Avenue and Lake Michigan.

## THE PEGGY NOTEBAERT NATURE MUSEUM
2430 N. Cannon Drive, Lincoln Park, 773-755-5100; www.chias.org
Be one with nature at the hands-on Notebaert. Watch more than 75 species of colorful butterflies set the Judy Istock Butterfly Haven aflutter year-round in the 2,700-square-foot greenhouse. Kids love the interactive River Works, a permanent exhibit where they can splash around while learning the mechanics of a river. For some fresh air, take a walk in the museum's gardens or watch the Lincoln Park action from the rooftop. The Notebaert also houses the Green City Market, the city's only sustainable green market, during early winter, so that you can get your fill of nature along with its bounty.
*Admission: adults $9, seniors and students $7, children 3-12. $6, children under 3 free. Free Thursday. Monday-Friday 9 a.m.-4:30 p.m., Saturday-Sunday 10 a.m.-5 p.m. Green City Market: November-late December, Wednesday and Saturday 8 a.m.-1 p.m.; January-April, days and times vary.*

## WHAT ARE THE BEST TOURS?

If you're going to do one sightseeing activity in Chicago, make it a tour. These options will help you cover the city in just a few hours.

There's nothing like seeing the city from the river, which flows through downtown. Board the **Chicago History Museum**'s *(465 N. McClurg Court, River North, 312-527-2002; www.chicagoline.com)* 90-minute architecture tour, where you'll see Mies van der Rohe's last major Chicago project (the IBM Building) and learn about Chicago's tie to the Ferris wheel. Obviously the CHM is all about history, but the tour also looks at Chicago's future.

If you're more interested in hearing about the city's sordid past, go on the **Chicago Architecture Foundation**'s *(224 S. Michigan Ave., Loop, 312-922-3432; www.architecture.org)* 3.25-hour Devil in the White City Companion Tour. First you'll get a slide show of photos taken during the 1893 Chicago World's Fair. Then you'll travel around by bus to the various sites mentioned in Erik Larson's best-selling nonfiction book of the same name about one of the nation's first serial killers, who struck during the fair.

Mob lore fans enjoy the **Untouchable Tours** *(Clark and Ohio streets, River North, 773-881-1195; www.gangstertour.com)*, which delves into Al Capone-era Chicago gangland. The two-hour tour takes you around the city explaining who got whacked by whom. While it's a bit cheesy—the guides dress in fedoras and adopt Italian accents—it's a fun time, and you get to see the sites of such grisly events as the St. Valentine's Day Massacre. *Chicago History Museum: For days and times, visit www.chicagoline.com. Tickets: adults $36, seniors $31, children 7-18 $21, children 6 and under free. Chicago Architecture Foundation: For days and times, visit www.architecture.org. Tickets: adults $55, seniors and students $50. Untouchables Tour: For days and times, visit www.gangstertour.com. Tickets: $28.*

## LAKEVIEW/WRIGLEYVILLE

Lakeview is the umbrella neighborhood that encompasses Wrigleyville—the surrounds of Wrigley Field—and Boystown, Chicago's main gay neighborhood. The area just off the Belmont El station is where Lakeview's heady mix of artsy and sporty happily collide in a blast of hip clothing stores, reliable neighborhood restaurants and raucous sports bars.

### GRACELAND CEMETERY TOUR
4001 N. Clark St., Lakeview, 773-525-1105;
www.gracelandcemetery.org

Graceland is called "The Cemetery of Architects" for being the final resting place for such acclaimed architects as Daniel Burnham, William Le Baron Jenney, Louis Sullivan and Ludwig Mies van der Rohe. But many of early Chicago's major players have their permanent home here as well, including businessman Marshall Field and power couple Potter (the business mogul who came up with the idea of store sales and policies such as money-back guarantees for any reason) and Bertha Palmer (the socialite trumped her hubby's accomplishments; she claimed to have invented the brownie). The cemetery, which is on the National Register of Historic Places, is also known for its artistry. A popular site on the grounds is *Eternal Silence*, a 1909 sculpture by Lorado Taft. Also called the Statute of Death, the haunting work features a black slab of granite fronted by a hooded bronze figure that menacingly covers his mouth and chin with his long robe. While the

CHICAGO BOTANIC GARDEN

cemetery doesn't offer tours, it provides a free map for those who want to have a go at it by themselves, and the Chicago Architecture Foundation *(312-922-8687; www.architecture.org)* and the Chicago History Museum *(312-642-4600; www.chicagohistory.com)* offer walking tours. Try planning a fall visit, when the colorful leaves make for a beautiful backdrop.

### MUSIC BOX THEATRE
3733 N. Southport Ave., Lakeview, 773-871-6604; www.musicboxtheatre.com

Built in 1929, the Music Box Theater was originally planned with an orchestra pit, in case "sound" films (new at the time) failed. They haven't, and neither has the Music Box. The theater has shown everything from Arabic feminist films exploring the oppression of women to *Sound of Music* sing-alongs. But for the last 20 years, the Music Box has been the premier Chicago spot to see independent and experimental films. Over the years, the theatre has also hosted movie premieres, such as *The Break-Up* and *(500) Days of Summer*, with the stars walking the red carpet beforehand. In 1991, the Music Box added a second, smaller theater, which sweetly tries to reproduce a small Italian garden with shabbily painted stars and clouds above and plaster side walls. You'll be quite close to the dozen or so people in the audience, but also likely to watch a great indie movie that you can name-drop at your next dinner party.

## SOUTH SIDE

The South Side is really the expansive region below the city center, which stretches from the South Loop all the way to the Indiana border. The area, which is vastly residential, has some of Chicago's most historically important and culturally diverse pockets, including Bronzeville *(35th Street and South King Drive)*, the center of Chicago's black renaissance; Hyde Park *(55th Street and Stony Island Avenue)*, home to the University of Chicago and the former site of the World's Columbian Exposition of 1893; Chinatown *(Cermak Road and Wentworth Avenue)*, the city's main Chinese enclave;

Bridgeport *(35th and Halsted streets)*, the stomping grounds of both the Chicago White Sox and the powerful Daley family; and Pilsen *(18th and Halsted streets)*, the gateway to the city's formidable Mexican-American community and a burgeoning arts area.

## DUSABLE MUSEUM OF AFRICAN-AMERICAN HISTORY
740 E. 56th St., Hyde Park, 773-947-0600; www.dusablemuseum.org

The DuSable Museum was created in 1961 when a local art teacher cleared out her living room furniture, replaced it with a collection of African-American art and artifacts, and hung a modest sign labeled simply "African-American Museum." Since then, it's grown quite a bit. Now in a building on the eastern side of Washington Park, the museum doesn't have the resources of, say, the Field Museum, but it holds a remarkable collection of more than 13,000 paintings, photographs and other artifacts. A large part of its collection focuses on local artists and history, with one wing dedicated to Chicago's first African-American mayor, Harold Washington. The exhibit, Red, White, Blue & Black: A History of Blacks in the Armed Forces, looks at how African-American military men struggled with enemies abroad and racism back home. The museum also hosts ongoing events, such as jazz concerts, poetry readings and film screenings.

*Admission: adults $3, seniors and students $2, children 6-12 $1, children under 6 free. Free Sunday. Monday-Saturday 10 a.m.-5 p.m. (closed Mondays June-January 2), Sunday noon-5 p.m.*

## MUSEUM OF SCIENCE AND INDUSTRY
57th Street and Lake Shore Drive, Hyde Park, 773-684-1414, 800-468-6674; www.msichicago.org

Opened in 1933, the MSI is the largest science museum in the Western Hemisphere—and it needs to be. It houses a full-size 727 airplane (board the plane and buckle up for a fake San Francisco-Chicago flight, complete with banter from an automated pilot); a full-scale coal mine, one of the museum's oldest displays with a great simulated trip into the depths of the mine; a refurbished Burlington Pioneer Zephyr train with interactive exhibits; the U-505 German submarine, which was captured in 1944 and has been given a new indoor arena that brings that era of American history to life; as well as farming, Internet and fairy castle-themed collections among its 2,000 exhibits. As if that weren't enough, there's the recently renovated Henry Crown Space Center in addition to its collections highlighting the history of space exploration.

*Admission: adults $15, seniors $14, children 3-11 $10. Memorial Day-Labor Day, Monday-Saturday 9:30 a.m.-5:30 p.m., Sunday 11 a.m.-5:30 p.m.; Labor Day-late May, Monday-Saturday 9:30 a.m.-4 p.m., Sunday 11 a.m.-4 p.m.*

## THE UNIVERSITY OF CHICAGO
5801 S. Ellis Ave., Hyde Park, 773-702-1234; www.uchicago.edu

You don't need to have high SAT scores to gain admittance to the grounds of one of America's premier universities. The Hyde Park campus features lovely collegiate buildings, in any number of which scholars are working to increase the U. of C.'s already large number of Nobel Prize winners. It was on these grounds that Enrico Fermi first sustained a nuclear reaction, that Milton Friedman created a generation of students championing his brand of economics, and that REM sleep was first discovered. The U. of C.'s Oriental

ARLINGTON PARK

Institute, devoted to art from the Near East, holds an outstanding collection of Ancient Egypt artifacts (like the gigantic 17-foot red quartzite statue of King Tut and the *Book of the Dead*, a collection of spells, hymns and prayers intended to secure for the deceased safe passage to the other world). And nearby is Frank Lloyd Wright's Robie House *(5757 S. Woodlawn Ave.)*, a Prairie-style house with dramatic overhangs and wide horizontal lines that, despite its design 90 years ago, revolutionized American architecture and looks as modern today as it did then.

### CHINATOWN
Cermak Road and Wentworth Avenue, Chinatown;
www.chicagochinatown.org
The Midwest's largest Chinatown is just a quick El ride from the Loop, and just seeing its architecture is worth the trip. The Chinatown Gate (Cermak Road and Wentworth Avenue) greets visitors with a hand-painted message that translates to "The world belongs to the commonwealth," reflecting the determination of the people—this 10-block commonwealth has more than 8,000 residents. Across from the gate, see the ornate "Nine Dragon Wall," a reproduction of the original in Beijing. Both dragons and the number nine are considered sacred among the Chinese, and the wall's vibrant gold, red and blue signify good fortune. The traditional Chinese design of the Pui Tak Center Building *(2216 S. Wentworth Ave., 312-328-1188; www.puitak.org)* makes for an interesting juxtaposition against the looming Willis Tower. Be sure to check if any seasonal events (January/February: Chinese New Year; fall: Dragon Boat Races) are taking place during your trip, but the main reason you'll want to visit Chinatown is to chow down. Eat dim sum at the always-packed Phoenix *(2131 S. Archer Ave., 312-328-0848; www.chinatownphoenix.com)*. For dessert, you can queue up for sweet, fruity bubble tea at Joy Yee's Noodle Shop *(2139 S. China Place, 312-328-0001; www.joyyee.com)* inside Chinatown Square, or grab some moon cakes from one of the many bakeries in the Square or along Wentworth Avenue and head to Ping Tom Memorial Park *(300 W. 19th*

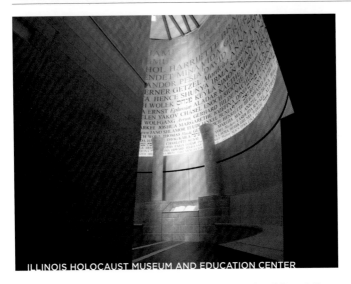

ILLINOIS HOLOCAUST MUSEUM AND EDUCATION CENTER

*St.)*, where you can get a view of the Chicago River and stroll through the Chinese-style landscaping. Afterward, buy some souvenirs. Ten Ren Tea & Ginseng Co. *(2247 S. Wentworth Ave., 312-842-1171, 888-650-1047; www. tenren.com)* offers a great selection of exotic teas and unusual teapots such as the whimsical ones modeled after Chinese zodiac animals. If you browse the many shops in the neighborhood, you can find hand-painted paper fans, jade plants and more only-in-Chinatown treats.

## SUBURBS

Chicagoans poke fun at the suburbs, but believe it or not, there are great reasons to venture beyond the city limits. For one, the suburbs offer an alternative to the faster pace of Chicago without necessarily forsaking the great things about Chicago: Oak Park on the West Side drips with culture and architecture (Ernest Hemingway was born here; Frank Lloyd Wright spent the first 20 years of his career here and plenty of his structures remain), while just north of the city, Evanston boasts amazing Lake Michigan vistas, Northwestern University and acclaimed restaurants. The western suburb Brookfield has the respected Brookfield Zoo, while Glencoe, on the North Shore, hosts the breathtaking Chicago Botanic Gardens.

### ARLINGTON PARK
2200 W. Euclid Ave., Arlington Heights, 847-385-7500;
www.arlingtonpark.com

With horse names like "Smack Daddy," "Heckofanacttofollow" and "Pass the Brandy," you don't need to be a gambler to enjoy thoroughbred racing in this six-story grandstand racetrack. Located in Chicago's northwest suburb, Arlington Heights, and only a 45 minute train ride outside the city, Arlington Park generates a diverse crowd of onlookers, from tranquil families soaking up a summer day to betters caught in the adrenaline rush of the race. With more than 50,000 seats and stables for over 2,000 horses, the dirt oval turf first made its appearance in 1927, thanks to founder Harry

D. "Curly" Brown. The park received national attention in 1981 when the winner of the Arlington Million purse race, legendary "John Henry," had a thrilling come-from-behind win over 40-1 long-shot "The Bart." The statue, "Against All Odds," located in the paddock, reveals the horse and his jockey, Bill Shoemaker, edging out "The Bart" by a nose. Stop by the paddock shortly before a race to see the horses being groomed
*See website for race schedules.*

## BROOKFIELD ZOO
**3300 Golf Road, Brookfield, 708-688-8000, 800-201-0784;**
**www.brookfieldzoo.com**

West-suburban Brookfield Zoo has the pioneering Midwestern spirit. It was the first zoo in the U.S. to have a mostly cageless facility—instead it uses natural barriers such as moats—and it was the first to exhibit giant pandas. The zoo also created Tropic World, the first indoor simulated rainforest in North America, where you see monkeys amid the treetops as waterfalls cascade nearby and fake thunderstorms growl overhead. If you're not a landlubber, check out the daily indoor dolphin shows, which star bottlenose dolphins doing Flipper-like feats. Set on 216 acres, the zoo is Chicagoland's largest and is home to more than 2,000 animals, including lions and tigers and binturongs.

*Admission: adults $13.50, seniors and children 3-11 $9.50. Free October-December, Tuesday and Thursday. Mid-May-Labor Day, Monday-Friday 9:30 a.m.-6 p.m., Sunday 9:30 a.m.-7:30 p.m.; Labor Day-mid-October and April-mid-May, Monday-Friday 10 a.m.-5 p.m., Saturday-Sunday 10 a.m.-6 p.m.; mid-October-March, daily 10 a.m.-5 p.m.*

## CHICAGO BOTANIC GARDEN
**1000 Lake Cook Road, Glencoe, 847-835-5440;**
**www.chicago-botanic.org**

Despite its name, the Chicago Botanic Garden is north of the city in Glencoe, but it is definitely worth the 20-mile car ride if you have a green thumb. (Just hop on I-94 W; you can't miss it.) Never the same on any two visits given the various blooms of its flowers, the garden is spread over 385 acres with 23 display gardens, along with small lakes, a prairie area and a woodland. Be sure to visit the Japanese Garden's three islands, where you can follow the curvy paths and find some Zen underneath the pruned trees. The garden also has a great café and offers a nice respite for those seeking a relaxing walk after several days of touring the city.

*Admission: Free. Labor Day-June, daily 8 a.m.-sunset; mid-June-Labor Day, daily 7 a.m.-9 p.m.*

## ILLINOIS HOLOCAUST MUSEUM AND EDUCATION CENTER
**9603 Wood Drive, Skokie, 847-967-4800;**
**www.iholocaustmuseum.com**

Opened in April 2009, the Illinois Holocaust Museum and Education Center is the largest one of its kind in the Midwest. The museum was originally housed in a small Skokie storefront in 1981, but with the large number of Holocaust survivors living in Skokie after World War II and the personal accounts and artifacts they willingly provided to the museum, more space was needed—65,000 square feet to be exact. Today, the sprawling museum is both somber and hopeful. In the Zev and Shifra Karkomi permanent exhibition, you can trace the Holocaust from pre-war Germany all the way to post-war life in Skokie. The walls of the Room of Remembrance are inscribed with names of some of the victims who died during the Holocaust, homage to the six million Jews who lost their lives. In addition to several interactive exhibits, artifacts like ghetto work permits, work camp uniforms and discarded luggage are also on view. Adopting the slogan "Remember the Past, Transform the Future," the museum is dedicated to preserving the memory of all those lost, while teaching younger generations about the need to prevent future genocides by fighting hatred and intolerance all over the world.

*Monday-Friday 10 a.m.-5 p.m., Saturday-Sunday 11 a.m.-4 p.m.*

ALINEA

# TASTES OF CHICAGO

Meat and potatoes rank right up there with Al Capone on the list of hardest to beat Chicago stereotypes. And that's not for lack of trying by the city's stellar culinary community. Everyone knows that some of the country's best, most innovative restaurants call Chicago home—including Charlie Trotter's, Alinea, Moto. The list goes on. But not everyone knows about the tucked-away gems in cozy neighborhoods such as Lincoln Square or Wicker Park, nor the modest but mind-bending pet projects of superstar chefs Rick Bayless, Paul Kahan and Graham Elliot. So although Chicago is proud of its "low-brow" dining history—deep-dish pizza and hot dogs are staples throughout the city—you'll never go hungry for award-winning and fine dining options. Neither will locals, who are more than happy to live in a place where dining comes in second to none.

## GOLD COAST/STREETERVILLE

### ★★★GIBSONS
1028 N. Rush St., Gold Coast, 312-266-8999;
www.gibsonssteakhouse.com

Pinky rings and massive steaks are the hallmark of Gibsons, a Gold Coast fixture since 1989. The walls are adorned with pictures of celebs ranging from Muhammad Ali to Clint Eastwood, but the restaurant is just as well-known as the haunt of local powerbrokers who make their deals over Gibsons' fishbowl-sized martinis and then celebrate with a gargantuan 24-ounce porterhouse. Big spenders go for the surf and turf, which features a huge Australian lobster tail served with a massive fillet. You could save room for dessert, but we're guessing you won't get too far into the famed macadamia turtle pie.
*Steak. Lunch, dinner. Reservations recommended. Bar. $36-85*

### ★★★LE COLONIAL
937 N. Rush St., Gold Coast, 312-255-0088;
www.lecolonialchicago.com

Chicago's Rush Street is a loud, bombastic avenue, often filled with rowdy revelers and tipsy tourists. But that's not the only reason the restrained elegance of Le Colonial stands out here. With its slowly rotating ceiling fans and potted palm trees, Le Colonial serves French-Vietnamese fare in a space that vividly evokes the feel of French colonial Southeast Asia. The authentic Vietnamese fare starts with pho, the popular beef soup with rice noodles and flavorful slivers of ginger and chilies. Then it's on to entrées like Ca Chien Saigon, a seared snapper in a sweet, spicy sauce, and Bo Bitet Tom Nuong, a grilled filet mignon with shrimp and tomato rice pilaf. Afterward, enjoy a cocktail in the sexy upstairs lounge, which is a pleasant way to savor the last drop of atmosphere before heading back out into the boisterous night.
*French, Vietnamese. Lunch, dinner. Bar. $36-85*

### ★★★★LES NOMADES
222 E. Ontario St., Streeterville, 312-649-9010; www.lesnomades.net

From its location in a former townhouse to the fresh flowers placed throughout the restaurant, Les Nomades is nothing but low-key elegance. Despite being a mere croissant's throw from nearby Michigan Avenue, the serene spot is

LES NOMADES

secluded, intimate and ideal for those seeking a romantic getaway within the city. That's not to say the French haute cuisine is an afterthought, though. From rack of lamb in a delicate mushroom soubise to roasted venison loin with sage braised root vegetables and prune confit, Les Nomades' prix fixe French fare is expertly prepared and perfectly fits the restaurant's elegant atmosphere. In keeping with the formal feel, jackets are required for men, and cell phones are strictly prohibited.

*French. Dinner. Closed Sunday-Monday. $86 and up*

### ★★★NOMI

Park Hyatt Chicago, 800 N. Michigan Ave., Gold Coast, 312-239-4030; www.nomirestaurant.com

When you first arrive at NoMI, you have to go through a glass-encased wine "cellar" and take several turns before entering the main dining room. It's almost as if they want to reward you for your efforts—and what a reward it is. The beautiful space, which offers stunning views of Michigan Avenue and the Water Tower across the street, matches executive chef Christophe David's cuisine: simple, unpretentious and elegant. Sushi makes up much of the menu, with à la carte pieces and larger plates of several rolls offered. David also presents entrées such as black truffle risotto, with a Perigord black truffle purée, soft poached egg and celery root. After your meal, the outdoor garden's gently pulsing lounge music, comfortable tables and spectacular view make a perfect environment for a relaxing after-dinner drink.

*French, Asian. Breakfast, lunch (Monday-Saturday), dinner, Sunday brunch. Reservations recommended. Bar. $36-85*

### ★★★RIA

Elysian, 11 E. Walton St., Gold Coast, 312-646-1300; www.elysianhotels.com

When Peking duck recently appeared on the menu at Ria, there was no indication (written, at least) that it was served as two courses: a traditional

sliced breast with crispy skin in a duck port sauce; then with the rich leg meat alongside pistachio-crusted foie gras in pear purée. At Ria, the presentation is as impressive as the food, which chef Jason McLeod (who manages both Ria and the more casual Balsan just across the hall at the Elysian hotel) takes great care to source and imaginatively prepare. The menu features several seafood courses, among other dishes. The seasonal five-course menu for $87 per person (the whole table must partcipate) is a great way to experience the restaurant. You might start with something like yellowfin tuna topped with caviar, before moving on to King crab, Alaskan halibut with sweetbreads, and milk-fed veal confit with foie gras. As for the wine, Dan Pilkey, the big-smile sommelier who's into surfing and yoga, will point you to just the right bottle. (If you're doing the tasting menu, wine pairings are an additional $45.) The pastries are heavenly and the overall experience—despite the fact that a cheese cart is wheeled over to your table before dessert—is never stuffy. The simple room shimmers with golds, greens and greys, silk wall coverings and metallic leather chairs, and has an intimate, private dining feel that's a welcome change from your typical hotel restaurant.
*American. Dinner. Closed Sunday-Monday. $36 and up*

### ★★★★SEASONS

**Four Seasons Hotel Chicago, 120 E. Delaware Place, Gold Coast, 312-649-2349; www.fourseasons.com**

Let other restaurants try to impress you with a stark, minimalist atmosphere. Seasons, located within the Four Seasons Hotel, goes the other way and spoils you with old-school luxury. How so? For starters, there's the marble fountain, armchair seats and deep mahogany wood trim. Then there is the French-leaning prix fixe five-course menu. The fare constantly changes to reflect availability of ingredients, but past favorites have included Tasmanian sea trout filled with slow-cooked Kobe short ribs, and rack of Colorado lamb wrapped in eggplant and scented with toasted cumin. After a day of Mag Mile shopping, no other place in the Gold Coast feels quite as decadently classic.
*Contemporary American, French. Dinner (Wednesday-Saturday), Sunday brunch. Reservations recommended. $86 and up*

### ★★★SPIAGGIA

**980 N. Michigan Ave., Gold Coast, 312-280-2750; www.spiaggiarestaurant.com**

Any talk of Chicago's high-end Italian restaurants begins (and arguably ends) with the gorgeous Spiaggia. How many restaurants have their own cheese cave? Exactly. The elegant setting matches the caliber of the

**CHARLIE TROTTER'S**

food: The multi-tiered restaurant, appropriately perched at the outset of the city's famed Magnificent Mile, offers a view of Lake Michigan and the city's most famous street. James Beard award-winning chef and partner Tony Mantuano offers an à la carte menu that includes hand rolled potato gnocchi with ricotta sauce and black truffles. There's also a tasting menu inspired by the island of Sicily, which includes items such as pasta sheets with wood-roasted sardines, fennel pollen and black currants, and desserts such as the espresso and marscapone cheese torte with caramel and Valrhona chocolate.

*Italian. Dinner. Jacket required. $86 and up*

### ★★★TABLE FIFTY-TWO
52 W. Elm St., Gold Coast, 312-573-4000; www.tablefifty-two.com
Art Smith will likely forever be known as Oprah's chef, although that's probably not such a bad thing. After all, it's given him the chance to open TABLE fifty-two, which provides a perfect outlet for his Southern-inflected cuisine. Each table begins the meal with piping hot, fluffy buttermilk biscuits pulled fresh from the oven. The menu boasts Smith's upgraded take on Southern classics, including fried green tomatoes with a romesco purée, pickled red bell pepper and orange crème frâiche, and cornmeal-crusted catfish with cheese grits and bacon-braised collard greens. Housed in a 19th century carriage house and featuring an open-hearth oven, Smith's restaurant is as cozy and comforting as his cuisine.

*American, Southern. Dinner. Reservations recommended. $36-85*

### ★★★★TRU
676 N. St. Clair St., Streeterville, 312-202-0001;
www.trurestaurant.com
If you want a stellar dining experience in a large, beautifully understated room with perfectly attuned service, make a reservation at Tru. The gorgeous surroundings include an original Andy Warhol, and the food is

**CHICAGO-STYLE HOT DOG**

## LET'S BE FRANK

Chicago has long been a hot dog town. The Chicago-style hot dog is world famous. You can still order the classic all around town, but today, the hot dog is getting considerably more fancy.

But, first things first. If you want to order the classic, there are a few things you need to know. For starters, the base is a poppy seed-studded bun and a boiled or steamed (not grilled nor charred) all-beef frank. Then come the seven key toppings: mustard, chopped onions, neon-green relish, sport peppers, tomato wedges, a quarter of a pickle cut lengthwise, and a sprinkling of celery salt. Woe to the vendor who squirts ketchup on it in the presence of a Chicago dog purist (and the city is crawling with them)— many believe that the tart sweetness of the red stuff clashes with the other toppings. To sample the classic invention, try Lincoln Park late-night spot **The Wieners Circle** (*2622 N. Clark St., 773-477-7444*), **Jim's Original** (*1250 S. Union Ave., 312-733-7820; www.jimsoriginal.com*), which is conveniently open 24 hours, seven days a week, or **SuperDawg** (*6363 N. Milwaukee Ave., 773-763-0660; www.superdawg.com*), a truly old-fashioned drive-in where uniformed servers bring your order out to your car.

A couple of more recent places, however, are venturing beyond the Chicago-style dog and offering gourmet sausages. There's always a line outside at **Hot Doug's** (*3324 N. California Ave., 773-279-9550; www. hotdougs.com*), which offers the classic dog as well as fancier sausage fare, and on Saturdays and Sundays, the popular duck-fat fries. At **Franks 'n' Dawgs** (*1863 N. Clybourn Ave., 312-281-5187; www.franksndawgs*), the gourmet sausages include a mystery corn dog (different sausages are used) made with a polenta breading. The chef is Joe Doren who used to work at Sixteen and Blackbird.

equally inspiring. Tru offers different ways to take advantage of executive chef Anthony Martin's work, including a three-course prix fixe and a six- or nine-course "collections" tasting menu. The offerings include a bacon-wrapped monkfish with fingerling potatoes and red wine reduction, and prime beef ribeye with grilled foie gras, chanterelle mushrooms and parsley. Practically anything at Tru will delight, but we especially recommend the caviar staircase appetizer, which serves several different types of roe on an elegant glass spiral stairway. Even the bathrooms here, with their sinks made up solely of large slanted glass panels, are a sight. Recently, the restaurant carved out room for a burger joint called M Burger, where locals and Mag Mile tourists line up for bugers, fries and shakes.

*Contemporary French. Dinner. Closed Sunday. Reservations recommended. Jacket required. $86 and up*

## ALSO RECOMMENDED
### BALSAN
Elysian, 11 E. Walton St., Gold Coast, 312-646-1300; www.elysianhotels.com

There's nothing not to love about Balsan, a place named after Étienne Balsan, who financed Coco Chanel's first hat shop, and which serves charcuterie, wood-fired pizzas and other tasty treats. Chef Jason McLeod (who also runs the Elysian hotel's fine-dining Ria just right across the hall) is passionate about discovering products from local farms and artisan purveyors, such as that perfect cheese from a small farm in Wisconsin, and turning out homemade dishes. McLeod and his team have even gone so far as to purchase land in Illinios to grow their own tomatoes to ensure they have enough for their housemade ketchup and tomato sauce. The kitchen also cures some of its own meats. A long white marble bar with an antique mirror dominates the chic eatery and large windows overlook the European-style courtyard.

*American. Breakfast, brunch (Saturday-Sunday), Lunch (Monday-Friday), dinner, late-night. $36-85*

### THE PURPLE PIG
500 N. Michigan Ave., 312-464-1744; www.thepurplepigchicago.com

With the motto, "Cheese, Swine & Wine" what is there not to like at this sliver of porky, cheesy goodness located on Michigan Avenue's Miracle Mile? The chain restaurants in this part of town are generally geared toward tourists walking off the double-decker buses nearby, but the Purple Pig aims higher. Developed by veteran Chicago restaurateurs Scott Harris and Jimmy Bannos, the menu is composed of a wide-selection of delicious small plates which are meant to be shared by a crowd. Smears run the gauntlet from the esoteric pork neck bone rillette to the more familiar (but no less tasty) whipped feta. Cured meats and cheese plates make for a quick bite paired with a quartino of wine—the menu includes a nice selection—while main plates such as milk-braised pork are more substantial and filling. The place is small and gets crowded. (Bonus: The restaurant is open late night.) The outdoor area—a rarity on shop-filled Michigan Avenue—is a great spot for dining and drinks when the weather is warm.

*Mediterranean. Lunch, dinner, late-night. Bar. $36-85*

AVENUES

## OLD TOWN/RIVER NORTH/RIVER WEST

### ★★★★AVENUES
**The Peninsula Chicago, 108 E. Superior St., River North, 312-573-6695;
www.chicago.peninsula.com**

Forget the plain name, and overlook the fact that the intimate Avenues is in a hotel (though the hotel is the Peninsula, one of the best in the city). You might have to tolerate a setting that's a little more staid than luxurious. Instead, try to focus on the food, as chef Curtis Duffy offers cuisine that manages to be both simple and extravagant. Duffy succeeded acclaimed toque Graham Elliot Bowles (who left to start his own eponymous River North restaurant). But Duffy, who was Grant Achatz's right-hand man at Alinea, has made Avenues all his own. He favors unusual pairings that work despite seeming contradictory: A grilled Wagyu steak comes with smoked coconut and African blue basil, and lamb is poached in tangerine oil with mint blossom. The best bet might be to take a seat at the bar in front of the open kitchen and watch Duffy work his magic.
*Contemporary American. Dinner. Closed Sunday-Monday. Reservations recommended. Bar. $86 and up*

### ★★★CHICAGO CHOP HOUSE
**60 W. Ontario St., River North, 312-787-7100;
www.chicagochophouse.com**

It's hard to capture authenticity—some places have it, while other spots feel like a couple of marketing majors drummed up a concept. But the Chop House has authenticity to spare, from the classic green awnings on the Victorian façade to the 1,400 pictures of Chicago icons on the walls. Of course, old-school charm is irrelevant if the food doesn't work—but the reasonably priced steaks here are wet-aged and perfectly prepared. The menu is light on perks, so don't expect anything fancy. Just start out with the prosciutto-wrapped asparagus before going for the massive New York strip (or the 64-ounce porterhouse, if you're up to it). The award-winning wine

## WHAT ARE THE TOP ROMANTIC RESTAURANTS?

**Café Absinthe**: The restaurant's dimly lit, romantic atmosphere is the perfect backdrop to the seasonal, American-oriented menu. Be sure to order the dark chocolate lava cake infused with Grand Marnier liqueur and served with a prickly-pear sauce.

**Les Nomades**: From its location in a former townhouse to the fresh flowers placed throughout the restaurant, Les Nomades is nothing but low-key elegance. The serene spot is secluded and intimate for those seeking a romantic getaway within the city.

**North Pond**: Situated in the middle of a pastoral setting in Lincoln Park, the restaurant's gorgeous Prairie-style building overlooks a small pond and provides a stunning view of the Chicago skyline. Almost as impeccable is chef Bruce Sherman's sustainable-minded fare.

list features more than 600 bottles, from Oregon pinot noirs to renowned French cabernets. Just be sure to leave the baseball caps and T-shirts at home; the dress code, while relatively relaxed, encourages smart attire.
*Steak. Dinner. Reservations recommended. Bar. $36-85*

### ★★★CROFTON ON WELLS
535 N. Wells St., River North, 312-755-1790; www.croftononwells.com
In a city that features such renowned chefs as Charlie Trotter and Grant Achatz, it's telling that Suzy Crofton's eponymous River North restaurant has survived—thrived, actually—since 1997. By leaving the foam and froth to others, Crofton has earned a truckload of awards for her elegant contemporary cuisine. Crofton's French-tinged cooking is elegant and thoughtful, without pretense. She puts as much thought into her appetizers—including the crab cake and sautée of wild mushrooms with bacon, cracked peppercorn and brioche—as she does on her farm chicken and pork tenderloin topped with her famous smoked-apple chutney. Vegetarians aren't relegated to a cursory dish at the corner of the menu—Crofton puts out a separate vegetarian menu, as well as several vegan options. Desserts include a delicious banana cream pie.
*Contemporary American. Dinner. Closed Sunday. Bar. $36-85*

### ★★★DAVID BURKE'S PRIMEHOUSE
The James Hotel, 616 N. Rush St., River North, 312-660-6000;
www.davidburke.com
Sure, many Chicago restaurants claim to be serious about their steaks, but we're guessing not many of them go as far as David Burke's Primehouse, which boasts its own salt-tiled aging room, in which the owners dry-age their own beef. Even more impressive: David Burke owns a stud steer in Kentucky whose offspring produce the meat for his aged steaks. These are just two of the reasons this spot stands apart from the herd. The room is a veritable ode to all things bovine: The chairs are a deep brown leather and the tables are wrapped in red leather. The steaks are the main draw, from the "South Side" bone-in filet to the châteaubriand for two. There are a respectable number of non-steak options as well, including a seared Alaskan king salmon and a wonderful roasted chicken. They're equally as

**FRONTERA GRILL**

good, though when else will you have a chance to trace the family tree of your prime rib? Burke is also famous for whimsical creations such as the cheesecake lollipop.

*Steak. Breakfast, lunch (Monday-Friday), dinner, Saturday-Sunday brunch. Bar. $36-85*

### ★★★FRONTERA GRILL

**445 N. Clark St., River North, 312-661-1434; www.rickbayless.com**

If you can't quite spring for the upscale offerings of Topolobampo next door—or maybe you want to save your money for Rick Bayless' acclaimed margaritas (we don't blame you)—you won't feel cheated if you opt for Frontera Grill. The always-popular spot has a festive atmosphere with colorful walls and hanging papier-mâché animals, which provides a perfect environment to enjoy the famous chef's housemade moles and freshly ground corn tortillas. The menu changes monthly but you may find such mouthwatering fare as Puerco Al Chipotle, a grilled pork loin in a red-bean chipotle sauce, and Carne Asada a la Oaxaquena, a grilled Angus rib steak marinated in red chile and served with black beans and plantains. Be forewarned: The restaurant takes reservations only for a limited number of tables, which explains the lines that form well before the doors open for dinner.

*Mexican. Lunch (Tuesday-Friday), dinner, Saturday brunch. Closed Sunday-Monday. Bar. $36-85*

### ★★★GENE & GEORGETTI

**500 N. Franklin St., River North, 312-527-3718; www.geneandgeorgetti.com**

Chicago's famed stockyards officially closed in 1971, but the city's carnivorous tradition is still going strong—and perhaps no stronger than at this timeless Italian steakhouse that's resided in the shadow of the El since 1941. From the pictures of Frank Sinatra and Bob Hope on the walls to the red vinyl chairs, G&G (as it's known) is old-school through and through.

---

**WHAT ARE THE BEST NEIGHBORHOOD RESTAURANTS?**

**Bistro Campagne**: This Lincoln Square bistro isn't exactly centrally situated, but the classic French fare and immaculate wine list make the cozy neighborhood spot well worth the trip to the North Side.

**Le Bouchon**: There's a reason this tiny storefront bistro has been packing in a crowd of regulars for more than 15 years: The food is delicious, the prices are reasonable, the mood is convivial, and the feeling is somehow unmistakably Parisian.

**West Town Tavern**: The contemporary American cuisine with a comfort-food touch is wonderful, and the specials—especially the fried chicken on Monday nights—can't be beat.

---

The waiters have as much character as the classic environs, and they're not exactly known for their geniality, but you'll forget their brusqueness the second you dig into the juicy wet-aged New York strip or the 18-ounce filet that stands some four inches tall.

*Italian, Steak. Lunch, dinner. Closed Sunday. Bar. $36-85*

### ★★★GRAHAM ELLIOT

217 W. Huron St., River North, 312-624-9975; www.grahamelliot.com

You'll either love or loathe the kookiness at acclaimed chef Graham Elliot Bowles' River North restaurant. The "informalized" dining room features '80s pop tunes (think Flock of Seagulls and Billy Ocean), and the snack between courses is popcorn (Parmesan-dusted and truffled popcorn, but popcorn nonetheless). Clad in jeans and Chuck Taylors, servers bring Bowles' playful haute cuisine (his opening menu included a duck leg confit served with Maytag blue cheese and Budweiser beer foam, and an aged cheddar risotto, featuring Pabst-glazed onions and Cheez-It crackers) that's divided into hot and cold appetizers and land and sea entrées. He tones it down a little for his entrées, as the grilled rack of pork features a massive loin tastefully infused with root-beer barbecue sauce, while the salmon BLT served with crispy bacon and fresh tomatoes is delicious—good enough, even, to endure the overly-loud Reagan-era jams.

*Contemporary American. Dinner. Closed Sunday. $36-85*

### ★★★JAPONAIS

600 W. Chicago Ave., River West, 312-822-9600;
www.japonaischicago.com

You'll need to cab it over to this gentrifying but not exactly glitzy part of town. But when you're enjoying Japanese-French fusion next to some of the city's most stylish foodies, you'll see why Japonais remains one of the hottest tables in town. Gently thumping lounge music and chic décor provide a perfect environment for the glammed-up crowd (Brad and Angelina dined here when she was filming *Wanted*) that can be found sipping on colorful drinks in the downstairs lounge and outdoor patio. If you're all about the food, you'll be just as pleased. The menu leans toward sushi but also includes a seven-spice Wagyu rib eye and Le Quack Japonais, a smoked duck served with hoisin sauce and chutney (yes, that's neither Japanese nor French, but trust us, it's delicious). If you like to play with your food, order The Rock, in which thinly sliced New York strip steak is cooked on a

## WHAT ARE THE BEST PLACES FOR A CASUAL LUNCH?

Big-name chefs are increasingly opening up more casual spots, so you always have access to delicious food when you're in town.

**Rick Bayless**—a chef, a businessman and a cookbook author—opened a few quick-service Mexican restaurants in 2007. **Frontera Fresco** (111 N. State Street, 312-781-1000; www.fronterafresco.com) boasts gourmet Mexican dishes comprised of the freshest ingredients from aromatic herbs to all-natural salsas to baked flatbreads. Striking a deal with Macy's department store, Bayless placed his fast-food restaurants in two great locations, offering both Chicago and Skokie shoppers a place to grab a bite, with plenty of space for their bags of goodies. The Top Chef Masters first season winner also opened up **XOCO** (located next door to Frontera Grill at 449 N. Clark St., 312-334-3688)—and people have been lined up since day one for the flavorful tortas (the wait can be up to an hour but it's worth it). You can also sample what has to be the world's best guacamole, order a Mexican chocolate or indulge in the homemade Mexican soft serve ice cream which comes with toppings such as crumbly pecans, caramel and bacon.

Fans of chef Graham Elliot Bowles can now stop in for a sandwich at **Grahamwich** (615 N. State, www.grahamwich.com). The shop offers a half-dozen sandwiches such as the tuna nicoise, five flavors of homemade soda and soft serve ice cream.

Chef **Marcus Samuelsson** had long been earning raves at Aquavit in New York City before opening up C-House at the Affinia Hotel in Chicago a few years ago. Recently, he also unveiled **Marc Burger** (111 N. State St., 312-781-3693) at the new food court at Macy's, where the signature burger is a juicy 10-ouncer topped with homemade steak sauce and a fried egg.

Another great burger is found at **DMK Burger Bar** (2954 N. Sheffield Ave., 773-360-8686) from chef Michael Kornick of MK, where you will find grass-fed beef, as well as lamb, turkey, veggie and portobella patties, topped with everything from chili-rubbed onion strings, olive tapenade and chipotle ketchup.

If it's Asian food you're craving, you have **Bill Kim** to thank for the affordable cuisine available at **Urban Belly** (3053 N. California Avenue, 773-583-0500; www.urbanbellychicago.com). Kim makes a pork belly and shitake pho ramen that's better than any cup of noodles you've ever tasted. He is, after all, a veteran chef who has worked all over the United States.

JAPONAIS

hot rock at your table. Whatever you order, be sure to add a side of fries, which come with a spicy sauce that's always a crowd pleaser. Cap off the night with an after-dinner drink in the downstairs lounge, where in summer months, you can sip on a patio overlooking the river.
*Japanese, French. Lunch (Monday-Friday), dinner. Bar. $36-85*

### ★★★LA MADIA

59 W. Grand Ave., River North, 312-329-0400; www.dinelamadia.com
You know a place is good when restaurant owners go there to eat. The heavenly pies served at this contemporary pizzeria have a crispy and slightly chewy crust and come in such interesting combinations as triple pepperoni with truffle oil and taleggio with three-hour roasted grapes. Unfortunately, everything else on the menu here is equally delicious, making ordering tough. Chef Jonathan Fox often uses ingredients he picked up at the market that morning which might inspire a lovely pumpkin pizza with crunchy pumpkin seeds or a whole new dish that might get added to the menu for a day, or a season. Menu standbys such as the impossibly tender short rib with creamy risotto and delicate homemade ricotta gnocchi with housemade sausage are also wonderfully satisfying.The wine list is vast and the chef's suggested pairings are spot on.
*American, Italian. Lunch, dinner. $36-85*

### ★★★MK

868 N. Franklin St., River North, 312-482-9179; www.mkchicago.com
Founder Michael Kornick is no longer preparing meals at his namesake restaurant (that falls to executive chef Erick Williams), but there's still a lot of substance beneath the style of this renowned loft-like spot with the brick walls and massive skylight. The chic lounge is a popular stop for a pre-dinner drink, while the spacious bi-level dining room provides a warm atmosphere for a classic contemporary American menu. Williams doesn't exactly reinvent the wheel, but we're not complaining: His specialties include grilled veal porterhouse in a cognac green peppercorn sauce, and bison rib eye with a cabernet

SIXTEEN

sauce. The dessert menu offers standbys like crème brûlée and sorbet, but you'll be glad to step outside the box for the Cake & Shake, which features layers of buttermilk chocolate cake, chocolate mousse, bittersweet chocolate pavé, chocolate meringue buttercream and a vanilla malted milkshake.
*Contemporary American. Dinner. $36-85*

### ★★NACIONAL 27
**325 W. Huron St., River North, 312-664-2727; www.nacional27.net**
The "27" in the name refers to the number of Latin American countries, but it also reflects this stylish restaurant's culinary diversity. In a large, dramatic space, Nacional 27 offers Nuevo Latino dishes that blend flavors and influences from throughout Central and South America. Starters include ceviche sampling platters with shrimp, scallops, ahi tuna and salmon. The menu also offers tapas (such as miniature lamb tacos with avocado salsa and smoked chicken empanadas), a four-course party menu (for four or more guests served family style), and à la carte dishes including a delicious grilled marinated skirt steak. There's also a tapas tasting menu Monday through Friday for $27 per person. If the food itself doesn't get you dancing, the restaurant's resident DJ will get you on the floor with weekend salsa and merengue music. (Have a mojito to best bring out your dance moves.)
*Latin American. Dinner. Closed Sunday. Bar. $36-85*

### ★★★NAHA
**500 N. Clark St., River North, 312-321-6242; www.naha-chicago.com**
In-the-know Chicagoans didn't need proof that NAHA, the creation of cousins Carrie and Michael Nahabedian, offers excellent contemporary cuisine with a Mediterranean flair. But that validation came anyway in the form of a 2008 James Beard award. Carrie's meals are served in an elegant, tranquil setting and emphasize locally grown, organic fare such as wood-grilled rib eye with spring onions, macaroni gratin, blue cheese and oxtail sauce, and honey-lacquered aged moulard duck breast with huckleberries and carrots. Not

## WHICH RESTAURANTS ARE BEST FOR A LIVELY SCENE?

**Epic:** This cavernous, loft-like space in River North includes a first-floor lounge, second-floor dining room and 3,000-square-foot rooftop deck with views of the city. Add in tasty cuisine and easy-to-sip cocktails, and it's easy to see why the place has been popular since it opened.

**Gibsons:** Gibsons fills up every night of the week with people looking for a fishbowl-sized martini and a giant steak.

**Landmark:** With its striking décor and boisterous crowd, you'd forgive the owners of Landmark if they concentrated a little less on the food. But it's equally worth going here for the barbecue glazed pork chop and braised short ribs, so go early.

**Nacional 27:** In a large, dramatic space, Nacional 27 offers Nuevo Latino fare along with excellent mojitos. The restaurant's resident DJ will get you on the floor with weekend salsa and merengue music.

**The Publican:** The space resembles a swank German beer hall, there's pork, oysters and beer on the menu, and everything is meant to be shared—the Publican is a perfect place for a fun dinner.

**Sable Kitchen & Bar:** The name pretty much sums it up. With at least as much focus on the drinks as the food, this is a good spot to start with dinner and then move on to cocktails in the sleek bar.

everything is such highbrow fare: The Angus hamburger served on a sea-salt crusted ciabatta bun with glazed onions wins raves as well, elevating the simple hamburger above its typical reputation. You have to get it for lunch, though. Otherwise, you're stuck ordering from the fantastic dinner menu.
*Contemporary American. Lunch (Monday-Friday), dinner. Closed Sunday. Reservations recommended. Bar. $36-85*

### ★★★★SIXTEEN
**401 N. Wabash Ave., River North, 312-588-8151; www.trumpchicagohotel.com**

As you might expect, everything at Sixteen (on the 16th floor of Donald Trump's hotel) is larger-than-life. The hostesses dress like they're about to walk down a Paris runway. The views of the city through the floor-to-ceiling windows are dazzling (and the ceiling in one of the three dining rooms is 30 feet high). Then there's the food. Chef Frank Brunacci meticulously crafts entrées like duck breasts in a date-and-kumquat chutney with black cumin, and pork with creamed corn, warm potato salad, collard greens and grilled peaches. (The menu changes daily.) The desserts—including chestnut meringue accompanied by port-wine ice cream and port reduction—take so much effort that it's recommended you order them at the start of your meal. All of this is almost enough to take your eyes off the gargantuan chandelier, which comprises more than 19,000 Swarovski crystals, or the views, which, from the 16th floor in the city's best location, are larger than life.
*Contemporary American. Breakfast, lunch, dinner, Sunday brunch. Reservations recommended. Bar. $86 and up*

## WHAT ARE THE BEST RESTAURANTS FOR AN UPSCALE LUNCH?

**Blackbird**: Lunch is the perfect time to enjoy chef Mike Sheerin's artisanal cooking. The three-course prix fixe includes a choice of appetizer, entrée and a dessert, with options like the pork belly sandwich with cabbage slaw and garlic frites.

**NAHA**: The excellent contemporary cuisine with a Mediterranean flair served at this elegant and tranquil restaurant is always wonderful. The Angus hamburger served on a sea-salt crusted ciabatta bun with glazed onions is one of the best in the city—and is only available at lunch.

### ★★★SHANGHAI TERRACE

**The Peninsula Chicago, 108 E. Superior St., River North, 312-573-6695; www.chicago.peninsula.com**

The main draw at the intimate Shanghai Terrace isn't the generous menu, with its emphasis on meticulous dim sum creations, or the elegantly appointed dining room with black lacquer chairs and daring red trim. The best reason to come here is the outdoor deck, with its stunning view of the soaring buildings that surround The Peninsula hotel. The alfresco area provides the perfect place to enjoy the delicious dim sum sampler, which includes spicy beef gyoza and foie gras and lobster dumplings. For a more complete meal, you can't go wrong with the traditional Peking duck, which offers five courses.
*Asian. Lunch, dinner. Closed Sunday. Bar. $36-85*

### ★★★TOPOLOBAMPO

**445 N. Clark St., River North, 312-661-1434; www.rickbayless.com**

You can't turn on a TV today without seeing chef Rick Bayless work his culinary magic with Mexican food—the ubiquitous chef from Chicago even won the first season of *Top Chef Masters*. But you don't have to just stare in awe if you make the trip to Topolobampo, the sleek, multicolored restaurant that serves Bayless' inventive cuisine with a monthly changing menu. Bayless isn't always in the kitchen (chef de cuisine Brian Enyart is the man in the toque here), but Bayless' influence is all over the menu, which uses sustainably raised veggies, meat and fish to craft stunningly imaginative Oaxacan cuisine. Favorites have included Puerco Pibil, achiote-marinated Maple Creek Farm pork served as a grill-roasted loin and a slow-cooked shoulder in banana leaves, and langosto al mojo de ajo, pan-roasted Maine lobster served with olive oil-poached garlic, giant butter beans and roasted fresh favas. It's the furthest thing from a taquería, but it's a lot more memorable.
*Mexican, Southwestern. Lunch (Tuesday-Friday), dinner. Closed Sunday-Monday. Reservations recommended. $36-85*

## ALSO RECOMMENDED

### BIN 36

**339 N. Dearborn St., River North, 312-755-9463; www.bin36.com**

Most restaurants serve food and enhance the experience with wine. At the cavernous Bin 36, it's the other way around. You'll see that love of the grape from the many wine flights served with dinner to the wine store on the premises that will sell you that wine you really liked with your dinner. "Wine Director" Brian Duncan—he refuses to be called a sommelier—offers some 50 wines by the glass, and about 300 bottles to choose from. Despite the hullaboo about vino, the menu is hardly an afterthought. Chef John

TOPOLOBAMPO

Caputo's contemporary American fare includes sautéed herb marinated prawns with white asparagus, saffron risotto cake and spanish chorizo, and grilled lamb with sauteed spinach, lentils, ricotta salata, mint oil and lamb jus. Bin 36 offers three different dining areas, depending on your mood: the bar, the cheese bar or at a standard table in the dining room. A sophisticated environment with options galore? We'll drink to that.

*Contemporary American. Breakfast, lunch, dinner. Bar. $36-85*

### BRASSERIE JO
59 W. Hubbard St., River North, 312-595-0800; www.brasseriejo.com

High ceilings and Art Deco accents aren't the only archetypal French elements at this River North fixture. With whimsical French accordion music constantly playing in the background, chef/owner Jean Joho's bistro has been a Chicago favorite since it opened in 1996, drawing adoring crowds with a casual Alsatian menu that features classics such as coq au vin and a juicy cut of steak topped with a heaping mound of frites. The value-conscious, however, don't need to venture beyond the tartes flambées, delicious pizzas topped with everything from Camembert Bleu and oven dried grapes to spinach, mushroom and Gruyère. A large beer and wine selection makes this the next best thing to being in Paris. Note: At press time, this restaurant was being reconcepted; see website for updates.

*French. Dinner. Bar. $36-85*

### PIZZERIA UNO
29 E. Ohio St., River North, 312-321-1000; www.unos.com

Despite the trendy thin-crust-pizza spots that have been popping up across Chicago lately, many still come to the city for chewy, gooey deep-dish pizza. There are many arguments about whose stuffed pizza is the best, but no matter who's doing the rating, Pizzeria Uno is almost always near the top. This standby—which actually served the world's first stuffed pizza, back in the 1940s—draws huge crowds, and it's not exactly spacious, so either

AVEC

arrive early (the restaurant doesn't take reservations) or be prepared for a long wait for a table (which will likely be cramped). But oh, how it's worth the wait: The cheese is melty, the tomato sauce is sweet but has a nice zip of garlic, and the crust is slightly crunchy. You'll quickly tune out the tourists that surround you as you dig in.

*Pizza. Lunch, dinner. $16-35*

### EPIC
112 W. Hubbard St., River North, 312-222-4940;
www.epicrestaurantchicago.com

Epic is perfect for, well, an epic-sized evening on the town. The cavernous, loft-like space includes a first-floor lounge, upstairs dining room and a rooftop space, a destination in itself with a special menu. It's a great place for drinks, dinner or both. Start in the lounge downstairs with a classic cocktail; head upstairs to dine on delicious plates of spiced lamb shank or crispy half chicken; and then make your way up to the roof with great views of the city for an after-dinner drink. With all this cocktailing, you may think the food takes a backseat. It doesn't. Stephen Wambach, the former corporate chef for Laurent Tourondel's BLT Restaurant Group in New York, is at the helm here. Be sure to try the signature appetizer of wild boar barbajuan (a fried ravioli filled with wild boar shoulder and housemade foie gras). Pastry Chef Christine McCabe prepares such heavenly desserts as the banana split made with a pineapple cake, malted chocolate, strawberry swirl and roasted banana ice creams and a cherry truffle on top. McCabe also bakes the housemade breads: a sourdough and a seasonally inspired selection. The wine list features a varied selection, with several wines available by the glass. There's also a large artisanal beer list and classic cocktails. With so many things to eat and drink, and so many spots within Epic from which to do so, it's no wonder the restaurant has been filling up since day one.

*American. Lunch (Monday-Friday), dinner. Bar opens at 2 p.m. $86 and up*

**WHAT ARE THE BEST STEAKHOUSES?**

**David Burke's Primehouse:** David Burke's Primehouse stands apart for many reasons. Two of these include having its own salt-tiled aging room and stud steer in Kentucky, whose offspring produce the meat for the aged steaks.

**Gibsons:** It may be a scene but the steaks at Gibsons are some of the best in town: thick, juicy and cooked to perfection.

## SABLE KITCHEN & BAR

Hotel Palomar, 505 North State Street, River North, 312-755-9704; www.sablechicago.com

With at least as much focus on the drinks as the food, this is one place you will not regret drinking your dinner. Many of the house-designed cocktails are prepared with locally sourced ingredients and paired with reputedly one of the largest brown liquor selections in the area. The interior is over-the-top with onyx, oxblood leather, oversized chandeliers and custom light fixtures. With all this excitement over master mixology and elaborate design, the food could be easily overlooked, but that would be a mistake. Executive Chef Heather Terhune has crafted a modern menu that pairs perfectly with the cocktails such as spicy buttermilk fried quail with blue cheese slaw and crispy pork belly B.L.T.'s.

*Contemporary American. Breakfast. Lunch. dinner. Bar $15-35*

# LOOP/WEST LOOP

### ★★★ARIA

The Fairmont Chicago, 200 N. Columbus Drive, Loop, 312-444-9494; www.ariachicago.com

Technically, Aria is located inside the Fairmont hotel, just east of tony Michigan Avenue. But the fact that the restaurant has its own entrance symbolizes how chef Brad Parsons wants his eclectic spot to separate itself from the norm. The globally influenced restaurant boasts its own tandoori oven for naan, and a hip sushi bar draws a lively crowd of saketini sippers. Those who want a globe-spanning culinary experience will have a great time in the dramatic dining room, which is filled with orchids and Tibetan artwork. The menu ranges from shrimp and chicken pad thai to a perfectly prepared New York strip steak to Hong Kong barbecue duck and lobster chow mein. The menu is all over the map, but it works.

*International. Breakfast, lunch, dinner. Bar. $36-85*

### ★★★ATWOOD CAFÉ

Hotel Burnham, 1 W. Washington St., Loop, 312-368-1900; www.atwoodcafe.com

You can't get much more centrally located than the Atwood Café, which sits in the heart of the action of Chicago's Loop and provides floor-to-ceiling views of bustling State Street. And you can't get much more comfortable than the food on the Atwood Café's menu, which presents new takes on classic American standbys. The expansive bar serves as an ideal place for a drink before heading to the nearby Theater District (we told you it was centrally located) for a show.

*Contemporary American. Breakfast (Monday-Saturday), lunch (Monday-Saturday), dinner, Sunday brunch. $36-85*

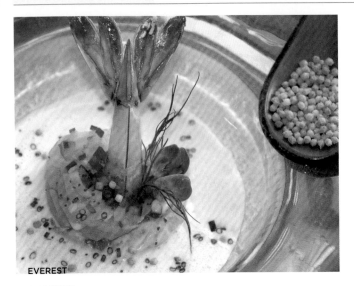
EVEREST

### ★★★AVEC

615 W. Randolph St., West Loop, 312-377-2002; www.avecrestaurant.com
Avec means "with" in French, which fits here because you're likely to end
up dining with complete strangers at one of the communal tables. You won't
mind, because the restaurant's Euro-Mediterranean fare and surprisingly
reasonable prices put you in such a good mood that you're happy to talk
with your neighbors about the amazing food in front of you. Co-owned by
chef Paul Kahan, Avec offers delicious fare prepared by chef de cuisine (and
recent James Beard award winner) Koren Grieveson. Popular items include
the chorizo-stuffed Medjool dates wrapped in smoked bacon and topped
with a piquillo pepper-tomato sauce, and the crispy focaccia with taleggio
cheese, truffle oil and fresh herbs. The menu, which is divided into large
and small plates, is always changing, which means this restaurant is worth
a trip every time you're in town. For example, in spring Grieveson might
whip up a heavenly English pea crostini with mint oil, roasted spring onion
vinaigrette and Pecorino; in fall, she might prepare the pork shoulder with
chestnut-bacon dumplings and butternut squash. The small room looks
almost sauna-like with its fully paneled cedar walls and ceiling, and its back
display of glass wine bottles is both colorful and whimsical. Speaking of
bottles, Avec offers some 130 wines from France, Italy, Spain and Portugal;
we recommend buying a bottle to share with the newfound friends you'll
undoubtedly meet at your table.
*Contemporary American, Mediterranean. Dinner. Bar. $36-85*

### ★★★BLACKBIRD

619 W. Randolph St., West Loop, 312-715-0708;
www.blackbirdrestaurant.com
When chef Mike Sheerin took over the reigns from chef/owner Paul Kahan,
no one knew quite what to expect; Kahan's food was beloved by foodies
everywhere. But Sheerin has not disappointed, bringing a slight element
of playfulness to Kahan's solid menu. Now, for instance, short ribs might

come with sesame gnocchi and ground cherries and "fried" chicken with a smoked potato salad. Foodies love it just as much as they always have. As for the restaurant itself, it's sleek and minimalist—but it's not exactly roomy. Tables are packed tightly together, but you won't mind overhearing a few conversations for food of this caliber. The prix fixe lunch menu, which includes three courses for $22, is one of the best deals in town.

*Contemporary American. Lunch (Monday-Friday), dinner. Closed Sunday. Reservations recommended. $36-85*

### ★★★CUSTOM HOUSE TAVERN

Hotel Blake, 500 S. Dearborn St., Loop, 312-523-0200; www.customhouse.cc

The old Custom House, a steakhouse helmed by chef Shawn McClain, has evolved into the Custom House Tavern, an upscale but comfortable urban tavern with hearty offerings. Executive chef Perry Hendrix takes a seasonal approach to urban American food with dishes such as smoked trout "rilletes" with cucumber and crème fraiche; roasted beets with Greek yogurt, lamb's lettuce and candied bacon; and gold rice risotto with ramps, wild mushrooms, sugar snap peas and pistachio. The main dining room is still elegant and refined; you can also settle into the comfortable lounge area where you'll find an expanded bar bites menu.

*Contemporary American. Lunch (Monday-Friday), dinner. Reservations recommended. Bar. $36-85*

### ★★★★EVEREST

440 S. LaSalle St., Loop, 312-663-8920; www.everestrestaurant.com

It takes a certain bravado to name a restaurant after the tallest mountain in the world—the damning reviews practically write themselves. Thankfully, chef Jean Joho's Everest has scaled the culinary heights and remains perched at the top of Chicago's fine-dining realm. Appropriately located on the 40th floor of the Chicago Stock Exchange, its magnificent city views (framed by floor-to-ceiling drapes) are a perfect companion for Joho's highbrow Alsatian cuisine. Served by an exceedingly polite waitstaff clad in suits, the menu includes a filet of wild sturgeon wrapped and roasted in cured ham, and venison served with wild huckleberries and braised pear. It's safe to say that a night at Everest will leave you feeling, well, on top of the world.

*French. Dinner. Closed Sunday-Monday. $86 and up*

---

**WHICH RESTAURANTS HAVE THE BEST VIEWS?**

**Everest**: Appropriately located on the 40th floor of the Chicago Stock Exchange, its magnificent city views (framed by floor-to-ceiling drapes) are a perfect companion for the highbrow Alsatian cuisine.

**NoMI**: The beautiful space, which offers lovely views of Michigan Avenue and the Water Tower across the street, is particular festive during the holidays when the lights on Michigan Avenue make everything twinkle.

**Sixteen**: Located on the 16th floor of Donald Trump's hotel, the views of the city through the floor-to-ceiling windows are dazzling (and the ceiling in one of the three dining rooms is 30 feet high).

## WHAT ARE SOME GREAT ETHNIC RESTAURANTS?

Some of the city's most popular eateries are nothing-to-look-at places that serve the most deliciously authentic (and inexpensive) food. Here are a few to try on your next visit to Chicago.

### 90 Miles Cuban Café

*3101 N. Clybourn Ave., Roscoe Village, 773-248-2822; 2540 W. Armitage, Logan Square, 773-227-2822; www.90milescubancafe.com*

Named after the number of miles between Miami and Cuba, this is the closest you'll get to Little Havana from Chicago. The owners quickly added a second location after the popularity of the first. Locals stop in for Cubanos and heavenly guava and cheese pastries. Throw down the house café con leche, and you'll be wired for days.

### Borinquen

*1720 N. California Ave., Humboldt Park, 773-227-6038; www.borinquenjibaro.com*

This Puerto Rican eatery—which sits in a predominantly Puerto Rican neighborhood west of Wicker Park—is so hot, it has opened two other locations. The original is still the most popular, for it's here that the café's famed jibarito—a steak sandwich in which crunchy pounded plantains stand in for bread slices—was born.

### Irazú

*1865 N. Milwaukee Ave., Bucktown, 773-252-5687; www.irazuchicago.com*

This Costa Rican gem has been a Bucktown fave since before the boutiques moved in, and it's easy to see—rather, taste—how the tiny restaurant stays in business. Don't leave without trying the thick, cinnamon-sprinkled oatmeal shake, the refreshing and hearty heart of palm salad, and the perfectly fried sweet plantains.

### Lao Szechuan

*2172 S. Archer Ave., Chinatown, 312-326-5040; www.tonygourmetgroup.com*

Local foodies head to this no-frills Szechuan in droves for the crispy eggplant with pork, ma po tofu and signature "chef's special" dry chili chicken (an addictive blend of wok-fried chicken, hot chili peppers, garlic and ginger). Chow down on the latter with plenty of cooling, complimentary tea, and you'll feel just like a regular.

### Nuevo León

*1515 W. 18th St., Pilsen, 312-421-1517; www.nuevoleonrestaurant.com*

The neighborhood of Pilsen is home to a sizable Mexican-American population and a growing art community. Both collide at this 49-year-old Mexican eatery. The harried waitstaff brings out a savory amuse-bouche while you peruse a menu teeming with classics, such as tamales and chorizo tacos. On Sundays, neighborhood regulars fill the seats for restorative menudo, a traditional Mexican tripe soup said to help with hangovers.

### Pho Xe Tang

*4953 N. Broadway, Uptown, 773-878-2253*

Most locals refer to this low-key but always-packed Vietnamese noodle house as Tank. We call it heaven in winter, thanks to the hearty, warming house specialty: pho, a Vietnamese soup that comes with meat (if you so desire), plus plates of add-ons like fresh lime, basil, chilies and sprouts.

ONE SIXTYBLUE

### ★★★GIRL & THE GOAT
809 W. Randolph St., West Loop, 312-492-6262;
www.girlandthegoat.com

The girl is Stephanie Izard, 2008 winner of Bravo's *Top Chef*; the goat appears in dishes like smoked goat pizza with sautéed kale and tart cherries. The renovated manufacturing space on the West Loop's restaurant row is ultra trendy, with lofted ceilings and an industrial vibe, but Izard is definitely the focus. She reportedly did it all for the 2010 opening, including having her own Washington state wine blended and an exclusive cheese made. Real foodies may be drawn to the wood oven roasted pig face, garnished with a sunny side egg; the less adventurous can choose from a bevy of seemingly simple vegetable dishes, such as roasted cauliflower with pine nuts and mint. Wash it all down with a meticulously concocted cocktail or crafted beer—Izard edited the extensive list of drafts and bottles herself. Be forewarned: Prepare for a wait, even with a reservation.

*American. Dinner. Outdoor seating. Bar. $36-85*

### ★★★MOTO
945 W. Fulton Market, West Loop, 312-491-0058;
www.motorestaurant.com

Moto's brilliant chef Homaro Cantu has repeatedly said he wants his customers to play with their food. But sometimes, when facing the concoction the renowned chef has created, the desire is to stare in awe rather than disrupt such a lavish creation. Cantu's whimsical dinners begin with an edible menu (vegetable inks on modified food starch) and go on to feature 10 to 20 courses, which may include inverted pumpkin pie or instant risotto. Some of Cantu's more celebrated dishes have included veal breast served with rice and runner beans, and fish cooked in an insulated box at the table. As you might expect, the presentation is both outrageous and practical. The "toro, sturgeon caviar, and utensil study," for instance, features a piece of tuna dabbed with caviar, served on a custom-made utensil for which the stem has been hollowed out

## WHICH RESTAURANTS SERVE THE BEST PIZZA?

**Coalfire:** Will thin-crust replace deep-dish as the quintessential Chicago pizza? This pizza restaurant aims to claim its place as the city's preferred pie.

**Crust:** Using organic flour and ingredients including fresh-pulled water buffalo mozzarella, Altenberg coaxes delicious pizzas from the tile-encrusted wood-burning oven.

**Great Lake:** This tiny pizza shop serves up some of the city's best pizza. The wait is long but oh-so-worth it.

**La Madia:** The heavenly pies served at this contemporary pizzeria have a crispy and slightly chewy crust and come in such interesting combinations as triple pepperoni with truffle oil.

**Piece:** Some of the combinations for toppings might sound strange (mashed potatoes and clams) but they somehow meld perfectly with the pizza's crunchy thin crust and tangy tomato sauce.

and filled with fresh thyme. Playful? Certainly. Sublime? Absolutely.
*International. Dinner. Closed Sunday-Monday. Reservations recommended. Bar. $86 and up*

### ★★★N9NE
**440 W. Randolph St., West Loop, 312-575-9900; www.n9negroup.com**
With its subtly changing light scheme and cosmo-sipping, air-kissing crowd, the slick N9NE occasionally gets criticized for being more of a scene than a restaurant. Whoever says that likely hasn't delved into the menu, which features huge, prime-aged steaks and chops, augmented with a Maine lobster tail or Alaskan crab legs for a reasonable $23. There's also a wide array of seafood options, including a miso-marinated cod with scallions and shiitake mushrooms. Bolstering the restaurant's argument is a caviar service, offering Russian caviar by the ounce. In any case, they must be doing something right, as this spot begat the N9NE/Ghost Bar in Las Vegas and Dallas.
*Steak. Lunch (Monday-Friday), dinner. Closed Sunday. $36-85*

### ★★★ONE SIXTYBLUE
**1400 W. Randolph St., West Loop, 312-850-0303;**
**www.onesixtyblue.com**
For many Chicagoans, One Sixtyblue is known only as the restaurant that features Michael Jordan as one of the owners. He's still known to occasionally drop in, which is enough to bring in a crowd hoping to shake hands with His Royal Airness. For everyone else, the contemporary American cuisine—which perfectly matches the quiet, romantic atmosphere of this converted former pickle factory—is the reason to eat here. Starters may include a housemade mozzarella with roasted red, golden and candy cane beets, baby arugula and red beet vinaigrette, while entrées might feature a grilled beef tenderloin with spring onion potato gratin. (The menu changes by season.) Even if you don't spot MJ, you'll be glad you stopped by—especially if you happen to catch one of the restaurant's many specials (namely on Wednesday nights when they serve fried chicken and champagne, for only $8 each).
*Contemporary American. Dinner. Closed Sunday. Bar. $36-85*

SEPIA

### ★★★OTOM

951 W. Fulton Market, West Loop, 312-491-5804;
www.otomrestaurant.com

The lower-priced, less-formal sister of haute cuisine standby Moto, Otom is a lively mix of minimalist elegance and playful mod, with orange plastic chairs and orange tableside flowers contrasting with the exposed brick walls. Décor aside, Otom stands out for its cuisine: Salmon ceviche on crispy wontons makes a perfect light start to the meal, and chef Thomas Elliot Bowman crafts clever fare for his entrées. You never know what you're doing to get but these have featured things like the "TV Dinner," which includes chicken-fried duck confit, carrot and edamame pie, and the popular fried beef cheek ravioli with saffron-parsnip purée. Despite its proximity to its more-famous sibling, Otom's moderate prices, unique atmosphere and excellent food make it a spot worthy of standing on its own.
*Contemporary American. Dinner. Closed Sunday-Monday. $36-85*

### ★★★THE PUBLICAN

837 W. Fulton Market, West Loop, 312-733-9555;
www.thepublicanrestaurant.com

At the Publican, the tastemakers behind Blackbird and Avec have turned their focus to pork, oysters and beer. The space resembles a swank German beer hall. If you want privacy, ask for one of the walnut booths, which have small salon doors. Dishes are served as soon as they are ready and are meant to be shared. The grilled chicken with frites is made especially tasty with a sprinkling of espelette pepper, a Basque spice that gives the dish a subtle heat. The frites with the sunny side egg may be tempting, but go for the addictive aioli instead. The family-style Sunday dinners are a great way to try the restaurant. One past menu featured a salad with a pancetta, basil and a poached farm egg, mussels with pork confit, whole roasted pig, and butterscotch pudding for dessert.
*Gastropub. Dinner, Sunday brunch. $36-85*

**WHICH RESTAURANTS HAVE THE MOST CUTTING-EDGE FOOD?**

**Alinea**: Some people call it sci-fi food. Chef Grant Achatz's food is indeed high-tech. The chef endlessly plays with food—the textures, the aromas, the flavors—as if he were in a chem lab, and yet it somehow manages to all feel familiar at the same time.

**Avenues**: Chef Curtis Duffy offers cuisine that manages to be both simple and extravagant. He favors unusual pairings that work despite seeming contradictory, such as the grilled Wagyu steak with smoked coconut and African blue basil.

**L20**: Chef Laurent Gras offers a French-oriented seafood menu in which hard-to-find varieties are prepared in interesting ways, say, lobster that has been vacuum-cooked or snapper smoked over cherry wood.

**Moto**: Chef Homaro Cantu of Moto keeps liquid nitrogen, helium and organic food-based inks sitting alongside pots, pans and spoons. After you order, the rice-paper menu itself is the first course (it tastes like risotto).

**Schwa**: Maverick chef Michael Carlson is bare bones—tiny room, no liquor license, the cooks also serve as the waitstaff—but the food is remarkably innovative. Carlson offers three- and nine-course menus that feature knockout dishes such as a savory beer cheese soup with a pretzel roll, and a gently-seared kona kampachi with galangal, lime and a tiny splash of maple syrup.

### ★★★SEPIA
123 N. Jefferson St., West Loop, 312-441-1920;
www.sepiachicago.com

Situated inside an 1890s print shop, Sepia's décor craftily mixes the old and new, much like contemporary American dishes rooted in tradition and quality products. Pork porterhouse with buttermilk mashed potatoes, grilled chicken with savory bread pudding or short ribs braised in Belgian ale are just a few examples of what you might find on the menu. When possible, ingredients are natural and organic, and the pasta, chutneys and jams are all homemade. Liquor aficionados come here for the creative cocktails, which feature handmade syrups and bitters.
*Contemporary American. Lunch (Monday-Friday), dinner. $36-85*

## ALSO RECOMMENDED
### THE GAGE
24 S. Michigan Ave., Loop, 312-372-4243; www.thegagechicago.com

From the elk ragout poutine to the Bison tartare to the roast elk with butter poached apples and ricotta, the Gage's pub grub is anything but common. Even the good ol' fish and chips get dressed up—in newspaper. The fringe-hugging menu combined with the hopping happy hour singles scene drew Christian Bale in while he was on location in the Windy City shooting *The Dark Knight*. Lunchtime service can get bogged down with larger groups meeting for business. Go elsewhere for a quick bite.
*Gastropub. Lunch, dinner, Saturday-Sunday brunch. Bar. $36-85*

L20

### PROVINCE
161 N. Jefferson, West Loop, 312-669-9900;
www.provincerestaurant.com

Located just west of downtown, Province is longtime former Nacional 27's chef Randy Zweiban's first restaurant. At Nacional 27, he focused on the worldly cuisine of 27 Latin American countries. It would seem that he has gone in a completely new direction at Province—the restaurant is a farm-to-table driven American restaurant with dishes such as a smoked pork belly sandwich and the signature ten-hour braised lamb. But his Spanish and South American influences are still seen in dishes throughout the extensive menu, such as rabbit confit with salsa verde and marcona almond emulsion. The layout of the menu is confusing as the dishes are separated into six different categories but regardless of whether you choose small, big or bigger dishes, the results will be delicious. House cocktails such as the Province martini or Absent Field Hand are smartly made and are a good idea before dinner.

*Contemporary American. Lunch. dinner. $36-85*

### SANTORINI
800 W. Adams St., West Loop, 312-829-8820;
www.santorinichicago.com

Chicago's Greektown is packed with restaurants that make a solid spanakopita and serve a decent flaming saganaki. But the rustic Santorini stands apart from the crowd with its fresh seafood, white walls with dark wood trim, and bi-level dining room featuring a large fireplace. The spot serves excellent versions of Greek standards, like melt-in-your-mouth center-cut lamb chops and juicy chicken baked with vegetables and zesty feta cheese in phyllo dough. The true don't-miss entrées here are the grilled octopus (a house specialty) and whole fish such as tender red snapper, which can be fileted tableside and served in a tangy simple sauce of olive oil and lemon juice.

*Greek. Lunch, dinner. $36-85*

## SUSHI WABI

842 W. Randolph St., West Loop, 312-563-1224; www.sushiwabi.com

From the industrial-chic exposed ductwork to the DJ spinning tunes above the dimly lit dining room, Sushi Wabi feels as much like a club as it does one of Chicago's most popular sushi restaurants. For every hipster reveling in the loft atmosphere and cool tunes, there's a sushi aficionado delving into the restaurant's fresh fish and unique creations. The maki rolls include the tried-and-true, from an expertly crafted dragon roll brushed with eel sauce to decadent specialties like the Tarantula, which bursts with soft-shell crab, avocado, chili sauce and masago mayo. Leave room for the green-tea cheesecake, which may be the world's most delicious way to enjoy antioxidants.

*Japanese. Lunch (Monday-Friday), dinner. Bar. $16-35*

## TRATTORIA NO. 10

10 N. Dearborn St., Loop, 312-984-1718; www.trattoriaten.com

Given its Loop location and subterranean, Old World feel, it's surprising to learn that Trattoria No. 10 chef Douglas D'Avico is fairly progressive with his menu: He features organic and locally grown ingredients in items like handcrafted ravioli filled with asparagus tips and aged provolone topped with sun-dried tomato sauce, and butternut and acorn squash in a sweet walnut-butter sauce. Although it's big with the lunch crowd, Trattoria No. 10's low ceilings, alfresco-style murals and textured walls help the restaurant overcome its substreet-level locale and create romantic, cozy environs for dinner in a decidedly non-cozy neighborhood.

*Italian. Lunch (Monday-Friday), dinner. Closed Sunday. $36-85*

## LINCOLN PARK

### ★★★★ALINEA

1723 N. Halsted St., Lincoln Park, 312-867-0110;
www.alinea-restaurant.com

Not only did Alinea's internationally respected chef Grant Achatz win the 2008 James Beard Outstanding Chef Award, he's also got a hell of a story to tell. In 2007, Achatz was diagnosed with tongue cancer, and doctors said he might lose his sense of taste forever. Thankfully, an aggressive treatment looks to have beaten the cancer, and Achatz's sense of taste was saved. So now he's back in the kitchen, creating some of the most wildly creative dishes in the country. Alinea, the Latin word for that funny little symbol (¶) indicating the need for a new paragraph—or a new train of thought—is at the forefront of the molecular gastronomy movement, which re-imagines familiar foods in stunningly innovative ways. Behind the restaurant's purposefully hidden entrance and up a floating glass-and-metal staircase, you'll be treated to breathtaking creations such as the black truffle explosion, featuring truffle-topped ravioli filled with truffle broth which "explodes" in your mouth. Another dish is duck served with mango and yogurt on a pillow of juniper air. The complex meals often require equally complicated instructions from the patient waitstaff, but trust us—you won't complain.

*Contemporary American. Dinner. Closed Monday-Tuesday. $86 and up*

ALINEA

### ★★★★★CHARLIE TROTTER'S
816 W. Armitage Ave., Lincoln Park, 773-248-6228;
www.charlietrotters.com

There's not much about internationally renowned chef Charlie Trotter that hasn't already been said. Awards? He has them in spades. Books? He's written them. TV shows? He stars in a cooking series. Which brings us back to Trotter's food, and for that he uses only naturally raised meats, line-caught fish and organic produce to craft his world-famous fare. The formal waitstaff speak in hushed tones when talking about Trotter's exactingly prepared menu, which includes dishes such as chilled trout with watercress and crayfish, and Crawford Farm lamb rack with chanterelle mushrooms and fermented black garlic. Housed in an unassuming brick building in the tony Lincoln Park neighborhood, the understated restaurant—there is no art on the walls, as Trotter believes any art should be on the plate—provides a tasteful environment for what is always a remarkable evening. For those who want to see the restaurant's inner workings firsthand, Trotter's offers a table in the kitchen that comes with its own custom-prepared menu.
*Contemporary American. Dinner. Closed Sunday-Monday. $86 and up*

### ★★★★L2O
2300 N. Lincoln Park West, Lincoln Park, 773-868-0002;
www.l2orestaurant.com

At L2O, acclaimed chef Laurent Gras offers a French-oriented seafood menu that's as sophisticated as the restaurant's beautiful décor, with the dining room separated by partitions of stainless-steel cables. The menu is divided into Raw, Warm and Main sections, with the four-course tasting option offering one of each, plus a dessert. The generous selections range from fluke with lemon vinegar, caviar and basil seeds to black bass in shellfish bouillon with saffron and Rhode Island mussels. Even the bread service is memorable, with offerings of bacon croissants, anchovy twists and demi-baguettes served with housemade butter. To get an idea of Gras's meticulous nature, seize the

NORTH POND

opportunity to take the optional tour of the painstakingly clean kitchen—and keep an eye out for his astounding array of spices.

*French, Contemporary American. Dinner. Closed Tuesday. $86 and up*

### ★★★LANDMARK

**1633 N. Halsted St., Lincoln Park, 312-587-1600; www.landmarkgrill.net**

With its striking décor and boisterous crowd, you'd forgive the owners of Landmark (who also run nearby Perennial and Boka) if they concentrated a little less on the food. But chef Kurt Guzowski ensures the fare remains a priority at this massive Lincoln Park favorite, committing to the details on his wide-ranging menu. Appetizer options include smoked ravioli with braised pork belly, and Kobe beef sliders with truffles, foie gras and Moroccan ketchup. Entrées including a lobster club sandwich and grilled black pepper ribeye with blue cheese potato gratin. We recommend going earlier in the evening, because the place gets packed at night with a throng that's clearly not there for the food.

*Contemporary American. Dinner. Closed Monday. Bar. $16-35*

### ★★★NORTH POND

**2610 N. Cannon Drive, Lincoln Park, 773-477-5845;**
**www.northpondrestaurant.com**

Talk about off the beaten path: North Pond is situated in the middle of a pastoral setting in Lincoln Park, surrounded by trees and blocks away from the neighborhood's occasionally lunkheaded bar scene. The restaurant's gorgeous Prairie-style building—originally built in 1912 as a lodge for ice-skaters—overlooks a small pond and provides a stunning view of the Chicago skyline. Almost as impeccable is chef Bruce Sherman's sustainable-minded fare, which emphasizes seasonal local items in dishes such as oil-poached Alaskan halibut with smoked caviar, and Dijon-crusted rib eye with roasted farro. Sherman puts the websites of local nonprofits on his menu, but with a meal this delicious—capped by wonderful desserts such as decadent chocolate panna cotta with bing cherries and red beet sorbet—you'll put up with a little political grandstanding.

*Contemporary American. Lunch (June-September, Tuesday-Friday), dinner, Sunday brunch. Closed Monday; also closed Tuesday from January-April. $36-85*

### ★★★PERENNIAL
1800 N. Lincoln Ave., Lincoln Park, 312-981-7070;
www.perennialchicago.com

The masterminds behind Chicago fixtures Boka and Landmark have transformed this space—formerly an unimaginative chain bar/restaurant—into a must-visit scene. With its canvas ceiling, birch trees in the center of the room, and floor-to-ceiling windows, Perennial's décor is as inviting as the perpetually smiling staff and the thoughtful cuisine prepared by chef Ryan Poli. The menu features crispy duck breast with savoy cabbage, duck confit and foie gras pithivier in a dried cherry sauce, and housemade linguini carbornara that's worth every fat gram. For dessert, be sure to order the crispy hazelnut bar with creme fraiche and chocolate caramel. The adjacent lounge provides an elegant spot for a post-dinner drink—provided you can get a seat, that is.

*Contemporary American. Dinner, brunch. Bar. $36-85*

## ALSO RECOMMENDED
### SAI CAFÉ
2010 N. Sheffield Ave., Lincoln Park, 773-472-8080; www.saicafe.com

There are plenty of neighborhood sushi restaurants in Chicago, but few offer fish that's as fresh—and generously portioned—as this Lincoln Park standby. The menu offers several different entrées, but it's the sushi that packs people into the restaurant's three laid-back rooms. Any of the sushi creations will delight you, but the rainbow maki with tuna, yellowtail, salmon and avocado delicately wrapped around rice and a crab stick is particularly fresh and delicious.

*Japanese. Dinner. $36-85*

## LINCOLN SQUARE/ANDERSONVILLE/NORTHWEST SIDE
### ★★★ARUN'S
4156 N. Kedzie Ave., Northwest Side, 773-539-1909;
www.arunsthai.com

Thai cuisine in Chicago was once consigned to BYOB storefronts, but owner Arun Sampanthavivat's gorgeous restaurant, which he opened in 1985, brought his native land's food to the level of haute cuisine. The 2,500-square-foot, bi-level dining room—its every nook and cranny filled with gorgeous Thai art (much of it painted by the owner's brother)—is located in far-flung Albany Park. The almost museum-like surroundings complement a dining experience that brilliantly combines heat and sweetness. The constantly changing offerings are part of a 12-course tasting menu consisting of six appetizers, four entrées and two desserts, and preparations range from a beef curry in a spicy sauce to whole tamarind snapper. The personable service is always ready to accommodate any preferences or tolerance for spiciness, and a meticulous wine-pairing is available for the asking.

*Thai. Dinner. Closed Monday. $86 and up*

### ★★★BISTRO CAMPAGNE
4518 N. Lincoln Ave., Lincoln Square, 773-271-6100;
www.bistrocampagne.com

We know this Lincoln Square bistro isn't exactly centrally situated, but the classic French fare and immaculate wine list make the cozy neighborhood spot well worth the trip to the North Side. Acclaimed chef Michael Altenberg is a vocal sustainable-food advocate, so he uses local, organic ingredients to create dishes like his flawless pan-seared salmon with braised lentils and succulent steak piled high with delicious fries. We can't talk about Bistro Campagne—let alone visit here—without mentioning Altenberg's steamed mussels, served in a tasty Belgian ale. The restaurant itself has a rustic feel with Prairie-style design touches and dark wood trim, while the outdoor space provides a beautiful mosaic fountain and a quaint cottage for a secluded retreat.

*French. Dinner, Sunday brunch. Bar. $36-85*

### ★★★SOLA
3868 N. Lincoln Ave., Northwest Side, 773-327-3868;
www.sola-restaurant.com

Drawing inspiration from the sun (sol), her own independence (solo) and her roots (she's so L.A., as her friends joke), chef/owner and former surfer Carol Wallack dove headfirst into Chicago's dining scene when she opened Sola in January 2006. Wallack's focus is on freshness, so she sources all her produce from local farmers and all her seafood from Hawaii. Perhaps you'll find the culmination of these ingredients brought to your table in the form of a salad of Asian greens, housemade bacon, pineapple, rosemary and black vinegar; or halibut atop a bed of soy beluga lentils and wilted watercress, dressed with a lobster butter sauce. If these inventive takes on island-style dishes aren't enough to make you feel like wearing a grass skirt in Chicago, nothing will be. Note: At press time, Sola was in works to move to a new location downtown and a new restaurant from Wallack would replace it; be sure to check their website for updates.

*Contemporary American, Hawaiian. Lunch (Thursday-Friday), dinner, Saturday-Sunday brunch. $36-85*

## ALSO RECOMMENDED
### GREAT LAKE
1477 West Balmoral Ave., Andersonville, 773-334-9270

It is easy to miss the unassuming storefront on a side street in Chicago's north side Andersonville neighborhood but that would be a mistake, as this intimate (read: tiny) "mom & pop" pizza shop serves up some of the city's best pizza. Due to the size and popularity of the place, and the fact that the chef/owner makes every single pizza that touches the lucky few diners' lips, the wait can be excruciatingly long. But do not let that deter you. There are three nightly pizza offerings and if the mushroom pie is on the menu, order it and you will be rewarded with an earthy, salty, cheesy slice of perfection. Capitalizing on locally sourced farm fresh ingredients, other toppings may include fresh spinach, herbs and tomatoes, as well as housemade sausage. A petit fresh green salad with choice of two dressings and scoops of locally made ice cream round out the sparse but well-edited menu. Great Lake is BYOB so put your name on the list and walk to grab a bottle of wine at nearby wine shop, In Fine Spirits.

*Pizza. Dinner. Closed Sunday-Tuesday. $16-35*

PERENNIAL

## UKRAINIAN VILLAGE/WEST TOWN

### ★★★GREEN ZEBRA

1460 W. Chicago Ave., Ukrainian Village, 312-243-7100;
www.greenzebrachicago.com

Vegetarians often feel like they get a raw deal at restaurants, with maybe a token eggplant dish tossed their way at the corner of the menu. Not so at Green Zebra, chef Shawn McClain's small-plates ode to non-carnivores. After all, even a filet fanatic would get hooked on slow-roasted shiitake mushrooms in a crispy potato with savoy cabbage, or grilled asparagus with Camembert beignets. The elegant, earth-toned décor is more upscale than granola; you're more likely to hear Joy Division than the Grateful Dead, and the service is efficient and refined. If you simply must eat meat, there are one or two non-vegetarian items on the menu—though considering the diverse and delicious plant-based options, why settle for chicken?
*Contemporary vegetarian. Dinner, Sunday brunch. $16-35*

### ★★★WEST TOWN TAVERN

1329 W. Chicago Ave., West Town, 312-666-6175; www.westtowntavern.com
You can get fried chicken just about anywhere, but for Susan Goss' great-grandmother's tried-and-true recipe, you have to come to the West Town Tavern. Co-owner Goss breaks out the recipe every week for the popular Fried Chicken (and Biscuit) Mondays, while serious carnivores make weekly pilgrimages here for the juicy, 10-ounce Wagyu beef creations (served on grilled focaccia with herbed mayo and grilled onions) on Burger Tuesdays. The restaurant's blond wood floors, exposed brick and warm lighting also provide a welcoming environment for the tavern's delicious contemporary American cuisine with a comfort-food touch, such as the pot roast that's braised in zinfandel, and the gently seared diver scallops served with a delicate mushroom-leek risotto.
*Contemporary American. Dinner. Closed Sunday. Bar. $36-85*

SPRING

## ALSO RECOMMENDED
### COALFIRE
1321 W. Grand Ave., West Town, 312-226-2625;
www.coalfirechicago.com

Chicago's reputation is changing dramatically these days: No one talks about Al Capone anymore, the Cubs are actually a good team and the city's pizza fans aren't all heading out for deep dish. Places like the unassuming, relatively new Coalfire are a big reason for this last shift. This restaurant bakes its pies in a coal-heated oven, which produces an eyebrow-singeing temperature of 800 degrees. This high heat delivers a smoky, slightly charred crust that's both crispy and chewy, while the housemade tomato sauce has the perfect amount of sweetness. The surprisingly spartan list of toppings includes prosciutto, red peppers and anchovies, but regulars swear by the simple margherita, which is made up of sauce, buffalo mozzarella, ricotta and freshly cut basil leaves.

*Pizza. Lunch (Saturday-Sunday), dinner. Closed Monday. $16-35*

## BUCKTOWN/WICKER PARK
### ★★★BOB SAN
1805-07 W. Division St., Wicker Park, 773-235-8888;
www.bob-san.com

Bob San's owner Bob Bee has created a veritable sushi empire throughout Chicago, giving the city fixtures like Sai Café, Sushi Naniwa and Hachi's Kitchen. But it's Wicker Park's bustling Bob San that's earned Bee his biggest buzz. The restaurant features lively lounge music, an open wooden-beam ceiling and playful fish-shaped lighting fixtures. But the focus here is the expansive menu, which features some 45 handcrafted rolls that include classics like the spider roll with soft-shell crab, avocado and cucumber. There are also a dozen entrées for non-sushi eaters, including a teriyaki New York strip steak. The tables are packed closely together, so if you're

## WHAT ARE THE BEST CELEBRITY CHEF RESTAURANTS?

**Frontera Grill**: The always-popular spot has a festive atmosphere with colorful walls and hanging papier-mâché animals, which provides a perfect environment to enjoy Rick Bayless's housemade moles and freshly ground corn tortillas.

**Table Fifty-Two**: Art Smith will likely forever be known as Oprah's chef, although that's probably not such a bad thing. The menu boasts Smith's upgraded take on Southern classics.

**Charlie Trotter's**: The master chef's eponymous Lincoln Park restaurant is a fixture in Chicago, consistently great year after year.

hoping for a romantic meal, try to get one of the tables by the window, close to the bar.
*Japanese. Dinner. Bar. $36-85*

### ★★★MIRAI SUSHI
2020 W. Division St., Wicker Park, 773-862-8500; www.miraisushi.com
Need to impress a sashimi aficionado? Head to Mirai, where the emphasis is solely on the fish. In-the-know sushi lovers flock here for the unagi trio, a roll with unagi, avocado and an unagi sauce. Chef/partner Jun Ichikawa also specializes in elegantly simple rolls, such as the tuna tuna salmon, which features poached salmon topped with tuna and drizzled with a light wasabi mayonnaise. Those who want something other than sushi won't be disappointed with offerings like the perfectly made teriyaki salmon or kani ebi korekke (shrimp and snow crab cakes). For a pre- (or post-) dinner cocktail, Mirai has a funky lounge upstairs.
*Japanese. Dinner. Bar. $36-85*

### ★★★RESTAURANT TAKASHI
1952 N. Damen Ave., Bucktown, 773-772-6170; www.takashichicago.com
It seemed like the pinnacle of chef Takashi Yagihashi's career: After putting together an award-winning résumé in Chicago and Detroit, he headed to Las Vegas to lead a restaurant in the Wynn Resort. Thankfully for Chicagoans, Yagihashi returned after 18 months to helm his namesake restaurant, a minimalist spot in Bucktown that expertly blends high-end American influences and French technique with the simplicity of Japanese fare. In a small, low-key room of gray walls accented with cherry wood, the menu offers hot and cold small plates that may feature fresh hamachi, salmon, tuna and other seafood. The more substantial large plates menu offers dishes such as roasted potato/prosciutto-crusted Atlantic salmon and a roasted New York strip with fresh wasabi and miso-glazed fingerling potatoes. In a neighborhood with more than a few so-so sushi spots, Takashi simultaneously expands the palate while refining the details of Japanese cuisine. If you're in the Loop, check out the chef's noodle bar in the food court of Macy's.
*Contemporary American, Japanese. Lunch (Sunday), dinner. Closed Monday. $36-85*

### ★★★SCHWA

**1466 N. Ashland Ave., Wicker Park, 773-252-1466;**
**www.schwarestaurant.com**

Maverick chef Michael Carlson is viewed as the enfant terrible of the Chicago dining world. His eccentric Schwa became the apple of Chicago foodies' eyes, but then he abruptly closed for four months and was vague about what he did in the meantime. Now, the restaurant has reopened and while its quixotic charms are still evident—tiny room, no liquor license, the cooks also serve as the waitstaff—the food is still remarkably innovative. The charismatic Carlson—who's likely to sprinkle a few uses of "dude" during your meal—offers three- and nine-course menus that feature organic ingredients and locally grown produce. The latter option includes such knockout dishes as a savory beer cheese soup with a pretzel roll, and a gently seared kona kampachi with galangal, lime and a tiny splash of maple syrup. It's a little pricey for what it is, but the cost of the meal is offset by the restaurant's BYOB policy, which allows you to carry in your own wine for a mere $2.50-per-person corkage fee. Just be sure to call ahead to snag a table; though Carlson may be unpredictable, the restaurant's popularity is not.
*Contemporary American. Dinner. Closed Sunday-Monday. $36-85*

### ★★★SPRING

**2039 W. North Ave., 773-395-7100, Wicker Park;**
**www.springrestaurant.net**

Spring is Chicago restaurant star Shawn McClain's first local outpost, and some still say it's his best. The spartan dining room—the building was once a Russian bathhouse, and some of the original white tiles are still on the walls—provides a relaxing environ for McClain's celebrated seafood-oriented, Asian-inflected fare, which may include such sophisticated fare as Maine sea scallop with braised oxtail, Arctic char with toasted sesame risotto and peekytoe crab, and organic roasted chicken with black garlic and ricotta dumplings. The honeydew sorbet in a plum soup makes the perfect light capper for a remarkable meal.
*Contemporary American. Dinner. Closed Monday. $36-85*

## ALSO RECOMMENDED
### BIG STAR

**1531 N. Damen, Wicker Park, 773-235-4039; www.bigstarchicago.com**

This gourmet honky tonk features tacos, whiskey and tequila. Those tacos are from chef Paul Kahan (of Blackbird, Avec and Publican fame) and are made with things such as pork belly and spit-roasted pork shoulder. Big Star took over the former Pontiac Cafe, a beloved—if run down—spot in Wicker Park that locals flocked to in the summer for its large outdoor patio out front (which is still there and has 125 seats). A square wooden bar takes up most of the interior; a few booths line the wall (only parties of four or more can sit there). Country music blares from a record player and they only take cash (there's an ATM on the premises). But the tacos make up for any inconvenience a lack of seating or no credit card policy may cause. The pork belly tacos are the best thing on the menu: rich, delicate and packed with flavor. The pork shoulder tacos are also very nice, as are the crispy fish tacos. You can also order guacamole and salads, and the whiskey and tequila selections are very good (if you don't prefer either, the house wine should do).
*Mexican. Lunch, dinner, late-night. $15 and under*

**BIG STAR**

## BONGO ROOM

1470 N. Milwaukee Ave., Wicker Park, 773-489-0690; 1152 S. Wabash Ave., South Loop, 312-291-0100

If you're looking for an imaginative breakfast in a playful environment, you'd better head to the Bongo Room early. Even 30 minutes before the doors open, the sidewalk outside this Wicker Park standby is packed with hungover urbanites anxiously awaiting a table. The breakfast burrito filled with guacamole and fluffy scrambled eggs is a favorite, but most come here for the outrageously sweet concoctions that mix breakfast with dessert, such as Oreo cookie pancakes or chocolate tower French toast. The spot is a little less crowded when lunchtime rolls around, when the kitchen offers inventive fare like a tasty maple-and-mustard-roasted pork loin sandwich and a delectable baby spinach, golden beet and duck confit salad. If you can't stomach the interminable brunch wait, try the South Loop location, where it's slightly—note, we said slightly—less crowded.

*Contemporary American. Breakfast, lunch, Saturday-Sunday brunch. $16-35*

## CAFÉ ABSINTHE

1958 W. North Ave., Wicker Park, 773-278-4488;
www.cafeabsinthechicago.com

It's telling that the entrance to this Wicker Park fave is not on teeming North Avenue but in an alley around the corner. The off-the-beaten-path entry likely keeps the tippling masses from stumbling in and disrupting the restaurant's dimly lit, romantic atmosphere. Chef Jose Garcia's seasonal, American-oriented menu changes daily, but a recent incarnation featured Australian herb-marinated lamb with sautéed watercress and rosemary jus, and horseradish-encrusted salmon with garlic mashed potatoes and cabernet butter sauce. The signature dessert is a dark chocolate lava cake infused with Grand Marnier liqueur in a prickly-pear sauce—a treat that's well worth a trip down any alley.

*Contemporary American. Dinner. Closed Monday. $36-85*

RIA

## CRUST

**2056 W. Division St., Wicker Park, 773-235-5511;**
**www.crustchicago.com**

With its stark white-brick walls and orange plastic chairs, Crust sure doesn't seem like it's at the forefront of a revolution. Yet the spot, helmed by Bistro Campagne's Michael Altenberg, has created the Midwest's first certified organic restaurant. Using organic flour and ingredients including fresh-pulled water buffalo mozzarella, Altenberg coaxes delicious pizzas (inexplicably called "wood-oven flatbreads" on the menu) from the tile-encrusted wood-burning oven. The surprisingly small menu features only 12 options, but the possibilities include such gourmet combinations as the Carbonara—topped with roasted slab bacon, peas and an egg sunny-side up—and the Mexicali blues—with provolone, mozzarella, roasted shrimp, cilantro and pico de gallo. Even some of the beer offerings are organic, letting you get soused as sustainably as possible.

*Pizza. Lunch, dinner. Closed Tuesday. $16-35*

## LE BOUCHON

**1958 N. Damen Ave., Bucktown, 773-862-6600;**
**www.lebouchonofchicago.com**

There's a reason this tiny storefront bistro has been packing in a crowd of regulars for more than 15 years. The food is delicious, the prices are reasonable, the mood is convivial, and the feeling is somehow unmistakably Parisian. The menu reflects owner Jean-Claude Poilevey's French roots (he's a native of Burgundy); Le Bouchon features standbys such as a creamy housemade pâté, beef Bourguignon over mashed potatoes, and white-wine poached salmon with cucumber and tomato beurre blanc. The onion tart—a classic intermingling of crispy pastry and tangy caramelized onions—is a signature dish. The closely packed tables and noisy room aren't for everyone, but those who seek out Le Bouchon's authentic environs will likely be glad they made the effort.

*French. Lunch, dinner. Closed Sunday. $16-35*

**PIECE**

1927 W. North Ave., Wicker Park, 773-772-4422;
www.piecechicago.com

Housed in a 5,800-square-foot former garage, Piece eschews classic deep-dish Chicago pizza in favor of a delicious thin-crust variety that was invented at the famed Sally's Apizza in New Haven, Connecticut. Piece (which is co-owned by Cheap Trick guitarist Rick Nielsen, who lent one of his five-necked guitars to the restaurant) serves huge rectangular pizzas featuring toppings that are both standard (pepperoni, onions) and not-so-standard (mashed potatoes, clams). Some of the combinations might sound strange but they somehow meld perfectly with the pizza's crunchy thin crust and tangy tomato sauce. The pizzas aren't the only reason that the massive space is always packed with a randy crowd checking out the game (and each other): Piece's onsite, handcrafted brews won the World Beer Cup's Small Brewpub Award in 2006.

*Pizza. Lunch, dinner. Bar. $16-35*

THE ELYSIAN

# SLEEP ON IT

It doesn't matter whether you're in town for a convention or for the latest outdoor music festival, you can rest easy knowing there's a hotel for you somewhere in this city. Chicago's lodging options are as diverse as they are vast. So decide what you're looking for—location? fabulous spa? boutique hotel?—and then pick the perfect one for your stay.

## GOLD COAST/STREETERVILLE

### ★★★THE ALLERTON HOTEL – MICHIGAN AVENUE

701 N. Michigan Ave., Streeterville, 312-440-1500, 877-701-8111; www.theallertonhotel.com

During the Roaring Twenties, the Allerton was one of the first high rises to pop up on the Chicago skyline. Now a designated landmark, the Michigan Avenue hotel retains some classic elements (such as its exterior sign that reads "Tip Top Tap"—the name of the popular cocktail lounge that closed in 1961) while adding some contemporary accents. The hotel had a makeover in May 2008 and the rooms are now in tip-top shape. The sophisticated spaces are done up in traditional navy blue and white, while modern touches, such as trendy patterned throw pillows, white upholstered headboards and iPod docking stations, are sprinkled throughout. Beware of the rooms labeled "Classic"—that's code for "tiny."

*443 rooms. Restaurant, bar. Fitness center. Business center. $151-250*

### ★★★THE AMBASSADOR EAST HOTEL

1301 N. State Parkway, Gold Coast, 312-787-7200, 888-506-3471; www.theambassadoreasthotel.com

Many celebs have checked into this Gold Coast hotel, including Vince Vaughn, Richard Gere and Frank Sinatra (who has a celebrity suite named after him). One reason for its popularity is its location. The hotel sits among residential buildings in a tony neighborhood, plus it's near the jogging trail and volleyball courts of Oak Street Beach. Another reason may be the famed Pump Room restaurant, where Old Hollywood stars flocked to its fabled Booth One, a table that only the most exclusive diners could snag. Robert Wagner and Natalie Wood toasted their wedding in that booth, as did Lauren Bacall and Humphrey Bogart when they got hitched. Frequent guest Judy Garland even paid tribute to the hot spot in her song *Chicago*: "Chicago, we'll meet at the Pump Room, Ambassador East." If you meet at the Pump Room today, you'll feast on contemporary American cuisine from executive chef Nick Sutton. Hotel impresario Ian Schraeger purchased the landmark in 2010 and is planning a massive renovation, so check with the front desk before visiting.

*285 rooms. Restaurant, bar. Fitness center. Business center. $151-250*

### ★★★THE DRAKE HOTEL CHICAGO

140 E. Walton Place, Gold Coast, 312-787-2200, 800-774-1500; www.thedrakehotel.com

The Drake is the hotel of choice for visiting politicians and dignitaries. Winston Churchill, Pope John Paul II and Princess Diana all roomed at the 1920 landmark hotel, ideally located at the beginning of North Michigan Avenue. But this old star could use some polish to regain its luster. While the public spaces still preserve the splendor of the past and some rooms got updated in early 2008, other guest rooms haven't yet gotten their makeovers. Avoid disappointment by asking for a newly renovated room (with gold and white linens and a flat-screen TV).

*535 rooms. Restaurant, bar. Fitness center. Business center. $251-350*

### ★★★★ELYSIAN
11 E. Walton, Gold Coast, 312-646-1300, 800-500-8511;
www.elysianhotels.com

If Madame Coco Chanel were alive today, she would most certainly feel at home at the Elysian. The chandeliers are inspired by her jewels, the drapes are patterned after her dress designs and the casual restaurant on the third floor, Balsan, is named after Étienne Balsan, the man who financed her first shop. Designed by Lucien Lagrange, the Parisian Art Deco jewel recalls a bygone era of travel with its old fashioned motor court, flawless service (note that the staff does not accept tips), and exquisite décor featuring white marble, velvet sofas, stacks of art books on antique tables and a sophisticated gray, white and black color palette. Guest rooms are spacious (there are only 10 per floor) with fireplaces, terraces, white marble baths and wet bars with handy refrigerator drawers. The hotel's two restaurants, the fine-dining Ria, and the more casual Balsan, are both sensational (the latter is a chic spot for cocktails and snacks). A handsome bar with wood paneling and leather seats is located on the second floor. The ground floor of the hotel is dedicated to the lavish spa, complete with Greek columns, mosaic pool and men's atelier.

*188 rooms. Restaurant, bar. Fitness center. Pool. Spa. $351 and up*

### ★★★EMBASSY SUITES CHICAGO - DOWNTOWN/LAKEFRONT
511 N. Columbus Drive, Streeterville, 312-836-5900, 888-903-8884;
www.chicagoembassy.com

Traveling families can spread out here and make it a home away from home. The two-room suites have a separate living room with a sofa bed and dining table, a microwave, a coffeemaker and a fridge. After a March 2008 renovation, the bland beige-hued suites got an upgrade with two flat-panel TVs per room and local artwork on the walls to add some Chicago flavor. If sticking close to your new home makes you stir-crazy, head to the atrium lounge, order a cocktail from the nearby bar and enjoy the soothing sound of the 70-foot cascading water wall. Or you can just wait until the free daily manager's reception to tipple and munch on some appetizers. Also be sure to take advantage of the complimentary made-to-order breakfast before rounding up the kids and trekking over to nearby Navy Pier—you'll need the energy.

*455 rooms. Restaurant, bar. Complimentary breakfast. Fitness center. Pool. Business center. $151-250*

### ★★★★★FOUR SEASONS HOTEL CHICAGO
120 E. Delaware Place, Gold Coast, 312-280-8800;
www.fourseasons.com/chicagofs

With its prime Mag Mile location and attractive, contemporary rooms, this luxe hotel is a top choice for visiting celebrities and those who appreciate the peace and quiet the polished staff practically guarantees. A recent renovation took the formerly traditional English country décor and transformed it by adding French deco style, with flowery prints replaced with rich chocolate, deep blue and shimmery silver hues, and new leather window

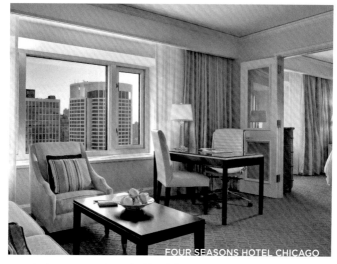

FOUR SEASONS HOTEL CHICAGO

seats in many rooms overlooking Lake Michigan and the Gold Coast. The lobby, grand ballroom, restaurants and the larger suites and apartments received updates in early 2009. Two things that haven't changed: the wonderful, personal service, and the location. It's situated just above Bloomingdale's and other stores such as Gucci, Williams-Sonoma and Michael Kors in the 900 North Michigan building.

*346 rooms. Restaurant, bar. Fitness center. Pool. Spa. Business center. $351 and up*

### ★★★HILTON SUITES CHICAGO/MAGNIFICENT MILE
**198 E. Delaware Place, Gold Coast, 312-664-1100; www.hilton.com**

This all-suite hotel is in the heart of downtown, making it a convenient choice for business travelers and families alike. The classic navy and maroon suites come with a separate living room complete with a flat-screen TV, mini-fridge and pullout sofa. But who would want to veg on the couch when you can head to the nearby Hancock Tower and peer out from the 94th-floor observatory or—even better—zip up to the 95th-floor Signature Lounge to relax with a sidecar and a vista of downtown? Go ahead and order another round or two; your hotel is within stumbling distance anyway.

*345 rooms. Restaurant. Fitness center. Pool. Business center. Pets accepted. $151-250*

### ★★★HOTEL INDIGO
**1244 N. Dearborn St., Gold Coast, 312-787-4980, 866-521-6950; www.goldcoastchicagohotel.com**

If you want something beyond a cookie-cutter hotel room bathed in banal beige, retreat to Hotel Indigo. The guest rooms are more like calming beach houses than typical hotel spaces. Hardwood floors, whitewashed furniture, teak benches, and navy and indigo blue dominate the rooms along with lime green accents, and vibrant wall-size photo murals of blueberries, irises and sky-blue cable-knit sweaters transform the space. Certain touches make it clear that it's not just another day at the beach: spa-style showerheads,

THE PENINSULA CHICAGO

sleek Melitta coffeemakers, Aveda toiletries and personal trainers at the fitness center.

*165 rooms. Restaurant, bar. Fitness center. Spa. Business center. Pets accepted. $251-350*

### ★★★HOTEL INTERCONTINENTAL

505 N. Michigan Ave., Streeterville, 312-944-4100, 800-628-2112; www.chicago.intercontinental.com

Originally the 1929 Medinah Athletic Club, Hotel InterContinental still maintains some of its old-time glory. Its 12th floor Art Deco Junior Olympic pool is where Olympic swimmer and *Tarzan* actor Johnny Weissmuller frequently escaped from the jungle to do some laps. The hotel now has a state-of-the-art three-story fitness center, one of the largest hotel gyms in the city. If you don't want to be quite that healthy, swing by ENO, where you can order wine flights accompanied by artisanal cheese or luscious chocolate. The rooms in the Main Building are plain-Jane with cream duvets, maroon throw pillows, and maroon-and-gold striped curtains. If you like Old World décor, you'll appreciate the historic tower's rooms, which use the same color palette, but replace mahogany headboards with carved ones and basic bedding with fancy patterned covers.

*790 rooms. Restaurant, bar. Fitness center. Pool. Business center. Pets accepted. $251-350*

### ★★★PARK HYATT CHICAGO

800 N. Michigan Ave., Gold Coast, 312-335-1234, 800-233-1234; www.parkchicago.hyatt.com

The luxe Park Hyatt showers guests with butlers, personal safes with laptop rechargers and storage for wardrobes (who can travel without that?). The chic décor is simple and understated with cherry wood-filled guest rooms, gold and mocha accents and leather chairs. Make sure to bathe in the oversized tub; as you soak you can slide open the wall to reveal the bedroom and views of the skyline or Lake Michigan. For more relaxation, pamper yourself at the onsite medispa Tiffani Kim Institute with a customized facial. If you're the sporty type, borrow one of the hotel's free bicycles and do some sightseeing while pedaling along Chicago's many bike paths. Afterward, complete the experience with dinner at NoMI, an excellent contemporary French-Asian restaurant overlooking Michigan Avenue.

*198 rooms. Restaurant, bar. Fitness center. Spa. Pool. Business center. Pets accepted. $351 and up*

### ★★★★★THE PENINSULA CHICAGO
**108 E. Superior St., Gold Coast, 312-337-2888, 866-288-8889; www.chicago.peninsula.com**

Stars like Ellen DeGeneres, Chris Rock and Brad Pitt and Angelina Jolie visit The Peninsula for its luxurious rooms and spa, but don't overlook it as a dining destination. The hotel is known for its highly acclaimed Shanghai Terrace and Avenues restaurants. There are also the afternoon teas, which offer exotic blends, including those made especially for The Peninsula, as well as a lavish chocolate buffet on Fridays and Saturdays. Even without the food options, The Peninsula stands out. The Peninsula Spa by ESPA offers a full menu of services and a relaxation lounge where you can doze under a comforter in a sectioned-off area and relax uninterrupted after your treatment. Luxurious guest rooms are bright with light wood and muted earth tones, and the marble bathrooms have roomy tubs where you can watch TV while you soak. A bedside control panel allows you to shut off the light and signal that you don't want to be disturbed, all without having to leave the comfort of your 300-thread-count sheets.

*339 rooms. Restaurant, bar. Fitness center. Spa. Pool. Business center. Pets accepted. $351 and up*

### ★★★★THE RITZ-CARLTON CHICAGO, A FOUR SEASONS HOTEL
**160 E. Pearson St., Gold Coast, 312-266-1000, 800-621-6906; www.fourseasons.com/chicagorc**

When you're at the Ritz, which rests atop shopping mecca Water Tower Place, the city view from the large-windowed rooms is hard to beat. The spacious guest rooms and executive suites were given a makeover in 2007, and floral-patterned duvets and dark wood furniture were replaced with crisp white linens and a soothing grey color palette. (Renovations were completed on all other suites in 2010.) If you don't want to leave, send up for the spa's in-room signature aromatherapy massage or have a customized fragranced bath drawn for you in your marble bathroom. After your treatment and soothing bath, you might want to rest your heavy head on the down pillow and bury yourself underneath the down blanket. But force yourself to grab a bite in Deca. The bar and restaurant on the 12th floor where ladies used to lunch is now a chic spot servings fizzy cocktails, oysters and bistro favorites such as duck confit.

*434 rooms. Restaurant, bar. Fitness center. Spa. Pool. Business center. Pets accepted. $351 and up*

### ★★★SOFITEL CHICAGO WATER TOWER
**20 E. Chestnut St., Gold Coast, 312-324-4000; www.sofitel.com**

You can't miss the stylish Sofitel—look for the triangle-shaped building near downtown. The glass and steel structure looks like it leapt out from the pages of an interior design magazine and into the Gold Coast. The rooms

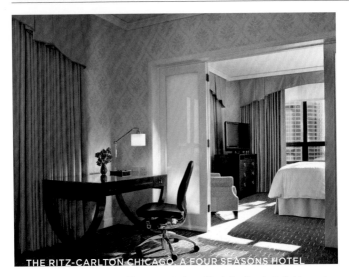
THE RITZ-CARLTON CHICAGO, A FOUR SEASONS HOTEL

aren't too shabby, either. They are a tad small but airy, thanks to light wood furniture, cream walls, bedding and mirrored closet doors. The bathrooms are roomier, with separate showers and tubs. This hotel goes Francophile all the way, with Café des Architectes, a French restaurant, and Le Bar, which has floor-to-ceiling glass walls and is the perfect place for a wine flight and a cheese plate.

*415 rooms. Restaurant, bar. Fitness center. Business center. Pets accepted. $251-350*

### ★★★THE SUTTON PLACE HOTEL – CHICAGO
**21 E. Bellevue Place, Gold Coast, 312-266-2100, 866-378-8866; www.suttonplace.com**
White is the shade of choice for the linens in the rooms here, while the drapes, carpeting and wallpaper are beige, replacing the old gloomy gray that used to dominate the rooms. The only vibrant color you'll see is a smattering of purple and bold blue in a stray chair or pillow. On the bright side, you can escape to The Whiskey Bar & Grill to unwind with some authentic Mexican fare; try the shrimp tacos and wash them down with a margarita or two, which will put some color in your cheeks if your room is without.

*246 rooms. Restaurant, bar. Business center. Fitness center. Pets accepted. $251-350*

### ★★★W CHICAGO - LAKESHORE
**644 N. Lake Shore Drive, Streeterville; 312-943-9200 www.starwoodhotels.com**
Business travelers who yawn at the usual tedious hotel environs will seek refuge at the W, which has a prime spot on Lake Shore Drive. After settling into your small, dimly lit but sophisticated room, which offers a mix of taupe and deep purples, head up to the hotel's eighth floor to pamper yourself with a treatment at Bliss, a cheerful spa that lives up to its name. There you can have a pedicure while you catch an episode of *Entourage* on your own personal TV. Afterward, return to your room, crawl under the goose-down

---

**WHAT ARE THE BEST BOUTIQUE HOTELS?**

**Dana Hotel:** To compete with the other boutique hotels, Dana offers guests some extras, including luxurious all-natural treatments at the spa and tasty bites from a floating sushi bar, luxe bathrooms featuring Italian rain showers roomy enough for two and stocked wine chillers in the rooms.

**The James Hotel:** This comfortable boutique hotel features rooms with full-size bars—not that you're likely to spend much time in your room considering that the bar and lounge are both hotspots, and David Burke's Primehouse is downstairs.

**The Wit:** The city's newest boutique hotel is located in the Loop in a stylish glass-encased tower. While rooms are contemporary and comfortable, the main draw here is the wildly popular rooftop bar.

---

duvet and watch a DVD from the lending library. Or go to the penthouse lounge, Whiskey Sky, where you sip a cocktail and admire the Lake Michigan views. Adjacent to Whiskey Sky is Altitude, a revolving banquet room that would be an impressive spot for a business meeting.

*520 rooms. Restaurant, bar. Business center. Fitness center. Pool. Spa. Pets accepted. $251-350*

### ★★★THE WESTIN MICHIGAN AVENUE
**909 N. Michigan Ave., Gold Coast, 312-943-7200, 800-937-8461; www.westin.com/michiganave**

The Westin tries to offer a little something for everyone. Shopaholics will love the hotel for its location across from Water Tower Place. Kids will enjoy the Kids Club, whose membership comes with a drawstring bag with a world map and make-your-own postcard kit upon check-in. Parents of newborns will appreciate getting their own drawstring bag filled with first-aid items, socket covers and a nightlight. Pets sleep soundly on their own beds. Joggers will lap up the Runner's World-approved maps of local running routes. And everyone will have a restful sleep on the hotel's legendary plush mattresses. As this hotel is constantly packed, it's no suprise that it shows a little wear.

*752 rooms. Restaurant, bar. Business center. Fitness center. Pets accepted. $251-350*

## ALSO RECOMMENDED
### FAIRFIELD INN AND SUITES CHICAGO DOWNTOWN
**216 E. Ontario St., Streeterville, 312-787-3777, 800-228-2800; www.fairfieldsuiteschicago.com**

The Fairfield, just steps from Michigan Avenue and a half mile from Oak Street Beach, is simply decorated and modestly sized, which suits its guests just fine—the proximity to the Mag Mile is the main draw. If you are looking for incentives, check out the packages: One for anyone who loves to shop includes a $50 gift card, plus a free breakfast and valet parking.

*185 rooms. Complimentary breakfast. Fitness center. Business center. $61-150*

### THE TREMONT CHICAGO
**100 E. Chestnut St., Gold Coast, 312-751-1900; www.tremontchicago.com**

The pale hues, dark wood and floral textiles in the small rooms aim for a romantic vibe, but they make this European-style hotel seem dated. The rooms also provide a strange juxtaposition to the hotel's restaurant, the decidedly unflowery Mike Ditka's Restaurant, owned by the legendary Bears coach. The two-floor steakhouse replaces the faux romanticism with a cigar lounge and a live Sinatra-esque singer. Odd pairings aside, the Tremont's best perk is its location; it's a half block away from Michigan Avenue, right near the Hancock Center and Water Tower Place shopping paradise.

*130 rooms. Restaurant, bar. Business Center $151-250*

## OLD TOWN/RIVER NORTH/RIVER WEST

### ★★★AMALFI HOTEL CHICAGO

**20 W. Kinzie St., River North, 312-395-9000, 877-262-5341;**
**www.amalfihotelchicago.com**

When you check into the Amalfi, you first sit for a consultation with your "Experience Designer" (or concierge) to discuss your stay. Then an "Impressionist" (doorman) brings your luggage up to your contemporary "Space" (room). This River North boutique hotel may be a bit pretentious, but it has the goods to back it up. You'll sleep well on the pillow-top mattresses and Egyptian cotton linens, and enjoy the multi-head showers and Aveda bath products. An in-room CD collection, the hotel's DVD library and the gratis breakfast on every floor make it feel like home. (Then the "Comfort Stylist" (housekeeper) knocks on the door and reminds you where you are.)

*215 rooms. Restaurant, bar. Complimentary breakfast. Business center. Fitness center. Pets accepted. $251-350*

### ★★★CONRAD CHICAGO

**521 N. Rush St., River North, 312-645-1500;**
**www.conradhotels.com**

Architecture buffs will want to check into the Conrad, located in the landmark McGraw-Hill Building. Be sure to take a look at the façade's sculpted zodiac panels, which make the Art Deco structure stand out. Although it's situated above shops such as A|X Armani Exchange and Nordstrom, this Magnificent Mile hotel can help you find some quiet. You'll discover tranquility in your room by lounging on 500 thread-count Pratesi linens while watching the 42-inch plasma TV, playing the Bose entertainment system or listening to your iPod on the room's docking station. A better escape is the rooftop Terrace at Conrad. It may only be five stories up, but it's still a swanky place where you can enjoy a cocktail and tapas underneath the Chicago sky while gazing at the skyscrapers.

*311 rooms. Restaurant, bar. Business center. Fitness center. Pets accepted. $251-350*

### ★★★DANA HOTEL

**660 N. State St., River North, 888-301-3262;**
**www.danahotelandspa.com**

Dana is relatively new to Chicago's boutique hotel scene, having opened in June 2008. To compete with the other boutique hotels, Dana offers guests some extras, including luxurious treatments at the Spa (try the hydramemory facial to treat jet-lagged skin) and tasty bites from a floating sushi bar. The rooms are filled with light wood and natural tones for a Zen vibe, and the luxe bathrooms feature Italian rain showers roomy enough for two. To unwind, dip into the stocked wine chiller in your room. Or if you want some scenery, visit the rooftop Vertigo Sky Lounge, which features a fire pit to

DANA HOTEL

keep you warm on those chilly Chicago nights.
*216 rooms. Restaurant, bar. Fitness center. Spa. Pets accepted. $251-350*

### ★★★EMBASSY SUITES CHICAGO – DOWNTOWN

600 N. State St., River North, 312-943-3800, 800-362-2779;
www.embassysuiteschicago.com

A less sophisticated alternative to its nearby sister inn in Streeterville, this outpost screams "hotel chain" with old-style comforters in mauves and blues and the obligatory generic framed landscapes in the bedrooms. What this place lacks in style, it makes up for in roominess. The spacious suites include a separate living room with a sofa, not to mention microwave, coffeemaker and fridge. If you don't feel like chowing down on a frozen dinner, stop off for a complimentary aperitif at the daily manager's reception (5:30-7:30 p.m.) before heading to the hotel's Osteria Via Stato & Enoteca for some Italian eats.

*367 rooms. Restaurant, bar. Complimentary breakfast. Business center. Fitness center. Pool. $151-250*

### ★★★HOTEL SAX

333 N. Dearborn St., River North, 312-245-0333;
www.hotelsaxchicago.com

Techies will blog about the high-end game room here, which is open to all guests and includes five Xbox 360 stations with wireless controllers, five Zune MP3 players preloaded with music and movies, and two laptops with Internet access. But gossip bloggers will write about the hotel's visiting celebrities, when famous DJs hit the red-hued Crimson Lounge. It's no wonder the hotel, which sits next to the House of Blues, draws such high-profile guests. The too-hip-to-handle slate-gray guest rooms are wallpapered with damask prints superimposed with fake shadows of candelabras, and textures abound with leather paisley headboards, suede throw pillows and chestnut furniture.

*354 rooms. Bar. Business center. Fitness center. $251-350*

### ★★★THE JAMES HOTEL
55 E. Ontario St., River North, 312-337-1000, 877-526-3755;
www.jameshotels.com

The James attracts more stars than an awards show: Jessica Simpson, Jennifer Hudson, Jeremy Piven and Jack Johnson have all checked into the hotel. The draw could be David Burke's Primehouse, which is known for its dry-aged steaks and whimsical desserts such as cheesecake lollipops. Or it could be popular nightspot J Bar. You also can't discount the attractive rooms: Dashes of brown, red or black give the all-white, contemporary design a mod slant, and features like vinyl headboards make this one chic spot. Forget your standard mini-bar. Each room here comes outfitted with a large bar of high-end liquors.

*297 rooms. Restaurant, bar. Fitness center. Business center. Pets accepted. $151-250*

### ★★★MARRIOTT CHICAGO DOWNTOWN MAGNIFICENT MILE
540 N. Michigan Ave., River North, 312-836-0100, 800-228-9290;
www.marriott.com

As its name implies, this Marriott is conveniently situated on the Magnificent Mile. But the harried shoppers below won't faze you when you've melted underneath the plush down comforter in your bold blue- and gold-colored room (courtesy of upgrades in spring 2006) for a nap. If you can't get any Z's, take a dip in the hotel pool, or give in and join the crowds at nearby Oak Street Beach. Those who are all work-and-no-play should head to the onsite Starbucks to get some java and free WiFi. Self-check out kiosks also will help business travelers on tight schedules.

*1,198 rooms. Restaurant, bar. Business center. Fitness center. Pool. $151-250*

### ★★★OMNI CHICAGO HOTEL
676 N. Michigan Ave., River North, 312-944-6664, 888-444-6664;
www.omnihotels.com

If the name sounds familiar, it's because Oprah puts up many of her show's guests at this all-suite hotel. The beige and cream suites offer roomy digs and plasma TVs. Kids get milk and cookies the first night, as well as a goodie bag at check-in. Ask for a free Get Fit Kit ($50 deposit is required), which includes a mat and weights so that you can work out in your hotel room while the little ones play. Afterward, head up to one of the two rooftop decks where you can catch some sun in warm weather.

*347 rooms. Restaurant, bar. Business center. Fitness center. Spa. Pool. Pets accepted. $251-350*

### ★★★★TRUMP INTERNATIONAL HOTEL AND TOWER
401 N. Wabash Ave., River North, 312-588-8000, 877-458-7867;
www.trumpchicagohotel.com

The Donald put his stamp on the Chicago skyline with his stainless-steel and iridescent glass hotel, which towers over the city at 92 stories. And he continues the splendor inside the tower. The modern, slate-gray rooms have floor-to-ceiling windows that give gorgeous vistas of the city, custom-designed furniture warms up the spaces, and chefs will come to your room to cook up a meal in your state-of-the-art kitchen. The lap-of-luxury treatment doesn't end there. You can get purifying massages using ruby and diamond-infused oils at the spa. If you don't opt for the in-room

TRUMP INTERNATIONAL HOTEL AND TOWER

chef, go to the restaurant Sixteen, which has a seasonally driven menu. Afterward, have a drink at the inviting Rebar, which offers a lovely view of the adjacent Chicago River.

*339 rooms. Restaurant, bar. Business center. Fitness center. Spa. Pool. $351 and up*

## ALSO RECOMMENDED
### HAMPTON INN CHICAGO AND SUITES
33 W. Illinois St., River North, 312-832-0330, 800-426-7866;
www.hamptoninnchicago.com

Business travelers and Internet junkies will be at home at Hampton Inn. Each room comes with a portable wooden laptop desk, so you can work or surf the web from the comfort of your bed. If you have to burn the midnight oil to get that big report done, the hotel offers free coffee 24 hours a day at a beverage station and you'll have a gratis hot breakfast waiting for you in the morning. Traveling for pleasure? Go for a meal at Ruth's Chris Steak House, lounge at nightspot Ballo, laze on the sundeck or check out the Frank Lloyd Wright-inspired lobby. The hotel brags that the rooms also are influenced by the architect's signature style, but really, Wright probably would have shrugged at the standard tan-and-cream-hued suites.

*230 rooms. Restaurant, bar. Complimentary breakfast. Business center. Fitness center. Pool. $61-150*

### HOMEWOOD SUITES CHICAGO DOWNTOWN
40 E. Grand Ave., River North, 312-644-2222;
www.homewoodsuiteschicago.com

Families will appreciate the roomy suites here, but the bedrooms have a cookie-cutter feel thanks to unimaginative tan décor. Although the living rooms are somewhat brighter with a red and gold sleeper sofa and chair, they're still generic. Yet the reason to come here is the full kitchen. It offers plenty of cupboard space, plates and accessories, a microwave, a fridge, a

dishwasher and more. If you're not in the mood to cook, there's a free daily breakfast buffet and complimentary receptions Monday through Thursday from 5 to 7 p.m. featuring a light meal and drinks.
*233 rooms. Complimentary breakfast. Business center. Fitness center. Pool. $61-150*

### HOTEL FELIX
**111 W Huron St., 312-447-3440; www.hotelfelixchicago.com**
Hotel Felix sets the mark for what an eco-friendly should be—not just LEED certified but chic and charming and relaxing, proving that helping the planet does not mean you have to sacrifice luxury or comfort. The guest rooms, while on the small size, make excellent use of their space, with flatscreen televisions, drawers in the platform beds and efficient workstations. The modern rooms have a cool silver and grey color palette, comfortable beds with super-soft linens, and bathrooms stocked with natural, water-based H20 products. Best of all, the hotel is a short walk to Michigan Avenue, the River North Galleries and some of the city's liveliest nightspots, but far enough away from the hustle and bustle to be a calm oasis. After enjoying Chicago's local attractions, take advantage of the hotel's full service spa or the seasonal restaurant Elate, before making your way to the cozy, dimly lit (from an interesting glass chandelier) lounge for a nightcap in front of the fire. All in all, Hotel Felix is a natural choice for anyone looking for a great value in the heart of downtown.
*225 rooms. Restaurant, bar. Fitness center. Spa. $151-250*

## TOO NEW TO REVIEW
### HOTEL PALOMAR CHICAGO
**505 N. State Street, River North, 312-755-9703, 877-731-0505;**
**www.hotelpalomarchicago.com**
Hotel Palomar Chicago is a welcome addition to the Chicago hotel scene, offering comfortable, affordable accommodations in the heart of downtown. The Kimpton Hotel features art-themed decor, an indoor rooftop pool, and a buzzing restaurant, Sable Kitchen & Bar. Guest rooms feature neutral tones

HOTEL FELIX

with pops of color and images from the 1993 Chicago World's Fair, floor-to-ceiling windows, complimentary wireless Internet and honor bars with organic products. The hotel is just two blocks from Michigan Avenue.
*261 rooms. Restaurant, bar. Business center. Fitness center. Pool. Pets accepted. $151-250*

## LOOP/WEST LOOP

### ★★★THE BLACKSTONE, A CHICAGO RENAISSANCE HOTEL
636 S. Michigan Ave., Loop, 312-447-0955, 800-468-3571;
www.blackstonerenaissance.com

If there's anything to that whole law of attraction business, that's reason enough to stay at The Blackstone. This 1910 Beaux-Arts hotel, listed on the National Register of Historic Places, has hosted presidents, royalty, sports icons and celebrities (including Rudolph Valentino, Joan Crawford, Spencer Tracy, Katharine Hepburn, Tennessee Williams, Truman Capote and Carl Sandburg). If you are not one to name names, though, the handsome renovation completed in the spring of 2008 will still convince you. Preserving the old-fashioned elegance and architectural integrity, Sage Hospitality Resources bought the long-dormant property, stripped it, then gave it a modern edge. The finished product features a grand gilded lobby with opulent designer details and extravagant extras like a video-generated computer art piece or the constantly changing lakefront landscape; a curated collection of more than 1,400 pieces of original art by Chicago artists is displayed on the walls. The guest rooms weren't forgotten either, tastefully adorned with black, white and red décor, rainshowers, Aveda bath amenities, Eames furniture, flat-screen TVs (and TVs integrated into the bathroom mirrors in upgraded rooms). Locals crowd the restaurant, Mercat a la Planxa, for delicious Catalan-inspired food and drinks.
*332 rooms. Restaurant, bar. Business center. Fitness center. $251-350*

HOTEL ALLEGRO

### ★★★THE FAIRMONT CHICAGO, MILLENNIUM PARK
200 N. Columbus Drive, Loop, 312-565-8000, 866-540-4408;
www.fairmont.com

The Fairmont wrapped up renovations in June 2008, and with them came a change from traditional chintzes and furniture to Mid-Century modern neutrals and large Warwick Orme floral images. Rooms are an updated retreat with flat-screen TVs and remodeled bathrooms with marble tile and rainshowers. Locals head to the new mySpa for treatments. The spa is all about the details: It uses vegan nail polish and pipes your iPod's music into the treatment room. Located in the lobby is Eno, a wine, chocolate and cheese room enclosed by a glass art wall in a bamboo pattern.

*687 rooms. Restaurant, bar. Fitness center. Pets accepted. $151-250*

### ★★★HARD ROCK HOTEL
230 N. Michigan Ave., Loop, 312-345-1000, 866-966-5166;
www.hardrockhotelchicago.com

Located in the landmark Carbide and Carbon Building, the Hard Rock gives some edge to the Art Deco skyscraper. Step into the lobby, which was recently renovated for a classic vibe. Be sure to tour the hotel's display cases, which show off noted musicians' outfits, instruments and other rock 'n' roll memorabilia. But the hotel is more sleek than kitschy. Its modern silver-gray rooms offer Aveda toiletries, pillow-top beds and laptop safes, and they keep to the music theme with bathroom murals of icons such as Bowie and the Beatles. Get the rock-star treatment by staying in the Extreme Suite, a 950-foot penthouse that's on its own floor with private elevator access.

*381 rooms. Restaurant, bar. Business center. Fitness center. Spa. Pets accepted. $151-250*

## WHICH HOTELS ARE MOST HISTORIC?

**The Blackstone:** This 1910 Beaux-Arts hotel, listed on the National Register of Historic Places, has hosted presidents, royalty, sports icons and celebrities (including Rudolph Valentino, Joan Crawford, Spencer Tracy, Katherine Hepburn, Tennessee Williams, Truman Capote and Carl Sandburg).

**The Drake Hotel Chicago:** Winston Churchill, Pope John Paul II and Princess Diana all roomed at the 1920 landmark hotel, ideally located at the beginning of North Michigan Avenue.

**Palmer House Hilton:** Named after business mogul Potter Palmer, the historic Palmer House is one of the longest continuously running hotels in the U.S., and also the first to be equipped with electric lights and telephones in each room.

### ★★★HILTON CHICAGO
720 S. Michigan Ave., South Loop, 312-922-4400;
www.hilton.com

Overlooking Grant Park, Lake Michigan and Millennium Park, this South Loop hotel is all about grandeur. The sumptuous Renaissance-style Great Hall is decorated in white with towering columns and gold accents to go along with intricate ceiling work. The theme tries to carry to the guest rooms with gold-trimmed wood dressers and cabinets and gold-tinged ornate duvets, but it doesn't translate as well in a smaller space. Still, the location across from Grant Park is superb, and if you're in town for St. Patrick's Day, onsite Kitty O'Shea's is the place to be.

*1,544 rooms. Restaurant, bar. Business center. Fitness center. Pool. Pets accepted. $151-250*

### ★★★HOTEL ALLEGRO
171 W. Randolph St., Loop, 312-236-0123, 800-643-1500;
www.allegrochicago.com

An early 2008 renovation has transformed Hotel Allegro into a stylish retreat. The blue and gray rooms have sleek geometric-patterned walls, 37-inch flat-screen TVs, zebra-print bathrobes in premier rooms and suites, Aveda toiletries and alarm clocks with iPod docking stations. Savor the soothing ambiance by indulging in an in-room spa treatment—go for the Calm Mind massage, which will fill the room with scents of lavender. If you can pry yourself out of your room, head to the gratis wine hour in the lobby. For sustenance, grab dinner at 312 Chicago for some delicious Italian eats, and then sip a pomegranate Mojito from Encore Liquid Lounge before catching a play at the Cadillac Palace Theatre next door.

*483 rooms. Restaurant, bar. Business center. Fitness center. Spa. Pets accepted. $251-350*

### ★★★HOTEL BLAKE
500 S. Dearborn St., Loop, 312-986-1234; www.hotelblake.com

Located in a 19th century building, Hotel Blake is a nice option in Printers Row. The contemporary, spacious rooms feature high ceilings, large windows (in some rooms they are floor to ceiling) and earth tones with splashes of red. For dinner, head to the hotel's equally sophisticated Custom House Tavern, where you'll find delicious American fare and an extensive bar menu if you're just looking for a quick bite after a day of meetings. The hotel is

near shopping on State Street, Grant Park and the Chicago Board of Trade.
*162 rooms. Restaurant, bar. Business center. Fitness center. Spa. $151-250*

### ★★★HOTEL BURNHAM
**1 W. Washington St., Loop, 312-782-1111, 877-294-9712;**
**www.burnhamhotel.com**
The landmark Hotel Burnham, the first precursor to modern skyscrapers, retains touches of its past life, with mosaic floors, marble ceilings and walls, and ornamental metal grills on the elevators and stairwells. The rooms, not so much: Decked out in navy and gold, they take on a nautical look, with the sunburst mirror and gold emblem on the deep-blue headboard mimicking a ship's wheel. Located across from the former Marshall Field's department store (now Macy's), the hotel is nestled in the middle of the Theater District. Before you catch a show, stop in the Atwood Café, an upscale American restaurant with an inviting jewel-tone dining room that resembles an old Parisian brasserie. Perks for pets are as swanky as those for guests: Animals get beds made of hypoallergenic fleece and cedar chips with an optional turndown service. If you left Fido at home and are feeling lonely, the hotel will lend you a goldfish to keep you company.
*122 rooms. Restaurant, bar. Fitness center. Pets accepted. $151-250*

### ★★★HOTEL MONACO
**225 N. Wabash Ave., Loop, 312-960-8500, 866-610-0081;**
**www.monaco-chicago.com**
It's om sweet om at the Hotel Monaco. Although the rooms feature whimsical Art Deco-inspired décor, with thick pistachio and butter cream striped walls, they are actually Zen dens. Each room comes with a meditation station, a large window with fluffy pillows meant for reflection. You can flip on the in-room yoga program and use the provided accessories to practice your sun salutation. If that doesn't work, take a bath with Aveda products. Then slip into the pillow bed and put the Relaxation Station on the TV, which will fill the room with soothing sounds and images. The Karen Neuburger suite is a retreat with a spacious living room and plush KN towels and soft bamboo-blend sheets. But if you don't do low-key, book the Rock and Roll Suite, which rolls out the zebra-print carpet with plush red velvet couches, a jukebox, guitar and amp.
*192 rooms. Restaurant, bar. Fitness center. Business center. $151-250*

### ★★★PALMER HOUSE HILTON
**17 E. Monroe St., Loop, 312-726-7500;**
**www.palmerhousehiltonhotel.com**
Named after business mogul Potter Palmer, the historic Palmer House is one of the longest continuously running hotels in the U.S., and also the first to be equipped with electric lights and telephones in each room. A 2008 renovation aimed to return the massive hotel to its roots, and thankfully it included more than just lights and phones; a health club and spa, standard elsewhere, were finally added. The rooms are now bathed in lavender, brown and sage, shades that mimic the lobby's original terrazzo flooring and opulent Beaux-Arts ceiling, but the décor is updated with monogrammed pillows, swirly and striped linens, and ebony headboards. Executive level rooms were renovated in 2009—they have a French Empire style with flowery pastels and ornate gold mirrors—and you get your own private concierge and a buffet of goodies such as the Palmer House

HOTEL BURNHAM

brownies, which is appropriate since Bertha Palmer invented the chocolate creation and the Palmer House debuted it at the 1893 World's Fair.

*1,639 rooms. Restaurant, bar. Business center. Fitness center. Pool. Pets accepted. $151-250*

### ★★★SHERATON CHICAGO HOTEL AND TOWERS

301 E. North Water St., Loop, 312-464-1000, 800-325-3535;
www.sheratonchicago.com

Overlooking the Chicago River, the Sheraton chain's flagship branch touts itself as the "premier convention and business hotel in the Midwest." In fact, its enormous size makes it seem more like a convention center than a luxury hotel. But the simply decorated cream and beige rooms with beds resting against wood-paneled walls are inviting, especially when you add in the calming views of the water. For a change of scenery, visit the surprisingly hip Chi Bar, where you can kick back in a cocoa-colored leather chair with a Chicago Sunset martini and forget about the conventioneers flitting around the rest of the hotel.

*1,209 rooms. Restaurant, bar. Business center. Fitness center. Pool. Pets accepted. $151-250*

### ★★★SWISSÔTEL CHICAGO

323 E. Wacker Drive, Loop, 312-565-0565, 800-637-9477;
www.swissotelchicago.com

After renovations in April 2008, the Swissôtel Chicago—the sole stateside outpost of the Swiss hotel chain—is more appealing to business travelers. Upgrades included larger desks, ergonomic chairs, tech docking stations to use various media devices simultaneously and 37-inch split-screen plasma TVs. And the hotel recently added more meeting space. Families will be at home here, too. Kid-friendly suites have double beds to match the theme of the room (Shedd Aquarium, Field Museum or Adler Planetaerium), toys, a play area and books. Parents can hunker down within the heather gray

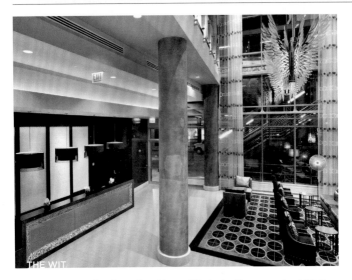

THE WIT

and ivory striped walls and rest in a white bed with an oversized fabric headboard. Whether you're there for business or pleasure, be sure to take a dip in the 45-foot indoor pool. It's on the 42nd floor and offers a nice view of Lake Michigan, as well as a wall that features a beautiful tiled mural of the Chicago skyline.

*661 rooms. Restaurant, bar. Business center. Fitness center. Pool. $251-350*

### ★★★W CHICAGO – CITY CENTER
172 W. Adams St., Loop, 312-332-1200, 877-946-8357;
www.whotels.com

Staying at the W is less about the rooms and amenities and more about the scene. Socialites and Loop workers crowd the bar for happy hour in the neo-gothic lobby, or the "Living Room," with long drapes at the entryways, and art projected on a wall set to music. The onsite Ristorante We serves Tuscan-inspired cuisine, and rooms are stylish and comfortable with pillow-top beds and eggplant comforters. The downside: if you want to visit the excellent Bliss spa, you'll have to head to the W's Lakeshore location.

*368 rooms. Restaurant, bar. Business center. Fitness center. Pets accepted. $251-350*

### ★★★THE WIT
201 N. State St., Loop, 312-467-0200; www.thewithotel.com

Wake-up calls from Barack Obama, Mayor Daley and Harry Caray are par for the course at The Wit (they are impersonators from The Second City improv troupe). And while they're just recordings, they give a feel for the tongue-in-cheek nature on display at this unique Loop hotel. Rooms are cheerful and contemporary, with pillow-top beds and down duvets, plus flat-screen TVs and in-room snack bars. When walking through the corridors, expect to hear birds chirping during the day and owls hooting at night (just another witty touch). You'll have to compete for a seat with the locals who crowd into ROOF, the 27th-floor rooftop lounge that offers incredible city views and cozy seating arranged around indoor fireplaces (be sure to walk out on what they call "the hangover," a portion of the roof that is suspended over the street; apparently it's a popular spot for proposals and has amazing views). If you can't get in at ROOF, head to the Phoenix Lounge which offers a live music series. The hotel also houses its own high-definition theater, Screen, which features comfortable recliners and cushy love seats and is available for private screenings, as well as a spa and two onsite restaurants, including the popular Cibo Matto. It's all part of the fun at this refreshing hotel.

*298 rooms. Restaurant, bar. Business center. Fitness center. Spa. $151-250*

SPA AT FOUR SEASONS

# URBAN RENEWAL

In a place where city dwellers are slapped with ice-cold winters and jungle-humid summers, it's no surprise that there are an abundance of soothing retreats. From the head-to-toe treatments at upscale spots like the Spa at Four Seasons to quick beauty rituals (such as expert acupuncture at Ruby Room Spa), there's something for everyone—because everyone needs pampering now and again.

## STAR-RATED SPAS

### ★★★★ELYSIAN SPA & HEALTH CLUB

**Elysian, 11 E. Walton, Gold Coast, 312-573-6860;**
**www.elysianhotels.com**

This beautiful Greek-inspired spa resides in the lavish Elysian hotel and features a mosiac-tiled lap pool, men's atelier and luxurious changing rooms with white stone, lacquered lockers and rich walnut wood. Unique treatments include the warm lava shell massage, the homepathic facial (there are also several age-defying facials) and the Elysian Cleanse, which combines water therapy, marine massage and a body treatment to renew the skin. The men's atelier (with flat-screen televisions) offers a traditional shave, facial treatments, manicures and pedicures and haircuts. (A monthly membership is available.) Ladies can have their hair and makeup done at the onsite salon. Fitness offerings include a pilates studios and personal trainers.

### ★★★★THE PENINSULA SPA BY ESPA

**The Peninsula Chicago, 108 E. Superior St., River North, 312-573-6860;**
**www.chicago.peninsula.com**

East meets Midwest at this 15,000-square-foot spa, where down-to-earth hospitality complements a full range of Asian and European-inspired treatments. To begin your visit, step through a giant oak door and enter the newly renovated Relaxation Lounge. The area's plush wooden beds, separated by individual curtains, set the mood for serious pampering. All treatments are exclusively designed by ESPA, an English product line focusing on high-quality, all-natural ingredients. Both mind and body get attention with the Chakra Balancing Massage, which uses smooth volcanic stones to ground and balance your energy. (Sounds wacky, feels great.) Post-treatment, swim in the spa's half-Olympic size pool; its floor-to-ceiling windows provide beautiful views and a chance to find your own moment of Zen.

### ★★★SPA AT THE CARLTON CLUB

**The Ritz-Carlton Chicago, 160 E. Pearson St., Gold Coast, 312-266-1000; www.fourseasons.com**

With names like Azalea, Magnolia and Lilac, treatment rooms at this elegant spa are all about organic luxury. Start your visit with a trip to the sophisticated locker room, which features a cedar sauna and private vanity areas. From there, try the Aroma-Tonic Body Envelopment, which begins with a full-body exfoliation and finishes with a clay and papaya cream mask to soothe dull, dry skin (perfect if you're here during the harsh winter). When the weather is nice, be sure to slather on the SPF before heading to the sun deck, where terrific views of the neighboring John Hancock Center make you feel like you're on top of the world. Considering the level of service you'll find here, it's more or less true.

### ★★★★SPA AT FOUR SEASONS
**Four Seasons Hotel Chicago, 120 E. Delaware Place, Gold Coast, 312-280-8800; www.fourseasons.com**

This spa's plush interior makes you feel right at home—that is, if fountains and marble floors are what you're used to. White suede wall panels and soundproofed treatment rooms add to the spa's elegant feel. Put on one of the spa's thick, silky robes and prepare for the royal treatment—literally. You can enjoy a facial massage with ruby-infused oil during the 80-minute Essence of Rubies Treatment. In gemstone therapy, rubies promote passion and well-being; in this treatment, they just make our muscles feel like jelly. Or try the Champagne Paraffin pedicure, which begins with an antioxidant-rich grape seed oil exfoliation, and ends with a glass of bubbly. (The heated massage chairs make this decadent pedicure more indulgent.) The gracious staff makes you feel even more relaxed. Extend your stay as much as possible by lounging in one of the day beds after your treatment.

### ★★★★THE SPA AT TRUMP
**Trump International Hotel and Tower, 401 N. Wabash Ave., River North, 312-588-8020; www.trumpchicagohotel.com**

The Donald wants to know your intentions—your spa intentions, that is. Whether you're looking to calm, balance, purify, heal or revitalize, you'll find what you need in this 23,000-square-foot den of relaxation. In concert with the property as a whole, the spa's décor is modern and sophisticated. Smooth blond wood, dim lighting and simple orchids create a comfortable, surprisingly unpretentious atmosphere. Still, it should come as no surprise that all the amenities here are the best: extra-spacious treatment rooms, deluge mood-enhancing showers (the shower lights up while water comes at you from everywhere) and an enormous health club boasting one of the most striking views in Chicago. As for the treatments, many of them focus on—what else—jewels. The Black Pearl Rejuvenation Facial combines crushed black pearls and mineral-packed oyster shell extracts to firm and tone your skin, while the Emerald Oasis Body Treatment uses mineral salt, mint and emerald-infused oils to exfoliate. If it's true that diamonds are a girl's best friend, maybe you should opt for the Purifying Diamonds Massage instead. The precious diamond and botanical essences will have you feeling engaged in Trump-style tranquility.

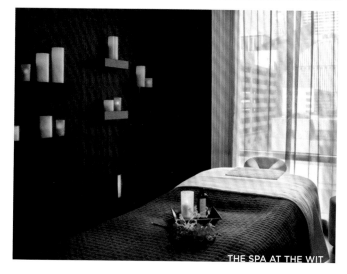

THE SPA AT THE WIT

## OTHER SPAS

### BLISS

W Chicago - Lakeshore, 644 N. Lake Shore Drive, Streeterville, 877-862-5477; www.blissworld.com

Cheerful and cheeky, the Chicago outpost of the New York-based spa rejects touchy-feely spa staples like piped-in new age music for a hipper, more upbeat environment. Each of its four nail stations has its own TV, where you can watch whatever you like while having your toes polished. The menu here is extensive and clever: try the Youth As We Know It Facial, which includes a mushroom enzyme peel. Or go for the Quadruple Thighpass Massage, an anti-cellulite treatment that uses a vacuum roller to leave your thighs dimple-free (or at least, less dimply) after six sessions. Instead of choking down diet food as you would at the average spa, you can nibble on brownies and cheese at Bliss, and after your treatment, step into a eucalyptus-infused steam shower—which, true to the spa's name, is pretty blissful indeed.

### SPA AT DANA HOTEL

Dana Hotel and Spa, 660 N. State St., River North, 888-301-3262; www.danahotelandspa.com

Green mosaic tiles shimmer in the oval-shaped lobby, while all treatment rooms include an iPod-ready Bose stereo—so you can be buffed and polished to your own beat. Signature treatments include the Aromasoul Massage, which incorporates essential oils from India, Asia, the Middle East and the Mediterranean. Or try the Nourishing Organics Manicure, which wraps hands in a mask made from pumpkin, tomato, artichoke and beet. Afterward, work up a sweat in the spa's cutting-edge gym—its ultra-sleek fitness equipment, called "Technogym," will give you a great workout.

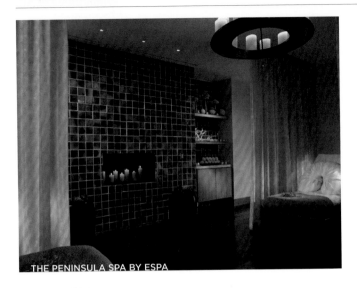

THE PENINSULA SPA BY ESPA

### EXHALE SPA
945 N. State St., Gold Coast, 312-753-6500; www.exhalespa.com

Pull up a yoga mat and start stretching at this New York City import, which combines fitness classes with traditional spa offerings. Choose from an extensive menu of holistic, Eastern-inspired spa treatments like cupping—a process in which heated glass cups are applied to skin to remove toxins. For something a little less exotic, try the Deep Flow Massage, which uses pulsating, wave-like movements to break up energy blocks. The effects are similar to a deep tissue massage, only you won't endure any pain. When you're knot-free, chill out in the spa's lounge, where herbal teas and chai-scented neck warmers await. If you're truly ambitious, you could partake in a Core Fusion class, which works the body's core muscles.

### KOHLER WATERS SPA
775 Village Center Drive, Burr Ridge, Suburbs, 630-323-7674;
www.kohlerwatersspa.com

Who knew that faucet manufacturers would turn out to be so adept at running a spa. The centerpiece of this recently opened space, located 20 miles from Chicago, is the Circle of Tranquility relaxation area. Inspired by Roman-style baths, the facility includes three showers, a 25-foot whirlpool, and even more ways to splash and soak. Let a thundering eight-foot waterfall massage your shoulders or, for a more comprehensive experience, try the 50-minute Go With The Flow Treatment. It begins with a Vichy shower, a French technique in which your therapist guides a five-headed shower bar over your body. After you're thoroughly soaked, the treatment finishes up with a full-body exfoliation and foot massage. This spa isn't too far from the city, but you'll feel like you're a world away.

WHICH SPAS HAVE THE BEST FACIALS?

**Spa at Four Seasons**: Facials here are ultra-luxe; ingredients include precious rubies and caviar for the ultimate in pampering.

**The Peninsula Spa by ESPA**: This spa's facials use high-quality ESPA products, which feel luxurious and cleansing; estheticians give you a gentle massage to give you the perfect glow.

## ELIZABETH ARDEN RED DOOR SPA

919 N. Michigan Ave., Gold Coast, 312-988-9191;
www.reddoorspas.com

Elizabeth Arden's famous red door reveals 15,000 square feet of pampering. With a staff of more than 100, this busy space includes 20 hairdressing stations, 16 treatment rooms and a café (which makes the spa popular with bridal parties). The signature massage uses rose oil essences, shea butter, acupressure and foot reflexology. The Red Door champagne and rose facial is a decadent treatment; while therapists pamper your skin, arms, neck and shoulders are massaged with warm stones. Bonus: This is Elizabeth Arden's spa, after all, so facials include a complimentary make-up refresher; just be sure to ask your esthetician to use a light hand, as they seem to practice the "more is more" philosophy when it comes to cosmetics. Couples won't have to be separated for their pampering; the spa added a couples' room in the fall of 2008.

## RUBY ROOM SPA

1743-45 W. Division St., Wicker Park, 773-235-2323;
www.rubyroom.com

This Wicker Park spa, yoga studio and salon focuses as much on inner healing as it does on outer beauty, incorporating new age philosophies into its offerings. In the Intuitive Blend Treatment, for example, you'll verbally work with an energy healer to balance your aura. Using a computer-generated photo of your aura, your healer will address possible issues in your life. Not in the mood for this kind of therapy? Go for a range of facials and massages, or choose a treatment with Chinese healing techniques like acupuncture and cupping. The Chakrassage Treatment is a combination of massage and energy work: therapists use both techniques to distribute blocked energy from head to toe. It all sounds a little hippie-dippy, but the overall experience is more posh than patchouli.

## SPA SOAK

1733 N. Milwaukee Ave., Bucktown, 773-395-9000; 2300 N. Lincoln Park West, Lincoln Park, 773-477-1144; www.spasoakchicago.com

With creaky wood floors and high-ceilinged suites, this homey spa gets rid of the frill and focuses on making you relax. Piano music sets the mood in the six treatment rooms, while pop tunes accompany manicures and pedicures. For breakfast on the go, try the Cereal Soak Pedicure. It begins with a milk foot bath and finishes with a vitamin-rich oats and honey mask. Along with nail services, this spa offers facials, waxing, massages and body treatments. The most comprehensive of them all may be the Look Better Naked Body Facial. After this 75-minute treatment, which uses clay and sea salt to buff your body, your skin will feel like butter.

THE SPA AT TRUMP

### THE SPA AT THE WIT
The Wit Hotel, 201 N. State St., Loop, 312-239-9402;
www.thewithotel.com

What the spa lacks in space—there are only three treatment rooms—it makes up for with a bevy of fun and relaxing treatments and top-notch organic products (which include Eminence, an all-organic skincare line from Hungary). Skin care treatments include age-defying, men's, even cocktail-inspired facials, while body care treatments run the gamut from a mimosa body polish to a traveler detox wrap. The soothing Wit signature massage combines Swedish massage, hot stones and aromatherapy. Nail treatments are also available and use Butter London nail polish. After your treatment, you can relax in the cozy lounge where you can sip water infused with cucumbers or fruit (it depends on the day) or organic hot tea and snack on granola. You can also get in a workout in the yoga studio, which has an iPod docking station, or in the well-equipped fitness center, where each piece of equipment has its own television screen. It may be small, but it seems they've thought of everything.

IKRAM

# LEADING THE CHARGE

Surely you've heard of Chicago's Michigan Avenue. You can find the latest of pretty much everything in the mixed bag of department stores and upscale shops that line the legendary strip. Step beyond this dowtown drag and you'll also happen upon unique boutiques with one-of-a-kind finds. Just be forewarned that Chicago has one the nation's highest sales tax—more than 9 percent, at press time—which doesn't seem to deter the many shoppers who flood Michigan Avenue on weekends. If you live in an area with a better tax rate, ask about having your purchases shipped to you to avoid the extra tariff.

## GOLD COAST/STREETERVILLE

### BARNEYS NEW YORK

15 E. Oak St., Gold Coast, 312-587-1700; www.barneys.com

The new Barneys harkens back to a time when visiting a department store was special, where you wore your best and prepared for a full-day event. This gleaming six-story building with marble floors and geometric staircases is full of beautiful clothes, shoes, purses, fragrances and cosmetics. Clerks dressed in black are ready to point you to the latest designer items, or you can take your sweet time pouring over the racks of Prada, Marc Jacobs, Lanvin, Chloé and Theory. The shoe selection is extensive, and there are dozens of beautiful handbags downstairs. Afterward, plan to spend a few blissful, lazy hours giggling over your purchases and sipping bubbly at Fred's, the store's penthouse restaurant complete with a lakeview terrace.
*Monday-Saturday 10 a.m.-7 p.m., Sunday 11 a.m.-6 p.m.*

### BLAKE

212 W. Chicago Ave., Gold Coast, 312-202-0047

A boutique with no sign, no posted hours and no website? What is this, a nightclub? Well, it's almost as exclusive—the only way to get in is by ringing a lone doorbell outside (it's a weird system, but go with it), and it's so sparse in its interior design, you may mistake it for a gallery, save for the suspended racks teeming with an immaculately assembled collection. Blake caters to no-nonsense fashionistas who appreciate French, British, Italian and Belgian designers like Dries van Noten (the boutique has the largest collection in the city), Marni, Louise Goldin, Rick Owens and Maurizio Pecoraro. Accessories are displayed neatly on white islands throughout the museum-like space, and much like a museum, the pieces—like a Chloé violet-gray snakeskin purse—are almost works of art.
*Monday-Friday 10:30 a.m.-7 p.m., Saturday 10:30 a.m.-6:30 p.m.*

### IKRAM

873 N. Rush St., Gold Coast, 312-587-1000; www.ikram.com

In 2001, Ikram Goldman took what she learned from being a salesperson for 10 years at the venerated Ultimo (a Chicago fixture for nearly 20 years before it recently closed its doors) and opened up her own store. It must have been one heck of an education in designer fashion, because to this day, Ikram remains a favorite among Chicago and national élite. (First Lady Michelle Obama is a fan.) Inside the contemporary-European-styled store, bathed in a gentle cream-and-gold palette, you'll run into an eye-popping collection of designers like Alexander McQueen, Jean Paul Gaultier and Junya Watanabe. To the right of the store, near a well-edited and carefully

SOFIA VINTAGE

assembled vintage collection, is the shoe selection, which almost solely consists of sharp-looking Azzedine Alaïa and Jimmy Choo pumps.
*Monday-Saturday 10 a.m.-6 p.m. and by appointment.*

### SOFIA VINTAGE
72 E. Oak St., Gold Coast, 312-640-0878; www.sofiavintage.com
Owned by two sisters with two completely different styles (one prefers a 70's boho-chic look, while the other is more traditional and conservative), Sophia Vintage is not what you would expect to see on tony Oak Street (home to Tod's, Prada, Jimmy Choo, etc., etc.). But the relative newcomer is most certainly a welcome addition. The shop offers men's and women's vintage clothing and accessories from the 1920s through the 1980s, which the two sisters find by scouring second-hand shops across the country (and sometimes even alter to make them more chic). Named after actress Sophia Lauren for her class and grace, the selection here may include Valentino and Lanvin dresses, Chanel handbags and Gucci ties. After you have scoured the perfect vintage bag or tie, browse all the other shops on Oak Street for that perfectly pulled together look. The owners may have different styles, but the store is classy all around.
*Monday–Saturday 11 a.m.–7 p.m., Sunday 12 p.m –5 p.m.*

## LOOP

### MACY'S
111 N. State St., Loop, 312-781-1000; www.visitmacyschicago.com
When Federated Department Stores (the owner of Macy's) decided that it was not going to retain Marshall Field's name and image after it bought the legendary Chicago department store in 2005, the announcement launched high-pitched outcries from locals. Despite all the commotion—and the wishes of disgruntled Field's loyalists who vowed never to set foot in Macy's—this State Street building is worth a visit regardless of who sells what inside. Opened for business in 1907 by Marshall Field & Company, the State Street store is pure nostalgia, with its soaring atrium, a gorgeous

MACY'S

Tiffany stained-glass ceiling and the historic "great clocks," which are still suspended on the corner of State and Washington and State and Randolph streets. Not much has changed inside, either—Macy's kept Field's favorites like the Merz Apothecary boutique on the ground floor and the exclusive 70-year-old 28 Shop on the third, which features a wide swath of designers, from Yves Saint Laurent to Marc Jacobs, as well as private elevator access and valet. You can still sit around the fountain in the historic Walnut Room restaurant, although a trip to the new food court next door is also definitely worth a visit. The upscale food court, Seven on State, features gourmet food stations from Rick Bayless (of Frontera Grill) and Marcus Samuelsson (Marc Burger).
*Monday-Saturday 10 a.m.-8 p.m., Sunday 11 a.m.-6 p.m.*

## LINCOLN PARK

### ART EFFECT
934 W. Armitage, Lincoln Park, 773-929-3600;
www.shoparteffect.com
Billing itself as "the modern day general store," Art Effect offers everything from great gifts (monogrammed soaps, candles, books), clothing, jewelry, toys, stationary, travel gear—you name it and this adorable shop pretty much has it. Best of all, the selection is well edited. Bath and body items feature Illume Yuzu, Tokyo Milk, and Sara Happ. Entertaining items (or lovely hostess gifts) might include marble cheese slicers and monogrammed old-fashioned glasses. You'll also find Alexis Bittar jewelry, Ella Moss clothing, and sparkly Moyna evening bags. Everything is packaged up at the end of a spree like the pretty little gifts that they are—even if you have just been treating yourself.
*Monday-Thursday 11 a.m.-7 p.m., Friday 11 a.m.-6 p.m., Saturday 10 a.m.-6 p.m., Sunday noon-5:00 p.m.*

# WHERE IS THE BEST SHOPPING ON MICHIGAN AVENUE?

On the Magnificent Mile's double-wide sidewalks, wide-eyed tourists mix with fashionistas, while businessmen duck into department stores and iPod-plugged hipsters navigate around the many street performers. Start on the southernmost point of the Mag Mile, where Michigan Avenue meets the Chicago River.

Your first stop is the **The Shops at North Bridge** (520 N. Michigan Ave.), which is anchored by **Nordstrom**. As any shopaholic with a sole addiction can tell you, the four-story department store has a huge shoe selection.

Cross Michigan Avenue and head inside the Midwestern flagship of **Gap** (555 N. Michigan Ave.), where you can find the chain's signature dependably comfortable clothes. Cross back to the left side of Michigan, where you can get timeless denim at **Levi's** (600 N. Michigan Ave.) and trendy, affordable clothing at the massive **Forever 21/XXI** (540 N. Michigan Ave).

At Ontario Street, boutiques such as **Cartier** (630 N. Michigan Ave.) and **Burberry** (633 N. Michigan Ave.) stand on either side of Michigan, while just down the block are jeweler **Van Cleef & Arpels** (636 N. Michigan Ave.), Italian fashion houses **Ermenegildo Zegna** (645 N. Michigan Ave.) and **Salvatore Ferragamo** (645 N. Michigan Ave.). Chicago-based housewares giant **Crate & Barrel** (646 N. Michigan Ave.) has its flagship on this block. Zip across the street to explore the colossal **Niketown** (669 N. Michigan Ave.) and the ultramodern cube that is the **Apple Store** (679 N. Michigan Ave.), where hands-on displays let you play with the latest gadgets.

The next block includes **Brooks Brothers** (713 N. Michigan Ave.). For an even larger selection of men's garments, stop in **Saks Fifth Avenue Men's Store** (717 N. Michigan Ave.); inside, you'll find everything from elegant silk ties and suits to deluxe grooming lines. For more of the same but for ladies, cross Michigan Avenue to **Saks Fifth Avenue** (700 N. Michigan Ave.).

On the following block north, gaze in the window at the imposing **Tiffany & Co.** (730 N. Michigan Ave.) before you're distracted by the goods just up the block: **Banana Republic** (744 N. Michigan Ave.) and **Ralph Lauren** (750 N. Michigan Ave.). For another kind of grandeur, go across Michigan to **Neiman Marcus** (737 N. Michigan Ave.); just don't forget your Neiman's credit card, AmEx or cash, as the legendary designer department store doesn't take checks or other credit cards.

On the last leg of the Mag Mile, you'll want to check out the approachable and increasingly fashionable **Water Tower Place** (835 N. Michigan Ave.), a shopping center that houses everything from **Custo Barcelona** to Neiman Marcus offshoot **Cusp** to kid cult favorite **American Girl Place**. Across the street from Water Tower is **Escada** (840 N. Michigan Ave.), which is the first in a series of markedly more upscale stores in the northernmost reaches of this shopping strip. North of Escada, on the east side of Michigan, you'll find sharply cut variations of the traditional white blouse at **Anne Fontaine** (909 N. Michigan Ave.); beautiful baubles from **Bulgari** (909 N. Michigan Ave.); classic-chic options from **St. John** and **J. Mendel** (919 N. Michigan Ave.); the ubiquitous monogrammed handbag and more at **Louis Vuitton** (919 N. Michigan Ave.); and the classic wool suit, fragrances and eyewear at **Chanel** (935 N. Michigan Ave.).

From here, cross the street and double back half a block to check out **The 900 Shops** (900 N. Michigan Ave.), a shopping center bookended by **Bloomingdale's**, and which also houses **MaxMara**, **Gucci**, **L'Occitane** and **Lululemon Athletica**.

# WHAT IS THE FASHION SCENE LIKE IN CHICAGO?

In cultivating homegrown designers and expanding sample sales and trunk shows, Chicago is finally trading in the sweatshirts and Zubaz for something a little more stylish.

Chicago isn't historically a fashion-forward city. In that respect, it usually fulfills the stereotypes of the pragmatic Midwest. Yet in the past few years, style has started to creep into the city's fabric more and more. Witness, for example, the success of sample sales that take place all over the city each month. Long a fixture in New York and L.A.'s fashion scenes, these events present the opportunity to own designer pieces for a fraction of the price. The catch is that the garments are either seasonal one-off test pieces—i.e., samples—that fashion houses produce to present to buyers, stylists and media, or simply overstock. Check out the popular **Beta Boutique** (*www. betaboutique.com*), which holds regular sample sales in various locations throughout the city, featuring designers such as Alice + Olivia, Milly and Rebecca Taylor.

Likewise, trunk shows are put on by designers to introduce a new collection to boutique owners and a select group of shoppers before they're available in stores. Usually, the designer is on hand to answer any questions about the garments. While big department stores (like Nordstrom and Saks) and smaller boutiques regularly host these events, the best way to find out about an upcoming trunk show is by signing up for newsletters—*Chicago* magazine's **Sales Check** (*www.chicagomag.com/Radar/Sales-Check*) has a reputable one.

Sometimes, finding undiscovered gems is more than half the fun, and to that end, it's best to turn to the city's emerging designers, such as Chicago darling **Lara Miller** (*www.laramiller.net*) whose deconstructed, multipurpose garments have earned her a loyal local following. You can find her pieces at Macy's on State Street, p.45 and other shops around Chicago (her clothing is also sold in many other cities). Other local talents include **Cynthia Ryba** (*www.cynthiaryba.com*), who uses conventional materials in a fresh new way, and **Diego Rocha** (*www.diegorocha.com*), who makes beautiful handbags. Also watch for the architecturally informed concoctions of **Apparatchik** (*www.apparatchikdesign.com*) and **Agga B.** (*www. aggab.com*), and the punk-rock aesthetic of **Bruiser** and **Brazen Judy** (*www.wolfbaitchicago.com*). **Chicago Fashion Resource** (*www.chicago-fashionresource.com/designers*) charts emerging designers, so sign up for its newsletter to keep tabs on the local fashion scene. They also put on the four-day annual **Fashion Focus Chicago** in October featuring fashion shows, free events, seminars and more. If you're in town in May, see the fashion program graduate shows at the **School of the Art Institute of Chicago** (*www.saic.edu*) or **Columbia College Chicago** (*www.colum.edu*)—risk-taking style mavens will love the heady hybrid of art and fashion that head down the runway.

To find unique designs, visit boutiques like **Habit** (*1951 W. Division St., 773-342-0093; www.habitchicago.com*) and **Renegade Handmade** (*1924 W. Division St., 773-227-2707; www.renegadecraft.com*), which do all the work for you by gathering local talent and showcasing their work. While the former features ethereal but wearable wares, the latter cultivates a strictly homegrown, indie style in the store and its annual Renegade Craft Fair (held in September). It's about time the Second City showed New York a thing or two about fashion.

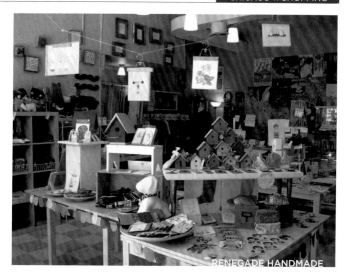

RENEGADE HANDMADE

## BARNEYS CO-OP

**2209-11 N. Halsted St., Lincoln Park, 773-248-0426; www.barneys.com**
If you regularly worship at the altar of Phillip Lim and Marc Jacobs, then Barneys New York's quirkier baby sister needs no introduction. Cult-brand devotees religiously come to this concrete-and-metal loftlike space in Lincoln Park to find the usual urban-chic suspects—that'd be the afore-mentioned (Lim constantly puts out Barneys-exclusive items), Alexander Wang and Acne jeans for ladies, and PS by Paul Smith, Prada Sport and J Brand jeans for men. The salespeople—who sport trendsetting haircuts and clothes that scream "amazing staff discounts"—are helpful and not cloying, especially around the well-stocked beauty bar, massive denim wall and tightly selected shoe collection. Those with handbag addictions should head to the gritty-girly bags by Marc Jacobs, soft leather slouches by Sissi Rossi and classic bowlers by Jas M.B., which are on display near the floor-to-ceiling windows up front.
*Monday-Saturday 11 a.m.-7 p.m., Sunday noon-6 p.m.*

## CYNTHIA ROWLEY

**810 W. Armitage Ave., Lincoln Park, 773-528-6160; 1653 N. Damen Ave., Bucktown, 773-276-9209; www.cynthiarowley.com**
It's only fitting that this designer's eponymous shop is in the heart of one of Chicago's hottest boutique-studded neighborhoods. Rowley—an Illinois native who sold her first collection while still a senior at the School of the Art Institute of Chicago—rolls out dynamic dresses, separates and sweaters without sacrificing girliness (achieved by using bold satins, soft leathers and sheer fabrics). Her quirky take on femininity translates into the boutique's pink-and-black motif and velvet monogrammed chairs. Head to the back for handbags and shoes, or make a beeline for Rowley's Bucktown store, which opened in late 2007 in response to that neighborhood's ever-growing shopping options.
*Monday-Saturday 11 a.m.-7 p.m., Sunday noon-5 p.m.*

P45

## LORI'S DESIGNER SHOES

824 W. Armitage Ave., Lincoln Park. 773-281-5655; www.lorisshoes.com
Don't even think of setting foot here on a Saturday or the first day of a
major sale (often twice a year, at the end of summer and fall). The no-frills
store—sales racks organized by shoe size line the perimeter of the space—
has a large selection of mid-range footwear, from traditional brands like
Calvin Klein, Franco Sarto and Charles David to funkier lines like Jeffrey
Campbell and Jessica Bennett, for less than you'd find them anywhere else
(sometimes up to 50 percent off). Don't expect much attention from the
sales staff, either; the no-return policy on sales items is strictly enforced.
*Monday-Thursday 11 a.m.-7 p.m., Friday 11 a.m.-6 p.m., Saturday 10 a.m.-6
p.m., Sunday noon-5 p.m.*

## VOSGES HAUT-CHOCOLAT

951 W. Armitage St., Lincoln Park, 773-296-9866;
www.vosgeschocolate.com
It's curious how a space so cozy and homey could whisk you to so many
exotic locales. But that's just what happens inside this pretty, purple-
hued chocolate-shop-cum-retail boutique. Owner and chocolatier Katrina
Markoff—a Chicagoan trained at Le Cordon Bleu—has made waves across
the nation with her surprising combinations, such as smoked bacon and
milk chocolate (Mo's Bacon Bar); Mexican chiles, Ceylon cinnamon and
dark chocolate (Red Fire Bar); and ginger, wasabi, sesame seeds and dark
chocolate (Black Pearl Bar). Indulge in any of her signature truffles, or opt for
gourmet ice cream from the dessert bar in the back. There are also Vosges

---

### WHICH BOUTIQUE HAS THE MOST UNIQUE ITEMS?

**Robin Richman**: Richman sells small quantities of limited-production wares
by emerging designers under the belief that items should be one-of-a-
kind. Richman also sells her own hand-knit sweaters and there is even an
in-house workshop.

## WHERE ARE THE BEST HOME STORES AND GALLERIES?

It turns out style can be bought—at least for your home. The River North neighborhood houses some of the most established galleries in the city, sleekest interior-décor shops and one colossal home-design warehouse.

In the mid-'70s, a group of upstart galleries started to move into store-fronts along Franklin, Wells, Superior and Huron streets—then a desolate, industrial part of town. More than 30 years later, this block boasts one of the largest concentrations of galleries in Chicago, regardless of the fact that the fare generally leans on traditional work and media. **David Weinberg Gallery** (*300 W. Superior St., 312-529-5090*) showcases fine art and photography with a socially conscious inclination, while **Ann Nathan Gallery** (*212 W. Superior St., 312-664-6622*), exhibits contemporary realist sculptures and paintings. For a taste of the nontraditional, visit **Judy A. Saslow Gallery** (*300 W. Superior St., 312-943-0530*)—the gallery specializes in outsider/intuit and folk art, like the eerily endearing works of Michel Nedjar or scenes of Chicago life from Winnifred Birts.

Next, take a stroll down Franklin Street and stop in at **Luminaire** (*301 W. Superior St., 312-664-9582*) and **Orange Skin** (*223 W. Erie St., 312-335-1033*). Both feature supremely slick furnishings, though the former also includes bathroom and kitchen fixtures and a housewares area, while the latter focuses on importing achingly chic Italian furniture. Standouts along Wells Street include the quirky home and personal accessories store **Elements** (*741 N. Wells St., 312-642-6574*) and **Chicago Luxury Beds** (*440 N. Wells St., 312-527-5337*) for gotta-sleep-on-it-to-believe-it beds whose price tags run as high as $70,000.

At the southern end of River North is the Art Deco-style **Merchandise Mart**—a building so big, it had its own zip code for 45 years. Unfortunately, the Mart is by and large an industry-only design playground above the ground-floor **LuxeHome** showrooms. (Which is no mean feat, mind you: You can find just about anything at LuxeHome, from custom, hand-finished antique reproductions at Birger Juell Ltd. to the latest in bathroom hardware at Kohler.) If you're really that curious about the goings-on upstairs, visit during **Artropolis**, the city's international art fair in late April and early May, which takes over multiple levels of the Mart and allows plebeians on the premises to gawk.

locations in the Shops at North Bridge and O'Hare's Terminal 1.
*Monday-Wednesday 10 a.m.-8 p.m., Thursday-Saturday 10 a.m.-9 p.m., Sunday 11 a.m.-6 p.m.*

# BUCKTOWN/WICKER PARK

## APARTMENT NUMBER 9

1804 N. Damen Ave., Bucktown, 773-395-2999;
www.apartmentnumber9.com

It's almost impossible to leave this somewhat-removed Bucktown boutique without looking dashing and polished—at least if you're a guy. The store is dedicated to styling men, and to do so, it mixes the classic with the cutting-edge. Expect to find crisp dress shirts by John Varvatos, Paul Smith and Dries van Noten mingling in the racks with Splendid Mills T-shirts and Fred Perry sweaters. Clean up your act with John Allan's grooming products or the solid selection of ties and belts that hang out in the back.
*Tuesday-Friday 11 a.m.-7 p.m., Saturday 11 a.m.-6 p.m., Sunday noon-5 p.m.*

## WHERE IS THE BEST SHOPPING IN WICKER PARK/BUCKTOWN?

You've heard all about the great local boutiques and hip designer shops in the Bucktown and Wicker Park neighborhoods. Don't know where to start?

Begin your shopping excursion at the "six corners"—the intersection of North, Milwaukee and Damen avenues. (The CTA Blue Line Damen stop is right there, and a cab ride from downtown is $15 or less.) Begin with **Niche | City Soles**, which is on the southwest corner of that intersection. Head north on Damen Avenue and you'll hit **p.45**, **Pagoda Red**, **Marc by Marc Jacobs**, **Apartment Number 9** and **Robin Richman** within six blocks. Double back to the six corners again (that is, head south again on Damen); at the six corners, head southeast on Milwaukee Avenue to hit **Eskell**, plus tons of other indie shops, salons, restaurants and bars. When you come across Ashland Avenue, make a right (so head south) and another quick right—you'll then be facing west on Division Street. Keep walking the double-wide sidewalks of Division, and you'll happen upon more cafés, boutiques and bakeries. As soon as you pass the intersection at Damen, you'll come across **Gamma Player**. Wrap up your shopping tour with a drink or a nibble at one of the area's many restaurants and bars.

## ESKELL

**1509 N. Milwaukee Ave., Wicker Park, 773-486-0830; www.eskell.com**

Nostalgia is a beautiful thing. Just ask local designers Kelly Whitesell and Elizabeth del Castillo, the designers behind Eskell. Their penchant and passion for vintage resulted in a line that masterfully incorporates retro prints into remixes of '60s- and '70s-inspired dresses, trousers, shorts and tops, as in a recently spied pretty, gathered-at-the-waist Louise blouse in a silk print with tiny rocking horses. Eskell's frocks hang side by side with other indie lines like Lorick, Samantha Pleet and In God We Trust. There's also an excellently curated rack of affordable vintage clothes near the fitting rooms and a good selection of jewelry and purses throughout the store.

*Tuesday-Saturday 11 a.m.-7 p.m., Sunday 11 a.m.-5 p.m.*

## GAMMA PLAYER

**2035 W. Division St., Wicker Park, 773-235-0755; www.gammaplayer.com**

Legendary techno DJ Jeff Mills and his wife, Yoko Uozumi, opened this razor-sharp boutique in spring 2007. The clothing is unpredictably edgy and decidedly high fashion, so shop with an open mind and an even more open wallet. Women, check out the risky designs by Tatsuya Shida, Jean Pierre Braganza, Veil, Reality Studio and Firma. You might see a shape-shifting, spider-web-inspired vest by the latter. Guys get equal double-take-nabbing pieces from brands such as Obscur, Julius and Odeur. If you happen to catch Mills at the store, stick around—you may just get a sample of his taste in tunes. After all, a shop that's named after one of his forward-thinking techno tracks has got to have hot music by design.

*Tuesday-Saturday 11 a.m.-7 p.m., Sunday noon-6 p.m.*

## NICHE | CITY SOLES

**1566 N. Damen Ave. or 2001 W. North Ave., Wicker Park, 773-489-2001, www.citysoles.com**

Hipsters with cash migrate in droves to this trendy footwear store with a

CITY SOLES

double-barreled name. Either side of the store—which occupies one of the Six Corners in buzzing Wicker Park—features fresh designer footwear for men and women, with American, European and Japanese brands such as Camper, Audley, Sendra, Biviel and Corso Como. The sales corridor in the Niche side offers hot discounts from last season's footwear, which, considering how fashion-forward the shoes here are, will probably hit mainstream appeal in the current seasons. (You might see a pair of mile-high Due Farina suede platform heels that look like they just walked off the Prada catwalk.) Accessories like sunglasses, colorful handbags and jewelry by local artists are also moderately represented, though the heart of the store centers on the soles. If you want to shop all night, call and ask when the next midnight madness sale is taking place.

*Monday-Wednesday 10 a.m.-7 p.m, Thursday-Friday 10 a.m.-8 p.m, Saturday 10 a.m.-7 p.m., Sunday 11 a.m.-6 p.m.*

## P.45

1643 N. Damen Ave., Bucktown, 773-862-4523; www.p45.com

The "p" in p.45 might just stand for "pioneer." When Bucktown was an up-and-coming neighborhood mainly populated by artists and musicians in

---

**WHAT ARE THE BEST BOUTIQUES?**

**Blake**: The shop caters to no-nonsense fashionistas who appreciate international designers like Dries Van Noten (the boutique has the largest collection in the city), Marni, Louise Goldin, Rick Owens and Maurizio Pecoraro.

**Ikram**: Ikram remains a favorite among Chicago's élite—First Lady Michelle Obama is a fan.

**p. 45**: The first fashion boutique to open in Bucktown way-back-when fills its racks with 3.1 Phillip Lim, Laila Azhar and more.

---

ROBIN RICHMAN

the '90s, this upscale store was among the first fashion boutiques to open. To this day, it offers simple and chic sleeveless tops, skirts, dresses and jewelry. Find 3.1 Phillip Lim and Laila Azhar on the roster of designers here, all of whom have one thing in common: understated cool elegance.

*Monday-Saturday 11 a.m.-7 p.m., Sunday noon-5 p.m. Open Thursday until 8 p.m. in November and December.*

### ROBIN RICHMAN
**2108 N. Damen Ave., Bucktown, 773-278-6150;**
**www.robinrichman.com**

Richman opened her eponymous boutique in 1998 to showcase her own hand-knit sweaters. A little over a decade later, her boutique buzzes with a creative vibe, thanks to an in-house workshop. Richman sells small quantities of limited-production wares by emerging designers under the belief that items should be one-of-a-kind. To that end, you will find dip-dyed pieces by Marc le Bihan, jewelry made from leather and metals by Tuscan designer Riccardo Goti, and handmade wooden heels by Marsèll.

*Tuesday-Saturday 11 a.m.-6 p.m., Sunday noon-5 p.m.*

### PAGODA RED
**1714 N. Damen Ave., Bucktown, 773-235-1188; www.pagodared.com**

You probably won't have the space to carry a pair of original Qing-era courtyard doors home with you, but there are so many gorgeous pieces of furniture and artifacts at this large Asian home décor showroom you're bound to come home with something. Many of the items—like a simple stool we recently saw replicated in a Crate & Barrel catalog or framed Chinese drawings depicting sexy, saucy vignettes—hold up surprisingly well to the test of time and taste. The pretty, Zen entrance alone is a free lesson in feng shui, if too many options (or airline weight restrictions) leave you empty-handed.

*Monday-Saturday 10 a.m.-6 p.m., Sunday noon-5 p.m.*

## WHAT ARE THE BEST SHOPS IN THE SOUTHPORT CORRIDOR?

Just a few blocks from Wrigley Field, this Northside strip of Southport Avenue incorporates a healthy blend of vintage homes, specialty boutiques and scrumptious restaurants. By the sheer number of strollers on the block at a given time, you'd think the corridor was lost to children's shops and mom-wear retailers, but Chicago's Northsiders don't take their shopping casually, and it shows with a plethora of stores offering upscale designer clothes at upscale prices.

Women seeking either casual outfits or chic eveningwear will find it a challenge to leave **Krista K** *(3458 N. Southport Ave., 773-248-1967; www. kristak.com)* without a shopping bag in hand. The well-edited collection includes designers such as James Perse, Laila Azhar and Twelfth St. by Cynthia Vincent. The downstairs denim selection is second-to-none on the Northside, thanks in part to an informed—and honest—sales staff. A sister store, Krista K Maternity + Baby, is just down the block, providing great quality wear for moms-to-be and a few cute baby gifts.

One of the newest boutiques on the block is the very chic **Perchance** *(3512 N. Southport Ave., 773-244-1300; www.perchanceboutique.com)*. The long, narrow space uses black and white displays and wall accents to promote the limited, but exceptional designer pieces. Pick up a sexy floral dress by Shoshanna and a cute MZ Wallace clutch to match, or prepare for winter with a stellar pair of Loeffler Randall boots. Don't be shy if you need a little fashion help; the staff is warm and eager to play dress up.

If you're looking for intimate apparel or swimwear that fits like a glove, walk right into **Trousseau** *(3543 N. Southport Ave., 773-472-2727)*. The stock ranges from racy lace get-ups to buttoned-up one-piece suits, as well as everything in between. You'll be spending a little more than you would at a department store, but the quality craftsmanship and custom fittings are worth it.

Women's boutiques aren't the only big business on the Southport Corridor. Along with a slew of bars and restaurants catering to both young families and energized Cubs fans, there is **Southport Grocery and Café** *(3552 N. Southport Ave., 773-665-0100; www.southportgrocery. com)*. Lines run around the block come Sunday morning for the famed brunch, but as the name dictates, it's also a grocery, with tasty offerings including specialty olive oils, handmade pastas, artisinal cheeses and wine and some of the best cupcakes in the city.

## UKRAINIAN VILLAGE/WEST TOWN
### SPROUT HOME
745 N. Damen Ave., Ukrainian Village, 312-226-5950;
www.sprouthome.com

You know that feeling you get when you wish you could just move into the most pretty store you know? Slap a bed in the middle of this housewares emporium and nursery, and you're home. The poured-concrete floor and wood accents give Sprout a sleek look, while the neat shelves contain playful accessories for home and garden: lampshades made of laminated Japanese silk, glazed terracotta bird feeders (with a ladder inside) and ultra-modern dinner chairs you'd never guess were made from recycled plastic. Take a stroll in the nursery, where urban gardeners get their pick of rare

## WHERE IS THE BEST SHOPPING ON OAK STREET?

Michigan Avenue is all well and good for High Street fashions, but for high fashion, there's nothing like Oak Street. Start your walk of this beautiful boutique road at Michigan Avenue and Oak. On the south side of the street, make a stop at **Tod's** *(121 E. Oak St., 312-943-0070)* for gorgeously hand-crafted leather handbags, shoes and accessories.

As expected, there's no shortage of gems and jewelry on Oak Street, so cross to the south side of the street again for a look inside **Trabert & Hoeffer** *(111 E. Oak St., 312-787-1654)*—if the gemstones inside don't make your heart skip a beat, then not to worry. **Graff Diamonds** *(103 E. Oak St., 312-604-1000)*, **Lester Lampert** *(57 E. Oak St., 312-944-6888)* and **David Yurman** *(40 E. Oak St., 312-787-7779)* are all just down the road.

Young girls will want to pop into **Juicy Couture** *(101 E. Oak St., 312-280-1637; www.juicycouture.com)*. Otherwise, back to mid-Oak: Make a stop at **Kate Spade** *(56 E. Oak St., 312-654-8853)* for ladylike touches, such as beautifully embossed thank-you cards or Martha's Vineyard-worthy wallets, then nip across Oak Street where shoe lovers can indulge in **Jimmy Choo**'s *(63 E. Oak St., 312-255-1170)* elegant, sexy heels. Lovers of everything streamlined and understated must stop in at **Jil Sander**'s *(48 E. Oak St., 312-335-0006)* museum-like digs, and makeup mavens would do well to stock up on **M.A.C.** *(40 E. Oak St., 312-951-7310)* cosmetics, which often collaborates with high-end designers (Liberty of London, Ungaro) on limited-edition makeup lines. Make sure you stop in at **Loro Piana** *(45 E. Oak St., 312-664-6644)* for luxurious knitwear.

Next, pay a visit to three formidable houses of style: **Vera Wang** *(34 E. Oak St., 312-787-4696)*, which specializes in wedding gowns (and is by appointment only); **Prada** *(30 E. Oak St., 312-951-1113)*, an ode to all things artistic; and **Hermès** *(25 E. Oak St., 312-787-8175)* which was in a smaller space down the street before it moved into the old Barneys space. The store is Chicago's only outpost of the prestigious French couture house. Wind down your walking tour at **Barneys New York** *(15 E. Oak St., 312-587-1700)*, which only a year ago moved into its gleaming new digs and now includes an outpost of the beloved eatery Fred's. Finally, if you're still not shopped out, there's a new **Marc Jacobs** *(11 E. Walton St.)* just down the block, which has a great selection of the designer's pieces for men, women and children.

**DETOUR: WALTON STREET** One street south, parallel to Oak Street, you'll find heaven for North Shore teens and college students. Here, you'll find West Coast-style purveyor **Samantha** *(64 E. Walton St., 312-951-5383)*, snowboarding outfitter **Burton** *(56 E. Walton St., 312-202-7900)*, the culty **AG Adriano Goldschmied Jeans** *(48 E. Walton St., 312-787-7680)*, basics giant **American Apparel** *(46 E. Walton St., 312-255-8360)*, trendy **Urban Outfitters** *(935 N. Rush St., 312-640-1919)* and **Diesel** *(923 N. Rush St., 312-255-0157)*.

**DETOUR: RUSH STREET** Starting at Chicago Avenue and walking north, you'll find luxury-clothing den **Ikram**; stylist fave **Intermix** *(40 E. Delaware Place, 312-640-2922)*; Australian boots-maker **Ugg** *(909 N. Rush St., 312-255-1280)*; athletic gear at **Adidas Originals** *(923 N. Rush St., 312-932-0651)*; ladylike cardigans at **Anthropologie** *(1120 N. State St., 312-255-1848)*; and travel accessories at **Flight 001** *(1133 N. State St., 312-944-1001)*.

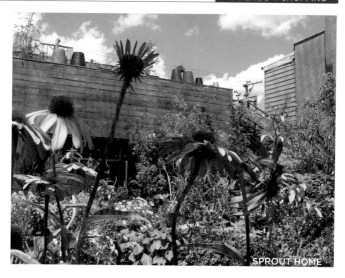

plants (passion flowers, anyone?), herbs and ornamental trees.
*Winter: Monday-Friday 10 a.m.-8 p.m., Saturday-Sunday 10 a.m.-7 p.m.*
*Spring/Summer: Monday-Friday 9 a.m.-8 p.m., Saturday-Sunday 9 a.m.-7*
*p.m.*

J BAR

# ON THE TOWN

Whether you're in the mood for lounging or dancing, Chicago's nightlife won't disappoint. Once darkness falls, dance floors light up with everything from Top 40 tunes to cutting-edge house and techno. If you prefer your music mainly for atmosphere, there are chic bars and lounges that put the focus on expertly mixed drinks, top-notch service and views. So raise a glass to the varied nightlife options—after a long day of meetings or sightseeing, you're going to need them.

## GOLD COAST/STREETERVILLE

### LE PASSAGE

937 N. Rush St., Gold Coast, 312-255-0022; www.lepassage.com

Any place that makes it this hard to find (you'll have to walk down a hidden brick alley, down a steep stairway and through a corridor) is bound to be a bit persnickety about who gets in. Once inside, you'll be glad for those hurdles, because they keep the riff-raff out and let a stylish crowd in. The slick space, outfitted in dark wood and potted tropical plants, gets its amber glow from dim lighting, and folks smart enough to reserve a table sit back and watch the action unfold on the dance floor. Don't feel like playing VIP? Hop up and get your own drink from one of the two bars—just make sure to bring sharp elbows, especially on weekends, when recent college grads descend on "Le Pas" to dance to Top 40 hits and hip-hop beats.

*Thursday-Friday 10 p.m.-4 a.m., Saturday 10 p.m.-5 a.m.*

## OLD TOWN/RIVER NORTH/RIVER WEST

### BULL & BEAR

431 N. Wells St., River North, 312-527-5973; www.bullbearbar.com

What used to house a home goods store in the River North gallery district is now a popular and stylish sports bar, thanks to a makeover in 2009 that saw the addition of oversized windows to let light stream in and an abundance of flat-screen TVs, which makes the bar popular with Chicago's sports-worshipping after-work crowd. Booths outfitted with table taps, which let you pour your own draft beer—a meter keeps track of your consumption and charges your tab accordingly—fill up quickly. Otherwise, slide into one of the hightops in the cozy, brick-walled space and order up one of seven different kinds of sliders (turkey sloppy joe, kobe beef, etc.), spicy chicken wings or a gruyère-topped bowl of onion soup from the comfort food-heavy menu while you listen to the fun tunes coming from the DJ booth.

*Monday-Friday 11 a.m.-2 a.m., Saturday-Sunday 11 a.m.-3 a.m.*

### DISTRICT

170 W. Ontario, River North, 312-337-3477;
www.districtbarchicago.com

Experience the best of several worlds at District. Many patrons are not sure if this new River North hot spot is a restaurant, a sports bar or a nightclub. It has been described as a "contemporary tavern," that promises to show every game that airs on television. While 40 flat-screens in the dining room are usually tuned in to ESPN, District's menu reflects more of an upscale dining experience than you would find at a typical sports bar. Forget cheese sticks and marinara sauce; the mozzarella log is topped with arugula, shaved fennel and sweet pickled red onions, served alongside smoked

LE PASSAGE

tomato fondue. Some of the specials include half-priced appetizers, half-priced bottles of wine and Sunday brunch. District's unique private event room is tucked away behind a secret bookcase entrance, giving you the feel of stepping into an underground speakeasy.

*Monday-Friday 11 a.m.-2 a.m., Saturday 11 a.m.-3 a.m., Sunday 10 a.m.-2 a.m.*

### ENGLISH

**444 N. La Salle Blvd., River North, 312-222-6200;**
**www.englishchicago.com**

With its dark, vaguely Victorian décor, this River North bar hints at the experience of drinking in an English pub. An open kitchen, menu of solidly American comfort food and oversized high-top tables, however, shifts the direction to this side of the pond, as does the preponderance of flat-screen TVs throughout the space. But whatever the influences, English is a comfortable space to settle in for an evening, just as you would at a proper British pub. On weeknights after work, the bar is perpetually packed with a young and stylish crowd who come to sip Pimm's Cups and take a turn on the pool table while listening to DJs spinning British rock.

*Monday-Friday 11 a.m.-2 a.m., Saturday 11 a.m.-3 a.m.*

### HOWL AT THE MOON

**26 W. Hubbard St., River North, 312-863-7427;**
**www.howlatthemoon.com**

At Howl at the Moon, dueling pianists play Billy Joel, Elton John and more, while encouraging the audience to sing along. It might sound hokey but the place is wildly popular—especially with a young crowd on weekends, who often wait upwards of an hour to get in. Signature drinks are comically named: X-Boyfriend, Double Agent Martini and Tradewind Punch. After a long wait, you'll need one. The place tends to attract raucous bachelorette parties on weekends.

*Monday-Friday 5 p.m.-2 a.m., Saturday 5 p.m.-3 a.m., Sunday 7 p.m.-2 a.m.*

## HUB 51
51 W. Hubbard St., River North, 312-828-0051;
www.hub51chicago.com

This lively spot on Hubbard (where you'll find scores of bars) is a great choice for both food and drink. The menu features everything from nachos and fish tacos to burgers and sushi (which is quite good here), and there's a nice wine list to accompany your meal. Desserts include butterscotch pudding and a delicious carrot cake. Once you've scored one of the high-top tables near the bar, stick around and enjoy some cocktails; the place fills up at night and there are televisions across the bar if you want to catch a game. Or, head downstairs to the reservations-only Sub 51 which features famous DJs.

*Monday-Tuesday 11 a.m.-midnight.; Wednesday-Friday 11 a.m.-2 a.m., Saturday 10 a.m.-3 a.m., Sunday 10 a.m.-10 p.m.*

## J BAR
James Hotel, 610 N. Rush St., River North, 312-660-7200;
www.jameshotels.com

Leather booths and mirrored walls skirt the periphery of the tiny, rectangle-shaped bar, and small, candlelit tables hold it down for high rollers (and the models who love them) with bottle service, especially on weekends, when the space reaches capacity well before midnight. If you can't manage to get a table, head to the bar, where trendy twenty- and thirty-somethings order up the potent and delicious cocktails, including the signature James Martini (a blend of raspberry vodka, elderflower liqueur, lime and fresh raspberries). Resident DJs spin house and dance music, but if beautiful-people-watching gets old, readjust your vision by watching video art installations on small plasma TVs embedded in the walls.

*Wednesday-Friday 6 p.m.-2 a.m., Saturday 8 p.m.-3 a.m.*

## LASALLE POWER CO.
500 N. Lasalle Blvd., River North, 312-661-1122;
www.lasallepowerco.com

Rock bar and music venue Lasalle Power Co. offers three floors of dining and music. Exposed brick walls, dark lighting and dim red candles make for a warm setting. You can catch both indie bands as well as national acts here, which have included the Chelsea Girls, Mandy Moore and Billy Corgan. Drinks are affordable ($4-6), while the menu features comfort foods from salads to a slider menu, as well as sandwiches and small plates. Check out the bathrooms—with quotes painted on the walls from rock legends like Keith Richards and Mick Jagger—to get you into the rock'n'roll frame of mind.

*Wednesday-Friday 4 p.m.-2 a.m., Saturday 4 p.m.-3 a.m.*

---

WHAT BARS HAVE THE MOST UNIQUE DÉCOR?

**The Violet Hour:** The elegant white and blue interior with high-backed seating, crystal chandeliers and parquet floors in a herringbone pattern is the perfect backdrop for the pre-Prohibition cocktails.

**Map Room:** Maps cover the walls and bookshelves are stocked with guidebooks at this quirky local favorite that boasts more than 200 brands of beer.

## WHAT ARE THE BEST BARS FOR BEER?

For every stereotype that Chicago tries to shrug off, there's an ounce of truth. And when it comes to beer, it's more like there's a pint of it. Chicagoans' love affair with beer is not a recent infatuation.

In fact, it's serious business that goes way back, from the Lager Beer Riot of 1855 (caused by then-mayor Levi Boone targeting German and Irish immigrant businesses by passing harsh liquor laws) to the debut of Pabst beer at the World's Columbian Exposition in 1893. Though most major breweries are located in Milwaukee or St. Louis, there have always been plenty of drinkers in the region to keep up demand for the stuff—witness the various turn-of-the-century buildings that bear the old Schlitz Brewing Company's logo in a concrete relief on their facade. You'll see early evidence of beer-related advertising on buildings such as **Schubas Tavern**, or an apartment building on 21st Street and Rockwell Avenue or at Damen and Grand avenues. (Coincidentally, Milwaukee's Schlitz only began to succeed in Chicago after the Great Fire of 1871, which destroyed many of the city's breweries and left the field open for aggressive tavern tie-ins and marketing schemes.)

Of course, if you want to combine an afternoon of bending elbows with a classic Chicago experience, there's no need to run around town looking for old buildings. Head to the lower level of Michigan Avenue, to the **Billy Goat Tavern** (430 N. Michigan Ave., 312-222-1525; www.billygoattavern. com). Legend has it that the Billy Goat's original owner, Bill Sianis, is the one who put an ironclad curse on the Chicago Cubs, but most people recognize this greasy spoon from John Belushi's Saturday Night Live lampooning of its hamburger-flipping counter guys. (Order a double "cheezborger," no fries, chips.) Duck in after 5 p.m., have an Old Style, and you might overhear reporters from the Tribune and Sun-Times discuss the latest sports news, city gossip or decrees from the mayor.

For a more contemporary taste of history, head to Wicker Park's **Rainbo Club** (1150 N. Damen Ave., 773-489-5999), where Miller High Life is cheap and local lore plentiful. After all, the dingy dive used to be the haunt of author Nelson Algren, and it's said that rocker Liz Phair's breakout Exile in Guyville album cover was shot in the Rainbo's photo booth.

Serious beer geeks with a taste for more than just mass-produced ales should reach for a bottle of Chicago's biggest local brewer, **Goose Island Beer Company and Brew Pub** (3535 N. Clark St., 773-832-9040; www. gooseisland.com). Since 1988, Goose Island has been putting out popular craft brews like the crisp and creamy 312 Urban Wheat and a biting, English Bitter-style Honker's Ale. In recent years, other independent brewers—such as Half Acre Beer Company and Two Brothers Brewing Company—have followed in Goose Island's footsteps in producing quality ales and lagers.

Chicago is also no slouch when it comes to beers brewed beyond the city limits, and for proof, tipplers should head to **Hopleaf** (5148 N. Clark St., 773-334-9851; www.hopleaf.com), a local favorite for its constantly rotating and expertly curated selection of Belgians; **Map Room** (1949 N. Hoyne Ave., 773-252-7636; www.maproom.com), which boasts 200 types of American and international beers; and **Sheffield's** (3258 N. Sheffield Ave., 773-281-4989; www.sheffieldschicago.com) a local institution for its North American beers as much as for its tremendous alfresco beer garden. Sun and suds—two things Chicago can't get enough of, yet luckily, you can find the latter around the city all year long.

RINO

## MANOR

642 N. Clark St., River North, 312-475-1390; www.manorchicago.com

You may not be a VIP, but you'll be treated like one with this club's focus on hospitality. The staff's been known to provide a hotel-like concierge service for anything from making dinner reservations or calling a car service to arranging accommodations for patrons at local hotels after one too many drinks. Once inside, settle in the booth-like benches that also serve as a storage area to hide your belongings (the dark wood and bordeaux accents of the place are warm and cozy).

*Thursday-Friday 10 p.m.-2 a.m., Saturday 10 p.m.-3 a.m. Hours may change.*

## OLD TOWN SOCIAL

455 West North Ave., Old Town, 312-266-2277;
www.oldtownsocial.com

This sophisticated bar bills itself as an old neighborhood spot with a classy Victorian/antique decor and flatscreen televisions, which can be hidden depending on the day's events (or lack thereof). The place is a little more upscale than your typical neighborhood joint, with offerings like handcrafted cocktails, craft beers and an upscale menu where you'd be hard-pressed to find nachos or chicken wings. The atmosphere is still laid-back and unpretentious and offers a great place to spend a few hours being social in the charming neighborhood of Old Town. The menu includes items such as Belgian-style hand cut fries with aioli, mussels, duck wings with a harissa sauce, housemade charcuterie, a BLT with pork belly and more. The beer menu features more than a half dozen offerings on draft and the cocktail menu changes depending on the season.

*Monday-Friday 5 p.m.-2 a.m., Saturday 10 a.m.-3 a.m., Sunday 10 a.m.-2 a.m.*

## REBAR

Trump International Hotel and Tower, 401 N. Wabash Ave., River North, 312-588-8100; www.trumpchicagohotel.com

Everyone knows that the word "subtle" is not in Donald Trump's vocabulary, and Rebar, the glitzy mezzanine-level bar at the Trump Hotel, falls right in line. Here, soaring 30-foot-tall windows overlook the Chicago River and Michigan Avenue Bridge, and the low lighting and even lower seating make for a sexy post-work or pre-dinner destination. Cocktails include the Wild Orchid, made of Trump vodka, sauvignon blanc and St. Germain garnished with a mini orchid and lime slice—a refreshing tipple for enjoying the alluring views.

*Monday-Wednesday 4 p.m.-midnight, Thursday-Friday 4 p.m.-1 a.m., Saturday 3 p.m.-1 a.m., Sunday 1 p.m.-midnight.*

## RINO

343 W. Erie St., River North, 312-587-3433; www.rinolounge.com

Pronounced like the horned animal and named after the River North territory in which it's set, RiNo is where the late-night party animals stampede to when the other clubs close. (RiNo is one of the few clubs to have the coveted 4 a.m./5 a.m. liquor license; most bars and clubs in the city have to stop serving at 2 a.m./3 a.m.). Sectioned-off leather seating surrounds the main floor next to windows giving perfect views of who's coming in and who's getting a drink at the bar. Bottle service is one way to survive the 2 a.m. swell of late-night partiers, but if you'd rather sit at the bar—made from a 200-year-old tree's midsection—one of the specialty martinis, like the potent Dirty Rino with vodka and olive juice, should tide you over for the night/morning.

*Wednesday-Friday 10 p.m.-4 a.m., Saturday 10 p.m.-5 a.m.*

## SUNDA

110 W. Illinois St., River North, 312-644-0500; www.sundachicago.com

This urbane bar and restaurant is the latest offering from the local nightlife impresario Billy Dec. The name refers to the Sunda Shelf, the water-covered landmass that stretches across and connects Southeast Asia, and with a menu (created by L.A.'s "Food Buddha" Rodelio Aglibot) that spans so many different Asian cuisines, it's appropriate. The room, dreamed up by renowned restaurant designer Tony Chi, is vast and visually dramatic, with plays on light and dark through the pairing of blond and black lacquered woods and splashes of bright colors. The four-sided sushi bar is crowned with a milky-way tangle of faux antlers, while a glossy, black bar hides the front lounge and its low candlelit tables. The main dining room is a mass of communal tables paired with comfy, persimmon settees that are perfect for lingering on through dessert (which should definitely be liquid, in the form of a lychee martini).

*Sunday-Wednesday 5 p.m.-midnight, Thursday-Saturday 5 p.m.-1 a.m.*

---

### WHICH LOUNGE HAS THE BEST VIEWS?

**Rebar**: Everyone knows that the word "subtle" is not in Donald Trump's vocabulary, and Rebar, the glitzy mezzanine-level bar at the Trump Hotel, falls right in line. Soaring 30-foot-tall windows overlook the Chicago River and Michigan Avenue Bridge, and the low lighting and even lower seating make for a sexy post-work or pre-dinner destination.

ZED451

### THE UNDERGROUND
56 W. Illinois St., River North, 312-644-7600;
www.theundergroundchicago.com

This supposedly secret spot isn't so secret—after all, Jeremy Piven and David Schwimmer have partied here. (If you need help finding it, just look for bouncers dressed in army fatigues.) Head downstairs to the military bunker-style main room, where dance, house and hip-hop music thunders from the speakers louder than an F-16. Two bars serve a crushing crowd, or you can lounge on low leather seating with bottle service. Unlike the club's entrance, people here desperately want to be seen—but you won't mind the scene after downing a Bunker Blues, made with raspberry and blueberry vodka, Pama Liqueur and pomegranate and cranberry juice.

*Thursday-Friday 9 p.m.-4 a.m., Saturday 9 p.m.-5 a.m., Sunday 10 p.m.-4 a.m.*

### ZED451
739 N. Clark St., River North, 312-266-6691; www.zed451.com

A one-stop shop for an evening of fun, ZED451 pretty much has your night planned from A to Z. Start off by making reservations for dinner. You'll find that even on a weekday, this bi-level restaurant and lounge fills up fast. But the big draw is the rooftop lounge that overlooks the downtown skyline; the queue can form as early as 5 p.m., but the views and no-pretense scene are worth the wait. If you prefer to stay indoors, the lower-level bar is a cozy spot, where you'll find business types mixed with young trendsetters sipping cocktails by the fireplace.

*Sunday-Thursday 4:30 p.m.-1 a.m., Friday-Saturday 4:30 p.m.-2 a.m. Rooftop opens at 2:30 p.m. Thursday-Friday and 11:30 a.m. Sunday.*

## LOOP/WEST LOOP

### BON V
1100 W. Randolph St., West Loop, 312-829-4805; www.bonvchicago.com

Bon V is a take on the French phrase meaning "good life." So what else

## WHAT ARE THE BEST BARS IN WRIGLEYVILLE?

If you're headed to a Cubs game (or even if you're not), there are plenty of options for pre-game and post-game partying in Wrigleyville. Win or lose, Wrigley bars are always overflowing with rowdy fans. So it's best to have a game day game plan, although sometimes it's fun to just follow the crowd.

Wrigleyville gets packed when there's a Cubs game, so it's best to arrive early to snag a table somewhere. Forget about driving unless you're willing to drive around for an hour looking for a parking spot. The El's Red Line stops about a half a block from the field at the Addison stop.

Start at the newly rebuilt **Sports Corner Bar & Grill** (956 W. Addison St.; www.cubbybear.com/sportscorner), a staple for Cubs fans since 1976, which sits on the Southeast corner of the park. What used to be a dumpy sports bar is now a sleek, three-level sports bar with an open-air rooftop. Start here with a few beers and some lunch. The menu features typical ballpark fare such as hot dogs, pizza puffs and nachos.

Next, head north to **Murphy's Bleacher's** (3655 N. Sheffield, 773-281-5356; www.murphysbleachers.com). Here you'll find almost the same setting, except the rooftop is rented out for private parties and the actual bar is a bit more cramped. But it's cozy and you never know who you might run into here—celebrities from Bill Murray and John Cusack to Billy Corgan have been spotted here on game days.

If you're looking for something a bit more upscale, head to **Rockit Bar & Grill Wrigleyville** (3700 N. Clark, 773-645-4400; www.rockitbarandgrill. com), the second installment from Billy Dec's Rockit Ranch Productions (the other one is in River North). The first floor features a bar and a lounge and upstairs, there is more seating for meals and a room with a pool table. The dining room was designed by Nate Berkus (Oprah's right-hand design man) and features more upscale bar grub, including the delicious Rockit Kobe beef burger with melted brie, fried shallots and medjool date aioli on a red onion brioche bun, which is served with truffle fries.

Just next door, you'll find the **Cubby Bear** (1059 W. Addison, 773-327-1662; www.cubbybear.com), probably Chicago's best known Wrigley bar. It's better to head to the Cubby Bear after the game, but hurry—the space fills up quick and usually features live music from both local and national acts. A bit further south on Clark, you'll find **Bernie's Tap & Grill** (3664 N. Clark St., 773-525-1898) and **Casey Moran's** (3660 N. Clark St., 773-755-4444; www.caseymorans.com), two always-crowded Wrigleyville spots that are located right next to each other with outdoor areas.

Then there's **Harry Caray's Tavern** (3551 N. Sheffield Ave., 773-327-7800; www.harrycaraystavern.com) on Sheffield, just a block southeast from the field. You'll find a younger crowd hanging at this tavern from the same group who own Harry Caray's Italian Steakhouse. A burger bar lets you design your own, from the preparation of the bun to which choice of beef (bison, Wagyu, free-range turkey, grass-fed beef and sirloin) you want. They also have signature martinis and cocktails like the Wrigley Rita and plenty of malts and whiskeys for an older, more distinguished crowd.

At most of the bars in Wrigleyville, you'll find beer tubs right inside the doors, plenty of game-day specials, outdoor seating and tons of rambunctious fans. Wherever you choose to go on game day, you're sure to find a good time, especially if the Chicago Cubs win—or even if they don't. After all, they don't call them the Loveable Losers for nothing.

LUMEN

would you expect but plush décor and attentive service? This bi-level nightclub is 7,500 square feet of lavishness, filled with chandeliers and a red-carpet welcome. With all the well-dressed dames and dapperly dressed men dancing to dance and top 40 tracks, you'd expect a snooty attitude from the staff. Amazingly enough, that's not the case. That's probably because Casey Urlacher—Chicago Bears football player Brian Urlacher's brother—is one of the owners, and he doesn't want to disappoint.
*Thursday-Friday 9 p.m.-2 a.m., Saturday 9 p.m.-3 a.m.*

## LUMEN

839 W. Fulton Market, West Loop, 312-733-2222;
www.lumen-chicago.com

At a glance, you'd wonder why anyone would venture down the dark, cobblestone streets of the industrial Fulton Market at night. But true to its name, Lumen illuminates this dingy area, both literally and figuratively. Featuring clean lines and an elevated VIP area, this lounge keeps it simple with one bar, great LED lighting effects and a sexy crowd. Since it opened in 2007, Lumen's made a name for itself as the home for fashion shows and must-go events with celebrity appearances, so make sure to dress your best. The finishing touch is at the bar: the Casablanca cocktail (vodka, a splash of sweet and sour, and white grape juice).
*Tuesday 10 p.m.-2 a.m., Friday 9 p.m.-2 a.m., Saturday 9 p.m.-3 a.m.*

## MARKET

1113 W. Randolph, 312-929-4787; www.marketbarchicago.com

Market is not your average sports bar. For starters, it's co-owned by White Sox GM Kenny Williams, and the space boasts chic, industrial décor. There are still plenty of TVs though—both inside as well as out in the Beer Garden—as well as a 92-inch projection screen. The Sidewalk Café is a great place to catch a quick bite, while the Rooftop Lounge provides an upscale experience with its cabanas and views of the city. The food is also

MARKET

more dressed up—you can still order sliders but here you could opt for braised beef and barbequed pork. A second-floor event room is equipped with its own bar, balcony and private restrooms.

*Monday-Friday 11-2 a.m., Saturday 11-3 a.m., Sunday 11-1 a.m.*

### VICTOR HOTEL

311 N. Sangamon St., West Loop, 312-733-6900;
www.victorhotelchicago.com

When you see the neon sign at the end of a dark, dead-end street, you may be wondering what you've gotten yourself into. But inside this West Loop club, the scene is chic, sleek and sophisticated. Sky-high ceilings and a black-on-white color scheme look straight out of film noir, and curtained-off rooms are gorgeous, with red walls and Mid-Century Modern furniture. You can sample sushi and mini-burgers while you sip your drink at the swanky bar with floor-to-ceiling shelves holding liquor bottles.

*Wednesday-Friday 8 p.m.-2 a.m., Saturday 8 p.m.-3 a.m., Sunday 10 p.m.-2 a.m.*

## UKRAINIAN VILLAGE/WEST TOWN

### DARKROOM

2210 W. Chicago Ave., Ukrainian Village, 773-276-1411;
www.darkroombar.com

While it promises to serve up tasty cocktails and frothy brews, the Darkroom's main focus, as the name suggests, is to feature local photographers. The bar was built as a photographer's light up box and the tabletops boast old film negatives to tie the whole concept together. Lit mostly by soft candle glows, the bar's dark décor is enhanced by red undertones. Local bands appear every so often and guest DJs spin new music.

*Hour vary; check website for exact times. Usually Sunday-Friday 9 p.m.-2 a.m., Saturday 9 p.m.-3 a.m.*

## WHAT ARE THE BEST PLACES FOR MUSIC?

**Lasalle Power Co.:** Booking mostly rock and alternative bands, you can catch both indie bands as well as national acts here, which have included the Chelsea Girls, Mandy Moore and Billy Corgan.

**The Underground:** International and celebrity DJs like DJ Momjeans (a.k.a. Danny Masterson) perform here on a regular basis, as do musicians such as Nick Cannon, Jermaine Dupri and Snow Patrol.

# BUCKTOWN/WICKER PARK

### MAP ROOM

**1949 N. Hoyne, Bucktown, 773-252-7636; www.maproom.com**

The map room bills itself as a "travelers tavern." Indeed, this is the place to come to make plans for your next trip, or simply dream of seeing the world as you choose from the more than 200 brands of beer at this cozy spot. The bar proudly boasts that it represents 36 different brewing styles. Locals love the selection (and the free WiFi). The place opens up early (6:30 a.m. Monday-Friday, and 7:30 a.m. on Saturday) to serve Intelligentsia coffee, pastries from Bennison's Bakery and sandwiches from The Goddess and Grocery. Alcohol is served beginning at 11 a.m. Keep in mind that the place is cash only; there's an ATM on the premises.
*Sunday-Friday 11 a.m.-2 a.m., Saturday 11 a.m.-3 a.m.*

### THE VIOLET HOUR

**1520 N. Damen Ave., Wicker Park, 773-252-1500; www.theviolethour.com**

If you're not paying attention, you'll breeze past this lounge with its unmarked wood-paneled entryway. The bar's name is a literary reference to T.S. Eliot's *The Waste Land*, as well as Bernard DeVoto's *The Hour*. The interior is hushed, relaxed and just as beautifully baffling as Eliot's poem: High-backed seating plays tricks on your eyes, while crystal chandeliers and parquet floors in a herringbone pattern are dizzyingly delightful. Even more mind-bending enjoyment comes courtesy of hand-mixed cocktails. Mixologists focus on pre-Prohibition libations, meticulously measuring the ingredients in jiggers. It's difficult to choose just one of these classics, but we recommend another literary nod: the Juliet & Romeo, made with gin, mint, cucumber and rose water.
*Sunday-Friday 6 p.m.-2 a.m., Saturday 6 p.m.-3 a.m.*

# LINCOLN PARK/LAKEVIEW/WRIGLEYVILLE

### D.O.C WINE BAR

**2602 N. Clark St., Lincoln Park, 773-883-5101; www.docwinebarchicago.com**

Situated on Clark Street between charming boutiques, restaurants and bars, not far from the park, this cozy neighborhood lounge-like bar and bistro is perfect for a romantic date. On a Friday evening, you'll find young professionals wining and dining after a busy week at the front bar or relaxing on couches by the fireplace. The front portion of the sleek bar is brighter, with light wood flooring, purple and cream couches and in the back, banquettes lining red walls and dim lighting. You don't have to be a wine connoisseur to feel comfortable here. The friendly and knowledgeable waitstaff will help

THE VIOLET HOUR

you choose from the lengthy wine list which spans the globe. Half bottles and wine flights are also available. The appetizing menu of paninis and pizzas is perfect to enjoy with your wine. For sharing with a group, choose the Butcher's Platter, which features bruschetta, cheese and meats of your choice (brie and apple bruschetta, aged gouda, sopresatta and prosciutto), along with a warm baguette, candied walnuts and jam. They also offer specials like discounted wine flights and half-off bottles, and events like wine tastings once a month (check website for calendar).
*Nightly 5 p.m.-2 a.m.*

### KINGSTON MINES
**2548 N. Halsted St., Lincoln Park, 773-477-4646;**
**www.kingstonmines.com**
If you can't make it to Buddy Guy Legends on the South Side, stop into this famed bar in Lincoln Park for a healthy dose of Chicago blues. Live bands occupy two stages every night of the week, while barbecued ribs from Doc's Rib Joint and bottles of Old Style set the tone for an evening of revelry. There is nothing fancy about the space—think dark and slightly dingy—but the dance floor is expansive and the music rarely stops. It can get crowded on weekends so aim for a visit midweek.
*Sunday-Thursday 8 p.m.-4 a.m., Friday 7 p.m.-4 a.m., Saturday 7 p.m.-5 a.m.*

### THE WILD HARE
**3530 N. Clark St., Wrigleyville, 773-327-0868;**
**www.wildharemusic.com**
This bright escape claims to be America's Reggae Capital, and judging by the droves of Jamaicans who crowd the place on a regular basis, we couldn't disagree. The Hare works hard to earn that title, too, with bright sunshine yellow walls, a wide dance floor, two bars and an elevated sound stage where international artists such as Julian Marley and Jah Roots play to a packed place. Although it isn't necessary to bring your sunglasses and

passport, you'll certainly forget that you're in Chicago once you step inside, especially with the fake palm trees next to the bar.

*Sunday-Friday 8 p.m.-2 a.m., Saturday 8 p.m.-3 a.m.*

## WILDE BAR & RESTAURANT

3130 N. Broadway, Lakeview, 773-244-0404; www.wildechicago.com

One thing Chicago has plenty of is Irish bars and pubs. But you won't find one quite like Wilde, located in Chicago's gay-friendly Boystown neighborhood. Named after the glorified Irish writer, Oscar Wilde, this restaurant and bar offers the community more of a "living room" to enjoy. The large bar features leather booths, high tables, stained-glass window skylights, photos and memorabilia of Oscar Wilde and Ireland, and there is an area set up like a library with a large fireplace, oriental carpets, chairs, and side tables. In warm weather, an outdoor sidewalk patio fills up fast with locals enjoying the pub grub and sunshine. The menu features typical Irish-American fare but pretty much anything you order will be tasty, from curried mussels and sweet potato fries to the whiskey-glazed burger and shepherd's pie. Late-night snacks, brunch and gluten-free menus are also available. As for the alcohol, Wilde has a lengthy beer list including specialty beers such as Delirium Tremens, Abita Purple Haze, Elliot Ness and Dogfish Head Indian Brown Ale along with the typical Irish selections like Guinness, Magners Irish Cider, Smithwicks and Harp. Specials are offered for every day of the week from half-price beers on Wednesday to half-price late-night menu items on Friday and Saturday.

*Monday-Friday 10 a.m.-2 a.m., Saturday 10 a.m.-3 a.m., Sunday 10 a.m.-2 a.m.*

THE CHICAGO THEATRE

# ON WITH THE SHOW

Some locals theorize that Chicago's arts and culture community owes a debt to the city's toe-freezing winters. How so? If the ground weren't frozen over for about half of the year, then artists, musicians, athletes and DJs wouldn't have the time to hone their skills and elevate Chicago's arts to new heights. It's just a theory, though, and with the quality work coming out of this city—from powerful plays by the Steppenwolf Theatre Company to powerhouse hits at the Friendly Confines and the Cell—we'll chalk it up to raw talent.

## WHAT ARE THE BEST PLACES TO SEE ART?

### CHICAGO ARTS DISTRICT

18th and Halsted streets, Pilsen; www.chicagoartsdistrict.org

The South Side doesn't see much action when it comes to art, but this rapidly gentrifying area of Pilsen is an exception to the rule. (The others are the Bronzeville Art District around 35th Street and South Martin Luther King Drive and the nascent Bridgeport Art District around Morgan and 32nd streets.) If you're the type to discover them while they're young and still starving, visit the Chicago Art Department *(1837 S. Halsted St., 312-725-4223; www.chicagoartdepartment.org)*—the gallery doubles as an art school. *Every second Friday of the month, the district's galleries and studios open to the public to showcase work or unveil new shows.*

### MONIQUE MELOCHE

2154 W. Division, West Town, 773-252-0299;
www.moniquemeloche.com

After cutting her teeth at the Museum of Contemporary Art, Monique Meloche decided to open her own gallery in the then-up-and-coming warehouse district just west of the Loop in 2001, before moving to her current location in West Town. The gallery focuses on contemporary artists—an eclectic bunch from Chicago, the U.S. and around the world—that showcase installations, mixed media pieces and paintings with a decidedly hip vibe. You might see anything from Kendall Carter's classic takes on street art to Carla Arocha's large-scale plexiglass creations.
*Tuesday-Saturday 11 a.m.-6 p.m.*

### RIVER NORTH GALLERIES

Franklin, Wells, Superior and Huron streets

Don't let the location under the El fool you—this slightly industrial strip is home to some of Chicago's most cutting edge galleries. The focus ranges from contemporary photography and outsider art to original masters' work and sculpture pieces.

### TONY WIGHT GALLERY

845 W. Washington Blvd., West Loop, 312-492-7261;
www.tonywightgallery.com

This spot—which used to be called Bodybuilder & Sportsman gallery—is the oldest in a building that also houses several other galleries and work studios (so make sure to wander around). Tony Wight features quirky, conceptually challenging pieces with a wisp of DIY aesthetic, such as Jason Salavon's digital prints and light and video installations or Scott Fife's cardboard-and-screws severed heads of Jackson Pollock.
*Tuesday-Saturday 11 a.m.-5 p.m.*

# WHAT ARE THE BEST COMEDY SHOWS?

## IO CHICAGO
### 3541 N. Clark St., Wrigleyville, 773-880-0199; www.ioimprov.com

Formerly Improv Olympics (the place was forced to change its name after the International Olympic Committee cried foul), this is the place for Chicago improv. Alumni include Mike Myers, Andy Richter and Amy Poehler, and talented improvisers still cut their teeth here on a nightly basis. The iO's signature show—created by one of the founding fathers of improv comedy, the late Del Close—is the long-form improvisation "the Harold," in which an improv team creates hilarious and often-convoluted "plots" with just one audience suggestion. However, it'd be a shame to miss the various other improv and sketch comedy shows at the Cabaret Theater or the Del Close Theater. The iO opened a Los Angeles branch a few years ago, a testament to its growing success on the stage as well as in Hollywood.
*Admission: $5-$20. Various show times; check website for details.*

## THE SECOND CITY
### 1616 N. Wells St., Old Town, 312-337-3992; www.secondcity.com

It's no joke: The Second City means serious funny business. How else could the theater have remained a top tourist attraction and a requisite for local comedians honing their skills (on stage and in workshops) since it was established in 1959? The Second City's brand of political and social satire still smarts, both on the mainstage and the gutsier e.t.c. stage next door—and even on TV (on shows like *Saturday Night Live* and *The Daily Show*) and film, as evident by famous, whip-smart grads such as Bill Murray, Steve Carell and Amy Sedaris. Donny's Skybox, the cabaret theater, serves as a performance space Thursday to Saturday for students.
*Admission: $12-$27 depending on show. Various show times; check website for details.*

# WHAT ARE THE TOP DANCE COMPANIES?

## HUBBARD STREET DANCE CHICAGO
### 1147 W. Jackson Blvd., West Loop, 312-850-9744;
### www.hubbardstreetdance.com

Founded in 1977 by Lou Conte, the HSDC is arguably the city's foremost dance company, specializing in contemporary modern dance. Under the leadership of current artistic director Glenn Edgerton (following Conte's retirement in 2000 and artistic director Jim Vincent's departure in 2009), the company moved from its jazz-centric beginnings into a worldlier repertoire, and is now known for brilliantly performing works by choreographers Nacho Duato, Toru Shimazaki and Jorma Elo. HSDC established the Hubbard Street Dance Center in 2006, which houses and administers the main company, along with Hubbard Street 2 (a company of young dancers), Lou Conte Dance Studio and HSDC's educational and community programs.
*Check website for details.*

## JOFFREY BALLET
### 10 E. Randolph St., Loop, 312-739-0120; www.joffrey.com

This is one of the country's preeminent ballet companies, and it's not hard to see why. Since its founding in New York City in 1956 by Robert Joffrey and Gerald Arpino (it moved permanently to Chicago in 1995), the company has built a reputation for supporting and staging contemporary American ballet pieces and choreographers, such as Twyla Tharp and Alvin Ailey.

The Devil's Alphabet

RIVER NORTH GALLERIES

To balance out its modern tendencies, it also leans heavily on the Ballet Russes tradition, so expect some works in that style, as well as more classic ballet pieces.

*Show times and ticket prices vary. Check website for details.*

## WHAT ARE THE BEST VENUES FOR LIVE MUSIC?

### BUDDY GUY'S LEGENDS

700 S. Wabash Ave., Loop, 312-427-1190; www.buddyguys.com

Buddy Guy's might have new digs, but that's about all that has changed at this Chicago institution. Drop in and you'll still be rewarded with classic, electrifying Chicago blues, sometimes courtesy of Guy himself. (He's in town the month of January, and on and off the rest of the year in between touring engagements.) There's a free acoustic blues set on Fridays from 5:30-8 p.m. and Saturdays from 6-8:30 p.m.; the full-on jams, however, start around 9:30 p.m. nightly, usually for a $10-$15 cover.

*Monday-Friday 11 a.m.-2 a.m., Saturday 5 p.m.-3 a.m., Sunday 6 p.m.-2 a.m.*

### EMPTY BOTTLE

1035 N. Western Ave., Ukrainian Village, 773-276-3600;
www.emptybottle.com

Consider yourself warned: This place is a dive. But this dark bar showcases some of the best up-and-coming bands in the country, whether it's straight-up rock, free jazz or experimental DJs, to a hipsterati crowd of twenty-somethings who are there first and foremost for the music. Occasionally, you'll get notable emerging international acts, too—for example, feisty UK rapper Lady Sovereign performed here a good four months before she was featured in *The Independent*. It's well worth the risk of braving the sticky floor to be able to say you saw the next big thing play here first.

*Monday-Wednesday 5 p.m.-2 a.m., Thursday-Friday 3 p.m.-2 a.m., Saturday noon-3 a.m., Sunday noon-2 a.m.*

HUBBARD STREET DANCE CHICAGO

## GREEN MILL

4802 N. Broadway, Lakeview (Uptown), 773-878-5552;
www.greenmilljazz.com

The Mill's legend goes beyond the fact that Al Capone and his cronies used to hang out at the bar in the '20s. After a brief decline in the '70s, current owner Dave Jemilo bought it in 1986 and restored its speakeasy décor, cool-cat vibe, and '30s- and '40s-inspired jazz sounds. On any day of the week, you can find discerning jazz fiends of all stripes: middle-aged suits be-bopping their heads alongside fresh-out-of-college hipsters. If you're lucky, you'll show up on the day of the week when resident and internationally recognized jazz vanguard Patricia Barber takes the stage. The Sabertooth Quartet still jams from midnight through 4 a.m. on Saturday nights, while the Uptown Poetry Slam showcases verses on Sunday nights. *Daily noon-4 a.m.*

## HOUSE OF BLUES

329 N. Dearborn St., River North, 312-923-2000; www.hob.com

Never mind the name: The only blues you'll find here is usually relegated to the small Back Porch Stage and presented in the form of Guy King and Jimmy Burns. What you'll find on the main stage is a cocktail of musical acts, including the likes of Cyndi Lauper, The Killers, Peter Frampton, Roger Daltrey and Jay-Z. It doesn't hurt that the Chicago outpost of this national chain is also smack-dab in the middle of the city and housed in a building that resembles a giant turtle shell—and it's even cooler for its lush sound system. Go ahead and splurge on balcony seats—the view of the stage is unbeatable, and it's a small price to pay to make sure you don't get accidentally swept into the thick standing-room-only crowd that rushes the stage downstairs.

*Show times and ticket prices vary. Check website for details.*

## JAY PRITZKER PAVILION

Millennium Park, Loop, 312-742-1168; www.millenniumpark.org

When the Pritzker Pavilion opened to much fanfare in 2004, there were murmurs that it would be Ravinia's undoing. A Frank Gehry-designed alfresco bandshell with mostly free programming in the heart of the city? Ravinia seemed like a distant memory. Luckily, both are coexisting just fine, although the Pritzker's dramatic look and sound are nothing to scoff about. The trellis over the lawn is laced with concert hall-quality speakers, so not an inch of the 7,000-capacity Great Lawn goes hard of hearing. (There are 4,000 permanent seats near the stage, which usually work on a first-come, first-served basis for free shows.) Though regular fare includes world music (Seu Jorge, Bajofondo Tango Club), jazz (Sonny Rollins), classical (Pinchas Zukerman) and experimental (Andrew Bird, Calexico), the Pritzker is also the summer home to the Grant Park Orchestra *(www.grantparkmusic festival.com)*.

*Concerts run from June to September. Check website for details.*

## LINCOLN HALL

2424 N. Lincoln Ave., Lincoln Park, 773-525-2501;
www.lincolnhallchicago.com

Though it's the newest addition to the live music scene, Lincoln Hall isn't without its share of Chicago history. After opening in 1912 as the Lincoln Theater, the building gained fame in 1934 when FBI sharpshooters positioned themselves on the roof to prevent John Dillinger's escape from the Biograph Theatre across the street. Dillinger didn't survive the night, but the hall did and has hosted everything from a garage to an arts cinema. Today, the bi-level, exposed brick space affords a surprisingly intimate arena for live bands such as The Walkmen and Mason Jennings and The Smoking Popes. The full bar and small plates menu round out the offerings. *Sunday-Friday noon-2 a.m., Saturday noon-3 a.m. See website for shows.*

## LYRIC OPERA

Civic Opera House, 20 N. Wacker Drive, Loop, 312-332-2244;
www.lyricopera.org

Considered one of the most classical opera houses in the country—when we say "classical," we're referring to its repertoire, Art Deco digs, resident orchestra and ornate costumes—the Lyric stages eight productions per season. In recent years, these have included Mozart's *The Marriage of Figaro* and Puccini's *Tosca*. Maybe it's a sign that Chicagoans like to stick to the basics, but the Lyric sells out to 95 percent capacity for all runs, so make sure to get your tickets early.

*Show times and ticket prices vary. Check website for details.*

## METRO/SMARTBAR

3730 N. Clark St., Wrigleyville, 773-549-0203;
www.metrochicago.com; www.smartbarchicago.com

For rock 'n' rollers and dance-music geeks, Metro and Smartbar have been delivering a deliciously deadly one-two punch for more than 25 years. Rock out upstairs at the worn-but-who-cares Metro, where the likes of R.E.M. and The Smashing Pumpkins played their earliest shows. (The caliber here remains—The White Stripes, Kanye West and Fall Out Boy were just a few of the headliners in recent years.) House-heads take it downstairs, where the focus is on Chicago, Detroit and international DJs (such as Jeff Mills,

RAVINIA FESTIVAL

Derrick Carter, Green Velvet and Telefon Tel Aviv) who play gigs to pulsating crowds hopped up on liquor and/or good vibes. Though Smartbar is in the basement, it's hardly a dungeon; a massive redesign in 2006 left in its wake one of the slickest specimens on the North Side, complete with the bombastic Funktion One sound system.

*Metro: Show dates and times vary; check website for details. Smartbar: Wednesday-Friday, Sunday 10 p.m.-4 a.m., Saturday 10 p.m.-5 a.m.*

## RAVINIA FESTIVAL
**Ravinia Park, Green Bay Road, Highland Park, 847-266-5100; www.ravinia.org**
This seasonal festival is one of the few things worth a trip into the suburbs if you're a strapped-for-time visitor. What began as the summer home for the Chicago Symphony Orchestra—still at the heart of Ravinia's programming—now showcases an outstanding repertoire of diverse acts. (Case in point: the 2010 season featured Sheryl Crow, Vince Gill, Sting, Carrie Underwood, Counting Crows and Nelly Furtado). But the music and the immaculate acoustics can hardly speak for the overall landscape. The expansive, tightly manicured lawn is the stuff of a Pottery Barn garden catalog, as are the picnics that patrons bring in (some replete with antique candelabras and free-flowing wine). The pricier seats of the 3,200-seat Ravinia Pavilion aren't shabby, either. Smaller acts (like chamber music groups and youth concerts) take place at the Martin Theatre and Bennett-Gordon Hall.
*Season runs June-September; check website for details.*

## SCHUBAS TAVERN
**3159 N. Southport Ave., Lakeview, 773-525-2508; www.schubas.com**
Chicago has a healthy indie-rock music scene, and Schubas is one of the best places to witness it first-hand, whether it's local acts or touring ones. Thankfully, it's not all indie navel-gazing and forlorn lyrics; the roster runs the gamut from honky-tonk and country to pop and jazz. Among those to

have graced the stage include Neko Case, Dave Matthews Band and Sufjan Stevens. If for some reason the backroom main stage isn't filling you up, check out the photo booth at the bar up front or head next door to the Harmony Grill for reliably good comfort food.

*Monday-Friday 11:30 a.m.-2 a.m., Saturday 11:30 a.m.-3 a.m., Sunday 11:30 a.m.-2 a.m.*

### SYMPHONY CENTER
**220 S. Michigan Ave., Loop, 312-294-3000; www.cso.org**

In early 2008, the Chicago Symphony Orchestra named a new director, Riccardo Muti, after its ninth one, Daniel Barenboim, left in 2006. Still, we've yet to see whether a new director signals a new direction: Muti's five-year contract starts with the 2010/2011 season, which means that until then, classical music fans will probably get more of the CSO's deep and brassy signature sound. It also doesn't hurt that the cavernous Symphony Center also serves as a concert hall for touring orchestras and organizations it runs, including the Civic Orchestra of Chicago and the Youth Symphony Orchestra.

*Admission: $12-$200 depending on show. Various show times; check website for details.*

## WHAT ARE THE CITY'S SPORTS TEAMS?

### CHICAGO BEARS
**Soldier Field, 1410 S. Museum Campus Drive, South Loop (Museum Campus), 847-295-6600; www.chicagobears.com**

Perhaps no other team is so loved across the city as "da Bears," which call Soldier Field home. Nobody will soon forget the glory days of the '80s, when the Super Bowl shuffle, William "Refrigerator" Perry and Mike Ditka made it all the way to the top. After a dry spell in the 1990s and early 2000s, the Bears made a comeback in 2007 (getting all the way to the Super Bowl before losing to the Indiana Colts) with formidable defense and a promising team of young players like Brian Urlacher, Matt Forte and Devin Hester.

### CHICAGO BULLS
**United Center, 1901 W. Madison St., West Loop, 312-455-4000; www.nba.com/bulls**

Basically immortalized across the globe by Michael Jordan, the Bulls are no longer that dream team from the '90s: they've suffered through years of losing seasons, but the late-2000s saw a batch of rookies changing the face of the team. Games now are fast-paced affairs that, although lacking the wow factor of the Jordan years, demonstrate just as much heart and action.

### CHICAGO CUBS
**Wrigley Field, 1060 W. Addison St., Wrigleyville, 773-404-2827; www.cubs.mlb.com**

The curse of the billy goat. Poor trades. And then there's the 2003 Steve Bartman fiasco. Since 1908, when the Cubs last won the World Series, the gods of baseball seem to conspire against these "lovable losers." (Though they came awfully close in 2008, only to be swept in the first round of play-offs.) Still, going to watch the "Cubbies" is a summertime rite of passage, one in which at least fans come out winning—just being inside the ivy-festooned, historic Wrigley Field is a stirring experience. (Wrigley

## BROADWAY IN CHICAGO

This production company has made a name for itself by bringing in big-ticket showstoppers like *Mamma Mia!*, *Rent* and, of course, *Chicago*. Most of the touring productions Broadway in Chicago brings in hit the stages of the **Bank of America Theatre** *(18 W. Monroe St., Loop, 312-986-6821)*—formerly the Shubert Theatre—and **Cadillac Palace Theatre** *(151 W. Randolph St., Loop, 312-986-5853)*. The **Ford Center for the Performing Arts, Oriental Theatre** *(24 W. Randolph St., Loop, 312-986-6863)* housed *Wicked* since its Chicago debut in June 2005 until January 2009, which was the highest-grossing Broadway musical in the city to date. The smash success is returning in December 2010 through January 23, 2011. The 2011 roster also promises other sure-to-be hits including *9 to 5: The Musical, Burn the Floor* and *Billy Elliot: The Musical*.

Even if you don't make a show, try to make some time for the Broadway in Chicago walking tour, which covers two of the three theaters on Saturday mornings. During the tour, you'll learn how Judy Garland got her stage name at the Oriental and how the Cadillac Palace chandeliers avoided being drafted during World War II, in addition to the history behind the vintage opulence of these working relics of a bygone era. Theater tours are $10 and depart from the Oriental Theatre at 11 a.m. on Saturday mornings; visit the Web site for details *(www.broadwayinchicago.com)*.

Many shows sell through Ticketmaster *(www.ticketmaster.com)*, though hefty fees add to the price, so you're probably better off calling theater box offices directly. The **League of Chicago Theatres** *(www.chicagoplays.com)* has a comprehensive online guide to what's on and at what time; it also administers **Hot Tix** *(www.hottix.org)*, where you can buy half-off tickets to select shows. Buy through the website or at two locations *(72 E. Randolph St. and at the Chicago Waterworks Visitor Center, 163 E. Pearson St.; closed Monday)*.

was built in 1914, and it still boasts a manual scoreboard; it installed lights to play night games only in 1988.) Try to get tickets in the bleachers, where drinking, sunning and socializing is just as important to some Cubs fans as the team finally winning a pennant would be. Can't get into the stadium? Celebrate in any of the dozens of watering holes around the Friendly Confines—thousands of fans tend to make game days all-day benders at popular bars like Cubby Bear *(1059 W. Addison St., 773-372-1662; www.cubbybear.com)* and Murphy's Bleachers *(3655 N. Sheffield Ave., 773-281-5356; www.murphysbleachers.com)*.

## CHICAGO WHITE SOX

**U.S. Cellular Field, 333 W. 35th St., Bridgeport, 312-674-1000;
www.whitesox.mlb.com**

The pride of the South Side, the Sox are often considered the Second City's second team, at least outside the confines of the city limits. Though the Sox's 2005 World Series victory seems to be turning the tides of popularity outside of Chicago, for fervent, lifelong fans here at home, it's business as usual. That means standing behind captain Paul Konerko, heavy hitters Jake Peavy, A.J. Pierzynski and Carlos Quentin, and jovial but foul-mouthed manager Ozzie Guillen as they try to keep the momentum going. The corporate-sounding name of the Sox's home, U.S. Cellular Field, is a good indication of what the stadium looks like—modern (it was completed in 1991), massive, in the middle of a sea of concrete, and by all counts a bit

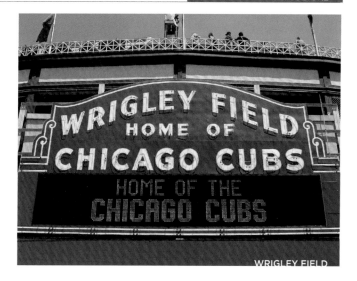

WRIGLEY FIELD

impersonal, especially in comparison to Wrigley. Still, fans have made "the new Comiskey" a bit friendlier by nicknaming it "the Cell". If that isn't cute and cuddly enough for you, head to Schaller's Pump *(3714 S. Halsted St., 773-376-6332)*, where the heart of the franchise—die-hard fans—gather for a pre-game drink.

## WHAT ARE SOME OF THE BEST THEATERS?

### AUDITORIUM THEATRE
50 E. Congress Parkway, Loop, 312-902-2110;
www.auditoriumtheatre.org

Opened in 1889, this gorgeous Louis Sullivan and Dankmar Adler-designed theater—a National Historic Landmark—regularly hosts dance, music and theater events, thanks in part to its splendid acoustics. It has hosted the Bolshoi Ballet, Alvin Ailey American Dance Theater and Kirov Ballet, and Chicago's Joffrey Ballet has a permanent home here. But it's not just about dance. The theater is no stranger to musicals and jazz shows. The gold-leaf interior, nature-landscape murals and soaring arch above the stage are reason enough to pay the entry fee.
*Show times and ticket prices vary. Check website for details.*

### THE CHICAGO THEATRE
175 N. State St., Loop, 312-462-6300; www.thechicagotheatre.com

Before "The Bean" and Navy Pier, and before the ritzy entertainment hub that was State Street hit the skids in the late '70s, this French Baroque-style theater with a colorful marquee was the stuff of postcards. Luckily, it is once again, thanks to the Loop's recent Theater District revival. On any given night, catch anything from national touring musicals and *So You Think You Can Dance* auditions to concerts by Steely Dan and Erykah Badu, and comedy shows by hometown gal Kathy Griffin—that is, if you're not too busy ooh-ing and ahh-ing at the lavish chandeliers and grand staircase.
*Show times and ticket prices vary. Check website for details.*

CHICAGO BLUES FESTIVAL

## HOW DID CHICAGO LEARN TO SING THE BLUES?

It all started in a small, lopsided former automobile parts factory at 2120 S. Michigan Ave., an address immortalized by the Rolling Stones in their bluesy instrumental of the same name. The building was purchased by the Chess brothers, and, from 1957 to 1967, it operated as the home of Chess Records, the recording studio that gave the world the sad, edgy sound of the "Chicago blues."

All the greats recorded here, or wanted to: Muddy Waters, Koko Taylor and Etta James. Junior Wells, whose harmonica playing—"harps," as it was called—influenced countless blues greats, including Junior's longtime friend and partner, Chicago legend Buddy Guy.

In the early days, Buddy was a red-hot backup musician. But as the years wore on, he became a showman, a flamboyant stylist who would hit his guitar against a microphone to get an acoustic sound, pluck its strings with his tongue, or hit the strings with a belt or drumstick to get a tone. He could coax any sound he wanted out of that thing, they said. Buddy made his guitar talk to you, they said. They said other things, too. Eric Clapton called him the greatest blues guitar player in the world and asked Buddy to play with him at Royal Albert Hall. The accolades inspired Guy's aptly titled album, *Damn Right I've Got the Blues*, the first of his four albums to win Grammys. Clapton wasn't the only rock star influenced by Guy, nor was he the first. The Rolling Stones asked Buddy and Junior Wells to open for them on their 1970 tour.

In 1989, Buddy opened a club on Chicago's South Side, **Buddy Guy's Legends**, so that blues artists would have a home in the Windy City. For more than 20 years, the venue has drawn blues fans from across the globe, eager to hear the gritty soulful sound of Chicago's up-and-coming blues artists and revered mainstays. If you're lucky, you might even see the legend himself, though his club drop-in's are becoming less frequent.

## THE GOODMAN THEATRE

170 N. Dearborn St., Loop, 312-443-3800; www.goodmantheatre.org

Under Tony Award-winning artistic director Robert Falls, this theater company—one of Chicago's most venerable at 80-plus years old—has put on classics (*Death of a Salesman*) and cutting-edge spins on classics (Mary Zimmerman's version of *The Odyssey*). That's not to say that the work here is stuffy: The Goodman also focuses on ethnically diverse lineups, staging works by African-American playwrights and a notable (but, sadly, only biennial) Latino theater festival. If you're the sentimental sort, don't miss its annual staging of *A Christmas Carol*; it's what every holiday production hopes to be.

*Show times and ticket prices vary. Check website for details.*

## THE HOUSE THEATRE OF CHICAGO

Chopin Theatre, 1543 W. Division St., Wicker Park, 773-251-2195; www.thehousetheatre.com

For a taste of the future of Chicago theater, do not miss a production by this rough-and-tumble storefront troupe. Expect lots of pop-culture references, rapid-fire delivery and action-film moves. The trilogy of plays that put this group on the map spanned several centuries and took place in the Wild West, feudal Japan and 1920s gangland Chicago.

*Show times and ticket prices vary. Check website for details.*

## STEPPENWOLF THEATRE COMPANY

1650 N. Halsted St., Lincoln Park, 312-335-1650; www.steppenwolf.org

Everyone has heard of The Steppenwolf's famous co-founder, Gary Sinise, and its legendary ensemble (John Malkovich, Joan Allen, Martha Plimpton, John Mahoney, et al). But this company—which started in the basement of a suburban church, with blokes and tough guys as prime subject matter—hasn't let fame, nor a slick space in Lincoln Park, go to its head. It still produces thought-provoking work with bite, like ensemble member Tracy Letts' 2008 Pulitzer Prize- and Tony Award-winning play, *August: Osage County*.

*Show times and ticket prices vary. Check website for details.*

# CHICAGO'S BEST FESTIVALS

Chicago's freezing winters mean only one thing—way too much to do during warmer months. Here's a primer to the city's best festivals.

## FALL

### Chicago Jazz Festival
*Grant Park, Loop; www.chicagojazzfestival.us*
This largely free fest features four full days of jazz courtesy of locals such as Kurt Elling and genre luminaries like Sonny Rollins and Ornette Coleman. Bring a blanket and camp out in front of the Petrillo Music Shell or the Pritzker Pavilion, but be warned that this is the city's longest-running music fest (30 years and counting) and super popular, so show up early for a good spot. *Labor Day weekend*

## SPRING

### St. Patrick's Day
*Downtown, Loop; www.chicagostpatsparade.com and South Side;*
*www.southsideirishparade.org*
The downtown celebration kicks off at 10:45 a.m. on the nearest Saturday to March 17 with the Chicago River being dyed a bright green hue, followed up with a parade. The South Side Irish St. Patrick's Day Parade Committee also hosts smaller events that celebrate the neighborhood's Irish heritage. (The long-held South Side parade was canceled in 2009 after much public drunkenness).
*March*

### Gospel Music Festival
*Millennium Park, Loop; www.chicagogospelmusicfestival.us*
Don't be surprised if you get goosebumps when you hear local musicians and seasoned performers belt out everything from classics to contemporary tunes. Past performers included Kirk Franklin, Maurice Griffin and *American Idol*'s Fantasia Barrino.
*Early June*

### Grant Park Music Festival
*Jay Pritzker Pavilion, Millennium Park, Loop; www.grantparkmusicfestival.com*
The country's only free, outdoor classical music series spans the city's warm months, and there's nothing like hearing Beethoven while sitting under the stars. Tickets for general seating aren't necessary (most concerts are free), and picnics are welcome and part of the fun.
*June to mid-August*

### Chicago Blues Festival
*Grant Park, Loop; www.chicagobluesfest.org*
There's some pressure for this festival—after all, this is Chicago, home of Muddy Waters and the electric blues, and that attracts more than half a million devotees to this event. Thankfully, its programmers do a consistently solid job with the lineup, which has included big acts like Grammy winner Buddy Guy and Mavis Staples and smaller local acts scattered over seven stages and venues.
*Second weekend in June*

### Old Town Art Fair
*N. Lincoln and W. Wisconsin avenues, Old Town; www.oldtownartfair.org*
You don't need to be an artist to appreciate the festivities at this juried fair, one of the oldest in the country. Come to see painting, sculpture, photography and ceramics by regional artists; stay to drink tall lemonades, chow down on food from nearby restaurants and listen to live music with the locals.
*Second weekend in June*

# SUMMER

### Chicago Pride Fest
*Boystown, Lakeview; www.chicagoevents.com*
Chicagoans celebrate the LGBT community with this weekend of performances, arts & crafts and food vendors. The crown jewel of the three-day event is the Pride Parade on Sunday, which features some of the wackiest and boldest outfits and floats this side of Mardi Gras.
*Fourth weekend in June*

### Taste of Chicago
*Grant Park, Loop; www.tasteofchicago.us*
At 10 days long and with 6 million visitors in attendance, this is the most bloated Chicago tradition. If you can navigate the molasses-thick crowds, you'll be rewarded with food from more than 70 city restaurants, and performances by the likes of Rob Thomas, Steve Miller Band, Los Lobos and Gavin Rossdale.
*Late June to early July*

### Independence Day Fireworks
*Grant Park, Loop; www.tasteofchicago.us*
The city's official Fourth of July fireworks happen around 9:30 p.m. along the lakefront. The best views are near the Taste of Chicago grounds or by the lakefront. Locals stake out spots as early as that morning.
*July 4*

### Lollapalooza
*Grant Park, Loop; www.lollapalooza.com*
Lolla—the brainchild of Jane's Addiction's Perry Farrell—took root in Chicago in the summer of 2005, and it looks like it's here to stay, at least until 2011 when its contract with the city ends. The giant music festival brings in bigger-than-life acts like Green Day, Lady Gaga, Soundgarden, and Kings of Leon, alongside emerging indie fare of the local variety (Andrew Bird, Hey Champ) and international ones (Bat for Lashes, Gomez) spread out over three days. Stay hydrated—it gets hot.
*First weekend in August*

### Bud Billiken Day Parade & Picnic
*39th Street and S. King Drive to Washington Park, South Side;*
*www.budbillikenparade.com*
This African-American parade started in 1929 by Chicago Defender founder Robert Abbott; it's now the largest of its kind in the nation. Held in honor of Chicago youth, the parade features more than 315 floats and has attracted celebrity participants such as Muhammad Ali, Oprah Winfrey, Michael Jordan and President Barack Obama. The parade meanders around the Hyde Park neighborhood and ends up with a barbecue at Washington Park.
*Second Saturday in August*

### Chicago Air & Water Show
*North Avenue Beach, Gold Coast; www.chicagoairandwatershow.us*
The U.S. Navy Blue Angels show off each summer with masterful aerial acrobatics. The best views are along North Avenue Beach. Actually, scratch that: The best views are from any of the skyscrapers facing Lake Michigan, so find yourself a friend with a condo on the lakefront.
*Mid-August*

MILWAUKEE ART MUSEUM

# MIDWEST BEST

Although there's an endless list of things to do in Chicago, the city's location along Lake Michigan and at the center of the tri-state area of Illinois, Indiana and Wisconsin makes it an ideal spot from which to tour some of the top parts of the Midwest. Just beyond Chicago's never-ending highway construction, you'll find beaches, art museums, concerts, festivals and, believe it or not, wineries, all within a 90-minute drive from the Windy City.

## WHAT IS THERE TO SEE AT THE INDIANA DUNES?

If you're tired of fighting for sand space on North Avenue Beach, head to **Indiana Dunes State Park** *(1100 N. Mineral Springs Road, Indiana, 219-926-7561; www.nps.gov/indu)* and make your monumental sand castle among the abundant sands of the dunes. Located 50 miles east of Chicago in Northwest Indiana, the park offers great hiking as well as year-round activities, from swimming and dune climbing in the summer to cross-country skiing and snowshoeing in the winter.

Before you go, visit **Fox & Obel Market** in River East (401 E. Illinois St., 312-410-7301; www.fox-obel.com) to pick up sandwiches and other treats to eat in the park.

Then hop onto I-90 east into Indiana and merge onto U.S. Highway 20 east toward Porter. Your first stop should be at the recently built **Dorothy Buell Memorial Visitor Center** *(U.S. Highway 20 and Indiana Route 49, Porter, Indiana, 219-926-7561)*, where you'll receive an overview of the woodlands and beach areas, as well as directions to good picnic spots. Begin the day with a romp through the deep sands of the dunes, then settle down for a picnic lunch along the three-mile beach, West Beach, where the Chicago skyline is visible from the shore on a clear day. Hiking the huge desert-like sand dunes is the reason to come here; the largest is Mount Baldy, whose 126-foot climb is a challenge. Don't be surprised if, like the poet Carl Sandburg, who often visited the dunes, you find bliss in the park's quiet, punctuated by the calls and songs of its more than 350 bird species.

There's much to do nearby, too. The historic **Chellberg Farm** *(U.S. Highway 20 and Mineral Springs Road, Porter, Indiana)* and home shows what farm life was like back in the 1880s for the Chellbergs, an immigrant Swedish family who lived in the area. For something a little more 21st century, there's always one of the nearby riverboat casinos, the most-well known of which (thanks to its ubiquitous road-side signs) is **Hammond's Horseshoe Casino** *(777 Casino Center Drive, Hammond, Indiana, 866-711-7463; www.horseshoehammond.com)*, whose size more than doubled after a 2008 renovation. After betting the farm on the craps tables, empty the sand out of your shoes and head back to Chicago.

*How to get there: If you're driving, get off at the U.S. 20/Indiana State Highway from Interstate 94 or the Indiana Toll Road. Or take the South Shore Line (there's a stop at Michigan Avenue and Randolph Street in downtown Chicago; www.nictd.com) to either the Miller, Portage/Ogden Dunes, Dune Park or Beverly Shores station in Indiana.*

## WHAT IS THERE TO SEE AND DO IN MILWAUKEE?

When Chicagoans want to unwind, they head to Milwaukee (just 90 minutes north of the city), where they can see groundbreaking art, take in amazing concerts and, most of all, just kick back with a frosty brew.

## WHAT'S THE BEST WAY TO SEE NEARBY WINERIES?

For your grape escape, you'll want to follow the **Lake Michigan Wine Trail**, a tour denoted by blue and white signs along the roads. First, download the wine trail map from www.miwinetrail.com. Eleven wineries dot the route, several off Interstate 94, but if you're short on time (or designated drivers), instead of tackling all of the wineries, pick a couple of spots to savor.

**St. Julian Winery** (716 S. Kalamazoo St., Paw Paw, Michigan, 800-732-6002; www.stjulian.com) is Michigan's oldest winery and one of its best. After taking a free tour of the grounds, head to the tasting room and snag some delicious riesling. If reds are more your thing, visit **Lemon Creek Winery and Fruit Farm** (533 E. Lemon Creek Road, Berrien Springs, Michigan, 269-471-1321; www.lemoncreekwinery.com) to sample its cabernets. While you're there, check out the farm stand and buy some of southwestern Michigan's luscious, plump fruit, such as blueberries, raspberries or cherries (if they are in season).

Get your last drop of vino at **Tabor Hill Winery & Restaurant** (185 Mount Tabor Road, Buchanan, Michigan, 800-283-3363; www.taborhill.com). After testing some vintages in the tasting room and taking the free tour of the grounds, eat a hearty meal to soak up the alcohol. The restaurant serves seasonal cuisine; pair the pecan breadcrumb-coated raspberry chicken and sweet potato succotash with demi-sec. As you dine in the honey-colored-wood dining room, you can drink in the beautiful view of the vineyard from the large windows before hitting your own trail back to Chicago.

*How to get there: Taking your taste buds to southwest Michigan for a wine-tasting trip is easy. Harbor Country (www.harborcountry.org), an eight-town region that hugs Lake Michigan, is only a 70-minute drive from downtown Chicago. To get there, take Interstate 90 east, merging onto Interstate 94 east. Follow Interstate 94 through Indiana into Michigan.*

If you devoured Chicago's Art Institute in a day and are hungry for more eye candy, visit the **Milwaukee Art Museum** (700 N. Art Museum Drive, Milwaukee, Wisconsin, 414-224-3200; www.mam.org), which was designed in part by world-renowned architect Santiago Calatrava. Against the backdrop of the lake, Calatrava designed a pedestrian bridge to the museum that looks like the sails of a boat leading to a one-story galleria, which evokes the shape of a wave. The collection of 20,000 works inside the building is outstanding, especially for fans of Wisconsin native Georgia O'Keeffe.

Milwaukee's lakefront also rocks with **Summerfest** (200 N. Harbor Drive, Milwaukee, Wisconsin; www.summerfest.com), a massive annual concert that draws music fans from across the U.S. to hear acts as varied as Stevie Wonder, No Doubt, Kenny Chesney, Flogging Molly, Bob Dylan and Lupe Fiasco. The 11-day noon-to-midnight behemoth is Milwaukee's best festival, but it gets some fierce competition from **German Fest** (200 N. Harbor Drive, Milwaukee, Wisconsin; www.germanfest.com), which cele-brates the city's roots (and its beer)—Milwaukee didn't get the nickname Brew City for nothing. You can guzzle steins of suds and chow down on sauerbraten while watching lederhosen-clad musicians belt out traditional Teutonic tunes.

The city's known for its German heritage and the breweries German families started here, including Pabst, Schlitz and Miller. Now called

FRANK LLOYD WRIGHT HOME AND STUDIO

**MillerCoors** *(4000 W. State St., Milwaukee, Wisconsin, 800-944-5483; www. millercoors.com)*, the company still offers the best brewery tour (it helps that the other mega-brewers have left town), which shows off how Miller started out at a small Plank Street property to become eventually the brand that fills out about half the commercials during any given football game. After the free hour-long tour, which looks at every stage of the brewing process, you're rewarded with some complimentary ale (for those over 21). For a taste of the smaller breweries bubbling up in the city, check out **Lakefront Brewery** *(1872 N. Commerce St., Milwaukee, Wisconsin, 414-372-8800; www.lakefrontbrewery.com)*. The brewery's tours are $6 and include a complimentary pint glass and four pours—yet more great reasons to plan a return trip to Brew City.

*How to get there: Take Interstate 94 from Chicago into Wisconsin, or take Amtrak's Hiawatha line (www.amtrakhiawatha.com) out of Union Station (225 S. Canal St., Chicago) to the Milwaukee Intermodal Station.*

## WHERE CAN YOU SEE FRANK LLOYD WRIGHT'S ARCHITECTURE?

Oak Park is best known for having the highest concentration of homes and buildings designed and built by Frank Lloyd Wright, the preeminent American architect whose streamlined style took on the once-prominent and ornate Victorian standard. Bibliophiles also head to Oak Park to see the birthplace of Ernest Hemingway and the local museum dedicated to his life and work.

If you happen to be driving there, slow down on Chicago Avenue just east of Harlem Avenue—along the street, keep an eye out for houses numbered 1019, 1027 and 1031, all of which are Wright's not-so-exciting early works. They followed the Queen Anne-type designs that were popular before Wright created the style that would make him famous.

The **Frank Lloyd Wright Home and Studio** *(951 Chicago Ave., Oak Park, Illinois, 708-848-1976; www.wrightplus.org)* is a must-see for any fan of

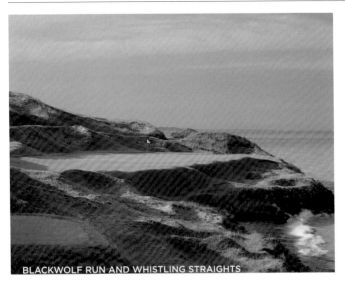

**BLACKWOLF RUN AND WHISTLING STRAIGHTS**

architecture. But you won't be able to peruse the museum on your own; entry is available with a 60-minute guided tour only (just be sure to reserve a ticket online beforehand since tours often sell out). The home served as Wright's workplace and residence for the first 20 years of his career. It's not his best work—he changed it frequently for practical purposes and it has little of the grace of sites he developed nearby—but the home shows off the evolution of his style as it changed to meet the needs of his growing family. In this house and the adjoining studio, Wright and his associates invented the Prairie School of architecture, designing 125 buildings along the way, including the **Unity Temple of Oak Park** *(875 W. Lake St., Oak Park, Illinois, 708-383-8873)*, where as a congregant, Wright was asked to design a replacement for the previously burned-down church. The exterior of the building is cold and uninviting, but the interior is still exciting to see and maintains a contemporary feel more than a century after its design. Using simple angles and stained wood instead of paint, Wright managed to design a church that was both "democratic," as he set out to do, and magisterial, befitting its role as a place of worship.

Very different in architectural style is the **Ernest Hemingway Birthplace** *(339 N. Oak Park Ave., Oak Park, Illinois, 708-848-2222; www.ehfop.org)*, a Victorian building refurbished to its turn-of-the-century style. The home contains some mementos from Hemingway's childhood and information about his birth and life here; understandably, it downplays the writer's characterization of Oak Park as a place of "wide lawns and narrow minds." A short walk away is the **Ernest Hemingway Museum** *(200 N. Oak Park Ave., Oak Park, Illinois, 708-524-5383)*, which has photos and Hemingway artifacts, including his childhood diary and earliest writing. The museum features a short documentary on his life and covers in detail his teenage years—good grist for parsing the psyche of this complicated man.

Beyond the Wright and Hemingway homes, there is much to do in Oak Park, which takes pride in its attention to the arts. Local art galleries show off some of the best works in the Chicagoland area. Check out **Ridge Art**

*(21 Harrison St., Oak Park, Illinois, 708-848-4062; www.ridgeart.com)*, which carries unusual Haitian pieces. With tree-lined streets and amiable proprietors of charming cafés and bakeries—take a final pit-stop at **Petersen's** *(1100 Chicago Ave., Oak Park, Illinois, 708-386-6130, www.petersenicecream.com)*, for some old-fashioned ice cream sundaes.

*How to get there: Just ten miles due west of downtown Chicago, Oak Park is easily accessible by car (or you can hop on the El's Green Line to the Oak Park stop). Take I-290 west to Harlem Avenue (Route 43). Turn north, and drive 1.5 miles to Chicago Avenue.*

## WHAT IS THERE TO SEE AND DO IN KOHLER, WISCONSIN?

There is a lot more to Wisconsin than delicious cheese and beautiful lakes. The small city of Kohler, located two and a half hours north of Chicago on the shores of Lake Michigan and the Sheboygan River, just happens to be the Midwest's golf mecca.

One of the nation's first planned communities, designed with the help of the Olmsted Brothers firm of Boston, Kohler began as a garden at the factory gate and headquarters for the country's largest plumbing manufacturer. Today, the city is all about recreation. The four world-class golf courses within **Blackwolf Run** and **Whistling Straits**, both designed by legendary Pete Dye, are challenging and scenic with 40-foot high dunes and miles of coastline. (The Straits course hosted the 2010 PGA Championship, which will return there in 2015. The Straits will also host the Ryder Cup in 2020.)

**The John Michael Kohler Arts Center** *(608 New York Ave., Kohler, 920-458-6144; www.jmkac.org)* is a nice alternative to hitting the links, with changing contemporary art exhibits, galleries and a theater, dance and concert series. A must-see for nature-lovers, the **River Wildlife** *(411 Highland Drive, Kohler, 920-457-0134)* is considered a "country club in the woods" with horseback riding, canoeing, fishing, hiking and camping all on a private 500-acre wildlife preserve.

Of course, you don't need to camp. One of the area's most luxurious resorts is right here. Forbes Four Star **The American Club** *(419 Highland Drive, Kohler, 920-457-8000; www.americanclub.com)* epitomizes country chic, offering upscale accommodations and warm customer service. The rooms are elegantly simple with wood-beamed ceilings, white duvets and Kohler bathrooms (of course). The Kohler Waters Spa is the centerpiece of the resort and sets a happy, relaxing atmosphere. You'll find guests padding around in spa robes throughout the day and into the evening, when everyone mingles in the lobby over wine, cheese and other tasty nibbles.

For a more complete meal, try **The Immigrant Restaurant and Winery Bar** *(419 Highland Drive, 920-457-8888)*. No expense was spared when it came to creating the space, originally remnants of Walter J. Kohler Sr.'s boarding house. Divided into six rooms, each of which represents the nationalities that populated Wisconsin in its early days—Dutch, German, Norman, Danish, French and English—the restaurant is elegant and cozy. You can't go wrong anywhere on the menu, which is why the tasting menu is a popular choice, offering such delicacies as olive oil-poached black cod in an orange emulsion and braised organic pork belly and New England lobster. For a more casual dining experience, try **Cucina** *(725 E. Woodlake Road, Kohler, 920-457-8888)*. The pastas are hearty and the view of Wood Lake is nice regardless of the season.

While the summer is the most popular time to visit, the fall can be equally enjoyable, thanks to vibrant changing foliage and special events. The **Kohler Food and Wine Experience** *(11 Upper Road, Kohler, 800-344-2838; www.destinationkohler.com)* is another good excuse to avoid the crowds and come in October, when the community is aflutter with cooking demonstrations, food and wine tastings and seminars. Or see how Wisconsin does winter, as the Traditional Holiday Illumination puts Kohler aglow with more than 200,000 lights on trees surrounding the Kohler village.

*How to get there: Kohler is about 2 1/2 hours from Chicago. Take Interstate 94 West from Chicago into Wisconsin; continue onto Interstate 43 North for 50 miles; Exit at 123 for Interstate 28 toward Sheboygan/Sheboygan Falls; Take that to Co Road A, and go right, then left at Co Road PP/Lower Road/ Lower Falls Road; then take the first right onto Highland Drive.*

WILLIS TOWER

## WHAT IS THE BEST WAY TO ARRIVE AND DEPART?

Two international airports serve Chicago: **O'Hare International Airport** (ORD) and **Midway International Airport** (MDW). O'Hare *(773-686-2200; www.flychicago.com)* lies about 20 miles northwest of the city center, and it's used by more than 70 million passengers a year. The airport has four terminals: 1, 2 and 3 serve mostly domestic flights, while Terminal 5 serves international arrivals and departures. O'Hare can be a nightmarish beehive for the uninitiated, so make sure you show up at least two hours before your flight, and double-check that you're going to the right terminal. Airport architects were wise to build in a Starbucks at baggage claim, too—this area alone can be enough to test your patience.

The Airport Transit System (ATS) provides transit between all terminals, long-term parking lots and the Metra station. Passengers can also access the Chicago Transit Authority (CTA) Blue Line El train, which provides 24-hour service to downtown Chicago for $2.25. There are also taxi ranks outside the baggage claim area of each terminal; rides downtown cost about $40 with tip, and usually take 30 minutes with no traffic (double that time during rush hour).

The recently renovated but smaller Midway International Airport *(773-686-2200; www.flychicago.com)* is 10 miles southwest of downtown. It serves mostly low-fare lines, in addition to a few major airlines, and though prone to busy periods, it's still a much smaller option than O'Hare, and thereby more manageable. You can access the CTA El train here as well; a $2.25 trip on the Orange Line to downtown takes about 35-40 minutes. Taxis are also available outside baggage claim and the 20- to 25-minute trip downtown costs $25-$35.

## WHAT ARE THE PUBLIC TRANSPORTATION OPTIONS?

The **Chicago Transit Authority** (CTA) is the state-run organization responsible for most city buses and the "El" (short for "Elevated Track," this is the mass-transit train line that crisscrosses the city). Aside from being safe, if somewhat rickety and old, the train system is also a good way to get around the city if you're going the four cardinal directions, and if you're not in a hurry. (Constant track repairs and train delays are part of the experience.) Don't ask us why the El's planners place most of the system above ground, in a city that's so cold for a solid three months. Locals put up with it because it's the cheapest way to zip across town—plus, it's a great way to get a bird's-eye view of neighborhoods and, in the Loop, practically a free architectural tour.

### HOW COLD IS CHICAGO?

Chicagoans often suffer through bone-chilling, face-smacking winters. The coldest months are January and February, where the wind-chill factor can plunge into double digits below zero degrees Fahrenheit. Summers are on the other extreme—hot and humid. Despite any humidity, though, the city is a summer playground for locals who flock to the beach and the many street fests. Spring and fall are also very pleasant, if a bit short sometimes: Spring realistically falls somewhere between March and June (though it can be in the 50 to 60 Fahrenheit range through May), while autumn usually sweeps in from September to November.

CHICAGO MARATHON

Most of the eight color-coordinated lines meet downtown. You can get maps and information at CTA station booths or at www.transitchicago.com; the website also has added bonuses like a trip planner (an itinerary builder fueled by Google maps) and CTA Bus Tracker (which tracks buses with GPS technology).

Fare cards can be bought at automated machines within 144 rail stations; likewise, most stations have information kiosks, but non-CTA personnel occasionally man these, and they don't sell fare cards. At press time, fares using a Transit Card were $2 per one-way ride on buses and $2.25 on trains, and transfers (two additional rides within two hours after first boarding) were $0.25 for the first transfer (the second transfer is free). Cash: $2.25 per ride for buses (you must have exact change and transfers are not issued when paying cash) and trains. You can also buy a Visitor Pass (one day, $5.75; three days, $14) and 7-Day Pass ($28) options. Just be mindful that the beleaguered CTA constantly battles budget shortages and service cuts, so prices are subject to change.

## ARE TAXIS AVAILABLE?

Taxis are plentiful in highly trafficked areas (the Loop, River North, Michigan Avenue, Lincoln Park, Lakeview, Wicker Park), and less so in strictly residential neighborhoods and the suburbs. If a cab has its lights on, it means it's unoccupied and ready to be flagged; when the light is off, it means it already has passengers. Fares start at $2.25 and increase by $0.20 for each 1/9 of a mile; the first additional passenger is $1 (after that, each additional passenger is $0.50). There is also a $1 fuel surcharge. There's no extra charge for your luggage, though a 15 to 20 percent tip at the end of your trip is expected.

## DO I NEED TO RENT A CAR?

Locals love to say how Chicago is a very drivable city, but unless you're staying far away from any public transportation, you really don't need a car. Depending on where you're staying, you might end up paying more for

**ADLER PLANETARIUM**

parking than you would for your flight or your rental car. If you do need a car, major car rental firms are available outside O'Hare and Midway; they include **Avis** *(800-331-1212; www.avis.com)*, **Budget** *(800-527-0700; www.budget. com)*, **Hertz** *(800-654-3131; www.hertz.com)* and **Enterprise** *(800-261-7331; www.enterprise.com)*. Visitors accustomed to driving in unpredictable city traffic won't have a problem navigating Chicago's streets.

## IS IT POSSIBLE TO WALK EVERYWHERE?

Walking is a great way to get to know the city. That said, it's probably not the smartest idea to try to walk from one neighborhood to another, as these can sometimes be spaced quite far apart. (Eight city blocks equals roughly about a mile.) Use this as a rule of thumb in orienting yourself: Chicago is on a grid system, with north-south State Street and east-west Madison Avenue being 0; one block north of Madison Avenue on State Street is 100 North State, two blocks west of State on Madison is 200 West Madison, and so on. Most street signs feature the name of the street and its numerical coordinate in this grid system.

## HOW SAFE IS CHICAGO?

Though Chicago is a safe city, avoid potentially dangerous areas, such as the Near West Side and some portions of the South Side. Certain well-lit and well-trodden neighborhoods, like Streeterville, the Gold Coast, Lincoln Park and Wicker Park, are safe to walk around in at any time of the day, though in general, don't draw attention to yourself in public and leave valuables in your hotel safe (including credit cards—carry only one and cash for what you need).

No matter what neighborhood you're in, you're likely to encounter panhandlers, whether they're opening a convenience store's door for spare change in Wicker Park or sitting with a sign in the Loop. Whether you donate a buck or two is up to you, but one of the most constructive ways to give is by buying a *StreetWise* magazine ($2) from vendors working throughout the city. The weekly publication—sold by homeless or near-homeless men and women—features articles and art by vendors and an editorial staff. Vendors make a $1.25 profit per magazine sold, and you get to give knowing that it's for a good cause.

## WHERE ARE THE CITY'S HOSPITALS?

Chicago is home to some of the foremost medical schools-cum-hospitals in the region. Among these institution-backed hospitals are **Northwestern Memorial Hospital** *(251 E. Huron St., 312-926-2000; www.nmh.org)*, **University of Chicago Medical Center** *(5841 S. Maryland Ave., 773-702-1000; www.uchospitals.edu)*, and **Rush University Medical Center** *(1653 W. Congress Parkway, 312-942-5000; www.rush.edu)*. The city's top-notch public hospital, **John H. Stroger, Jr. Hospital of Cook County** *(1901 W. Harrison St., 312-864-6000; www.cchil.org)*—a.k.a "County" to Chicagoans—treats emergencies as well, though the wait can stretch for hours.

## WHAT ARE THE LOCAL MEDIA OUTLETS?

Chicago's major newspapers are the venerable *Chicago Tribune (www. chicagotribune.com)*—owned by media heavyweight Tribune Company—and the grittier *Chicago Sun-Times (www.suntimes.com)*.

Weeklies include the *Chicago Reader (www.chicagoreader.com)*—a 40-year-old alt-weekly—and *Time Out Chicago (www.timeout.com/chicago)*. Both hit the streets on Thursday and obsessively cover local arts, theater, film, nightlife, restaurants and more. Other publications include the online music-centric *UR Chicago (www.urchicago.com)* and monthly lifestyle magazine *Chicago* magazine *(www.chicagomag.com)*.

CHICAGO SKYLINE

# CHICAGO OVERVIEW

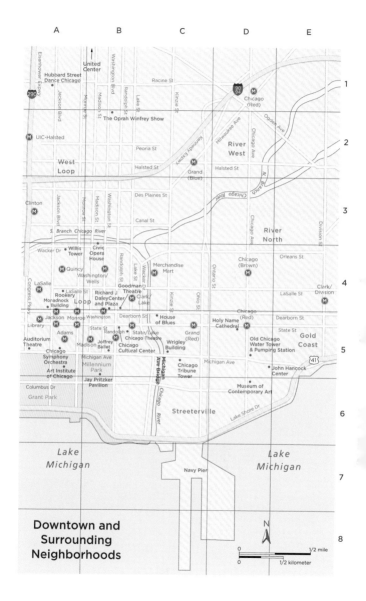

Downtown and
Surrounding
Neighborhoods

179

Near North and
North Side

Northwest
Side

Andersonville

Foster Ave

Lawrence Ave

Lincoln
Square

Green
Mill

Western

Damen

Montrose

Irving Park Rd

Irving
Park

Addison St

Music Box
Theater

Addison
Brown

Paulina

Belmont Ave

Diversey Ave

Elston Ave

Kennedy Expressway

Fullerton Ave

Milwaukee Ave

Western
O'Hare

Bucktown

North Ave

Damen
O'Hare

Wicker Park

House Theatre of Chicago
Chopin Theatre

Empty
Bottle

Ukrainian
Village

West
Town

Thorndale

Bryn Mawr

Berwyn

Argyle

Lawrence

Wilson

Graceland
Cemetery

Sheridan

Wrigley
Field

Metro/
Smartbar
Wrigleyville

Addison Red

IO
Chicago

Belmont

Schubas
Tavern

Lakeview

Diversy

Peggy Notebaert
Nature Museum

Fullerton

Armitage

Steppenwolf
Theatre
Company

North/
Clybourn

Division

Chicago
Blue

Lincoln
Park

Lincoln Park
Zoo

The
Second City

Chicago
History
Museum

Sedgwick

Old Town

Clark/
Division

Chicago Ave

Chicago
Brown

Chicago
Red

Lake Michigan

Montrose
Harbor

Lincoln Park

Belmont Harbor

Diversey
Harbor

0                    1 mile

0              1 kilometer

N

180

# South Loop, Printers Row & South Side

N

0 — 1 mile
0 — 1 kilometer

Eisenhower Expwy
290

Jackson Blvd
Harrison

Buddy Guy's Legends
Printers Row

Grant Park

Roosevelt Rd
Roosevelt

Shedd Aquarium

Adler Planetarium

Field Museum of Natural History

South Loop

Soldier Field

18th St

90 94

Prairie Avenue Historic District

Chinatown

Cermak Rd

Cermak-Chinatown

Archer Ave

55

Stevenson Expwy

Lake Michigan

35th St

Sox-35th

35th-Bronzeville-IIT

U.S. Cellular Field

Pershing Rd

41

Burnham Park

Indiana

South Side

43rd St

43rd

47th (Red)

47th (Green)

51st St

Hyde Park Blvd

51st

Washington Park

DuSable Museum of African-American History

Garfield St

Garfield (Red)

Garfield (Green)

55th St

Museum of Science and Industry

University of Chicago

Midway Plaisance Park

60th St

63rd St

Jackson Park

Halsted

King Drive

East 63rd

94

90

Marquette Rd

Halsted St
Canal St
S. Branch
Chicago River
Michigan Ave
Lake Shore Dr
Wentworth Ave
State St
Michigan Ave
Martin Luther King Jr Dr
Dan Ryan Expwy
State St
Drexel Ave
Woodlawn Ave

FERRIS WHEEL AT NAVY PIER

CHICAGO RIVER

MODERN WING AT THE CHICAGO ART INSTITUTE

MILLENNIUM PARK

## PHOTO CREDITS

Pg. 8 : Chicago River Tour
    © City of Chicago /
    GRC
Pg. 11 : Marina City © City of
    Chicago/GRC
Pg. 12 : Buckingham Fountain ©
    City of Chicago/GRC
Pg. 14 : Michigan Avenue Bridge
    © City of
    Chicago/GRC
Pg. 17 : Chicago Bungalows
    © City of Chicago/GRC
Pg. 18 : Chicago Lake Front
    © iStock
Pg. 20 : Farmers Market at
    Daley Plaza © City of
    Chicago/GRC
Pg. 20 : Downtown EL Train
    © City of Chicago/GRC
Pg. 24 : Downtown Chicago
    © iStockphoto
Pg. 26 : Cloud Gate © City of
    Chicago/GRC
Pg. 28 : Museum of Contempo-
    rary Art © Museum of
    Contemporary Art
Pg. 31 : The Art Institute of
    Chicago. McKinlock
    Court, Courtesy of the
    Art Institute of Chicago.
Pg. 32 : Chicago Cultural
    Center © City of
    Chicago / GRC
Pg. 36 : Jay Pritzker Pavilion at
    Millennium Park © City
    of Chicago / GRC
Pg. 39 : Field Museum of
    Natural History © City
    of Chicago/GRC
Pg 41 : Brookfield Zoo
    © City of Chicago/GRC
Pg. 43 : Robie House © Frank
    Lloyd Wright: Tim
    Long/Frank Lloyd
    Wright Preservation
    Trust